GLASS SHORE

GLASS SHORE

STEFAN JACKSON

Elsewhen Press

Glass Shore
First published in Great Britain by Elsewhen Press, 2014
An imprint of Alnpete Limited

Elsewhen Press, PO Box 757, Dartford, Kent DA2 7TQ
www.elsewhen.press

British Library Cataloguing in Publication Data.
A catalogue record for this book is available from the British Library.
ISBN 978-1-908168-48-1 Print edition
ISBN 978-1-908168-58-0 eBook edition

Designed and formatted by Elsewhen Press

For Angeliki and Isabella – Two of a perfect pair.

Selfish behavior and economic incentives rule every
aspect of life.

–Chicago School of Economics. Circa 1950s

PROLOGUE

Puget Sound. July 15, 2062.

A murderous bullwhip crack shattered the sound barrier.

In that instant planes, birds, trees, flesh, bone, rock, fish, metal, concrete, dirt, candy, love – all things become undone.

In that instant sand was pounded and melted to perfection.

Vitrified.

Super-cooled.

In that instant a pristine sandy coast was turned to miles of solid and smooth dull crystal shoreline.

1

Manhattan 2076

5:45 AM. The ring on Nikki's pinky finger vibrates.

Her eyes snap open and her mind fires on all cylinders. She removes the ring from her finger and sets it on the contoured alloy charging cradle, shutting down the alarm.

She checks her phone. No coordinates yet. The pinky alarm had been synced with her phone. She had expected to awaken to instructions on what to do next. Now she is on hold. She doesn't like being on hold. Nikki is a girl on the move. A woman in constant motion.

She slides out of bed and walks over to the translucent screen on the east wall of the rented apartment. She pushes the small yellow button that activates the device. The translucent wall becomes a three dimensional, real time image of the outside world. The device is designed for spaces that have no real windows. She places her forefinger on the wall and calls up the east view. The window displays the still and verdant corner of Henderson and Broad streets. Outside is soft blue-gray and quiet. The sun is on a slow rise, a soft yellow flare on the horizon. She enjoys this time of the morning more than any other time of the day. She had read that the magical energies of the morning sun blast away the negative residue from the preceding day. So each day is fresh and clean. And those who set their path in the wake of that healing wash can own the day. It is something she believes. And so, more often than not, she is successful in her endeavors.

The lower left corner of the window reads: 41°F. Wind: 10 NW. Nikki uses her finger to slide the panel from east to north, then to the south and to the west. She finds it is a peaceful morning in all four corners of the city. She moves the window back to the east.

Walking into the bathroom Nikki looks in the bathroom mirror – *Twinkle*. (You are loved.) She sits on the toilet, content.

Later, Nikki washes her hands and again looks in the mirror – *Twinkle*. (Life is good. You have the power to make it better.)

She grabs a sleeveless, knee length, open back Basesuit from her black satchel, stands before the full-length mirror – *Twinkle* (You are beautiful) – and inspects her body. Her breasts are more than a mouthful and nicely shaped. They get attention and elicit smiles from both men and women. Nikki likes that.

Nikki works her slender form into the black, skintight body garment made of live fibers that mimic and mold to wardrobe programs.

She walks over to her laptop computer, opens her wardrobe folder and searches for the perfect outfit. Nikki is not happy with her current stock but she doesn't have time to shop now. She settles for a dress she has not worn in years, a long black sleeveless number with a swooping open v-back. She double clicks SHOW/RUN. A life-sized image of the dress is projected next to Nikki. She steps into the projection and looks at herself in the mirror. She likes the way the dress falls at the back; it really accents her firm butt.

Nikki steps out of the projection and grabs the belt off the countertop. She removes the marker from the belt and slips it into the coding slot on her laptop computer. The belt icon (a smiling woman with a bright yellow jumpsuit) appears on the computer monitor. Nikki opens the icon, removes a few wardrobe programs from the marker, then uploads the black dress. She returns the marker into its niche on the belt. She presses a tiny chrome button on the belt. The black dress she selected a moment ago envelopes her body. She taps the SELECT button and calls up her work outfits; finally choses black denim pants and a black shirt with a chrome spine and blue-laced trim on the collar and sleeves. She puts on her flat-soled, closed-toed shoes, which the wardrobe program converts to black peep-toed pumps. (Nikki selects Mickey Mouse Red for her toenail color.)

Nikki pops the wand free from her laptop. She taps the end, activating the eyelash detail.

Her phone rings. She looks at the screen and notes the code. Time to go.

I'm not right.

I feel a frost of mind and grit in my veins. I feel like a deliberate melody with a dragging bastard beat. A nagging, unwanted but proud vibe. I want to be free of it. I want to feel free in body and mind. Yet I can't jump the tricky beat. I can't find the time.

I run my fingers over the nape of my neck and locate my mjac. I plug into Aliceon and set my authorization code. *00:01 running* appears as a quiet ghost before my eyes. I fade the Aliceon timer.

I tap the audio icon and select jazz, play all. The city is beautiful and quiet at this time of morning, save for the dozens of *personals* moving about. I drive south on Seventh Avenue. The stores of Chelsea are bright and empty with the exception of a few window dressers working on their displays.

03:01 complete flashes three times and quits. Then *Clean* appears and fades away.

I still feel like hell. I unplug Aliceon, running my fingers along the nape of my neck, blindly manipulating my skin and securing the port.

Buzz-buzz emits from the dashboard of the mot. The call is from Nikki. Little Miss Fun. I press the speaker icon and say, "Yo."

"Hi, Lover. Whachadoin'?"

"Dealing with my mind."

"Still? Damn. Did you run a diag?"

"Yeah. Aliceon says I'm clean."

"I'll give you a proper scan when I see you. I got the call."

"I'll be there in five."

"Cool. See you soon."

"Yep."

Nikki disconnects.

Suddenly my mot and I are scanned by a palm-sized

personal. Once the unit has verified occupancy, it displays Olympic champion Bosnit Pota winning the one hundred meter men's dash in seven-one wearing Naide's Pulsewear. Naide is my preferred brand of sportswear.

I drive my mot into the horseshoe drive of Nikki's apartment complex. She rushes from the lobby when she sees me. I come to a stop and she gets in the vehicle. Nikki is sweet on the eyes and havoc on the imagination. She has caramel dipped skin, a clean oval face accented with thick eyebrows and cushy lips lightened with warm and smiling amber eyes. Her thick black hair is captured in a ponytail that curls at length's end. She uses her hands to talk and she pinches and punches, slaps, hugs and touches.

"Okay, turn around." Nikki orders as she pulls her laptop from her black messenger bag.

I do as instructed. I feel Nikki peel away the fabric that mocks skin at the nape of my neck. She inserts a plug into my mjac.

"Running," Nikki states.

"So, you gonna tell me what the gig is?" I ask.

"Quiet," she snaps. "Let me do this in peace."

We sit quietly and listen to *Cerulean Sea*.

"I have to meet your original designer one day. You have some funky codes. You are clear and clean but I don't like the dress of your programs. You're tricky."

She removes the plug and closes my skin.

I run my fingers over the sealed mjac port. "I'll bring you along the next time I reach out to my creator."

I watch her secure her laptop within her messenger bag. She then draws a flash drive from a niche in her bag. "Where to?" I ask.

"Eastern Long Island," she replies as she inserts the flash drive into the dashboard port. The menu appears and she drags the address into the travel bin. She presses the walking man icon.

"Journey loading," says the mot. Then a heartbeat later, "Destination confirmed."

Nikki reclaims the flash drive and places it in her bag.

I tap the green button and the mot drives.

"What are we looking for?" I ask.

"My holy grail," she says flatly.

I nod. "Is this gonna get messy?"

"Probably. That's why I called you. Otherwise, I'd do this myself."

"Can you give me an idea of what I'm up against?"

"No. I honestly don't know. I just know where it is and that we have to get it now."

Damn. I hate this type of gig. I can't properly prepare, which means I need to think in extremes so that I can minimize the surprises that reality will hurl at me.

My mot is scanned by numerous *personals* as we move down the avenue. A large square-shaped translucent flatware appears quickly on my left and features the forever-cool Arsenio Rodríguez and the always glamorous Sparta Rie sharing coffee at a Havana café. Arsenio lights Sparta's cigarette, then he lights his own. They smoke *Página 53. Un producto Cubano fino.*

A full sized star-shaped *personal* on our right shows a platinum-haired woman with exquisitely sharp cheekbones wielding a neon green lasso to stop an evildoer. The heroine wears tight-fitting, thigh-high boots made of *S*-Leather exclusive for Prini.

Before my mot, dozens of exotic models parade to and fro in colorfully elegant gowns as they display fresh flesh and dazzling jewels. "First Water estate diamonds and gems from the eighteenth, nineteenth and twentieth centuries, only at Rubin's," each model states as she rotates to center position in the advert. *Global Certified Consignments* flashes at the bottom edge of the ad.

We continue down the avenue as legion of *personals* suggest people, corporations, services and items of necessity and fantasy specific for Nikki and me.

4

The single door has long ago been removed from its hinges and stored somewhere in this severe indoor landfill.

Cascading mountains of decades old newsprint, magazines, comics, porn, posters, printed cardboard, plain, colored, and printed-paper choke the entire warehouse. White and brown spider webs are thick in the corners, on the walls, from ceiling to floor, a faux netting stretching across the columns of paper, covering meter after meter of the warehouse's French windows. The vermin leave behind evidence that they rule this place. The stench of mold and decay worms into the tongue, it's like chewing on burning hair. This pervasive smell can't be from decaying paper alone. No doubt many things have died here and I have no desire to become part of that mix.

Nikki's phone loudly pings. Looks like we've located her holy grail.

We struggle with the junk. Then we extract a bundle of manila folders bound by thin twine. Nikki's phone emits a single loud drone. She turns it off.

"This is it," Nikki says low and hard. No question or disappointment in her voice, yet, it feels as though she can't believe it.

I see the black chip and rip it from the top folder. I crush the electronic tag with my boot heel.

"What's that noise?" Nikki asks. "You hear that? Sounds like a drunkard playing a Theremin."

"I know what it is – brace for impact!" I reach for Nikki but too late. The concussion hurtles us to the floor of the filthy room.

I'm on my feet a heartbeat later.

Nikki is not. She's on her hands and knees for a moment then lands on her ass and stares at me. She blinks. I can see she is gathering her thoughts.

Continued sounds of destruction erupt from the quarters

below us. I hear heavy and steady noises of rude, uninvited people.

I expected this.

I do not believe in surprises and accidents so I knew we'd have company sooner or later. Nikki is of the same mind. That's why she hired me. Now her flesh is my priority.

Life is simple when your agenda is clear.

I turn away from my client and pull out my gun, a blunt-nosed thirty-eight caliber Smith and Wesson. A classic. Guaranteed to stop and drop. I ease toward the lone exit of this room.

I crouch behind a precarious stack of newspapers and peek around the column to get a look down the hall. No sightlines, so I listen.

Nikki, stuffs the bundle of precious documents into her black messenger bag, snaps the catch and cinches the strap.

Nikki says, "These documents are more important than me. Keep the documents safe and secure above all else."

So the cold side of my mind says I don't need her breathing to get paid. I'm sure I can find a market for what she holds dear in that black messenger bag. Of course the warm side of my mind says I must honor our original deal, using all my resources and going to any extreme to keep her alive and well.

Now I hear one … two … three … distinct sets of footfalls ascending the near stairwell. This is a close-quarters confrontation. I feel the situation works to my advantage.

I motion with my free hand for Nikki to stay low and train my gun toward the top of the stairwell. I have a damn good idea what these guys are here for. Secure the files that Nikki took possession of just moments ago. Astronomical odds against something else of value being hidden in this indoor dump.

These guys were either in tune with the same beacon that brought Nikki and me here, or they followed us here.

I'm sure they have orders to kill first and don't ask questions later. That's something I have to respect. I was trained the same way. Follow orders. Be quiet.

A bright yellow POD emerges from another room and floats chest high down the crowded passage. I blast its eye and duck back into the room, covering Nikki. The Peace Officer Drone fires rubber pellets then ejects a short burst of foam upon stacks of newsprint. The POD hums in mid-air, inert, senses dead and out of ammo, it falls to the floor and a moment later the foamed fused tower of newsprint crashes atop it.

Great, now I have to clear the exit.

"Stay low", I tell Nikki as I spring up and return to my former position.

I set my foot on the POD / paper blockage and force it away from the door. Now, I'm loath to do it, but I use my hands to shove the pile down the hall, opposite to the exit stairwell. It's like relocating mud in the rain yet I eke out enough space for a smooth exit. Okay, smooth is not the appropriate word but we can get over the heap and out of the room.

I look about, as best as is allowed by these narrow sightlines.

The lead man appears at the top of the stairs. I fire my gun. The bullet hits him in the chest and he lights up a bright orange and staggers back a step.

Shields, of course. Conventional weapons are useless. I put my gun back in my shoulder holster.

"Alright, you know you can't hurt us so c'mon out," a husky-voiced solider states.

"Confirm Sarge, we got resistance on the second floor. POD is down," another voice says.

I hear more feet ascend the stairs. I look at Nikki. I try to calm her with my eyes. I put on my black leather gloves.

"You know, Apollo, you've got style," she says with a grin, "That Torque blue shirt is slamming but you're the prissiest Black man I've ever known." Nikki smiles at me as she looks away from my eyes to my gloved hands.

"My hands take care of me. I take care of my hands."

"Yeah, okay," she chuckles.

I cut her laugh short when I pull out my Bolt. I place the slender black metal unit in the palm of my right hand. Nikki's eyes narrow with concern as the Bolt melds with the glove. I'm pretty sure she has never seen this type of weapon. It's a specialized firearm and illegal for anyone to own. The weapon channels my Qi into a physical force. The angrier or more aggressive I am, the more potent the charge. A Bolt works well underwater and in zero-g, and as long as I'm breathing I can keep shooting. Aside from my wits, it's the best damn weapon I own.

Nikki stares at the Bolt. "What is that?"

"This will penetrate most body armor and incapacitate the solider."

"Most", she replies calm and easy.

"Yeah, most, as in majority. These guys don't look like regular army. They look like an alphabet group. They may not be that well-equipped."

I step out into the hallway and twice push the trigger on the silent weapon. One pellet strikes the chest of the soldier in the foreground and the second pellet slams the other soldier in the head. Both men crash to the floor with violent urgency: like hyper-kinetic voodoo dancers that first lose skeletal support and then motor skills. I fire two more pellets, striking the next two soldiers in line and they both drop with the rapid energy of ruthlessly discarded marionettes.

Four quiet bodies clog the travel-challenging hallway.

A soldier yells, "He's got a Bolt", and troops kiss the steps. A couple of soldiers spray the second floor with bullets. It's a flash outburst because the soldiers realize that firing into dense newsprint produces misty confetti that clouds the hallway.

Nikki sneezes as the funky confetti cloud rains down upon us. I'll need a very long hot shower in order to clean off the stink of this place. Nikki sneezes again, then stands and walks toward the far set of large windows. I watch her pick up a stack of newspapers and then toss the pile through the windows.

I hear footsteps rush over the stairs, away from us.

"Smart girl. That may buy us a moment."

"That's the plan," she replies. She pulls a tiny vial from a small pocket on the front flap of her bag. She yanks the cork free and spills the liquid from the vial over stacks of paper. She smashes the vial to the ground. The smell of kerosene fills the room. Nikki pulls out a lighter and sets flame to the wetted papers. The fire envelops the paper with an envious passion. Blue and orange flames, slow and deliberate, licking and reaching and teasing the ready pulp. The flame expresses nasty greed and want and hunger, the cornerstones of a good romance. I'm a content voyeur as I watch the fire consume the literary graveyard.

"Get me outta here, bodyguard," Nikki says with an easy smile on her lips and hard urgency in her eyes. That's Nikki. Little Miss Fun.

I grab her hand. "Step lively and stay close to me. And don't be shy about stepping on the men lying in the hallway."

"Are they dead?"

"No."

"When will they recover?"

"Long after we're gone." No need to burden her with the fact that recovery from a Bolt strike is a long and painful process. Unfortunately Bolt strikes don't kill. Damage depends on the shooter's energy, with bodily harm ranging from severe muscular degeneration to extreme neurological dysfunction.

We walk over the soldiers without pause. Nikki doesn't seem to have a problem with it. I keep my Bolt at the ready as we hit the metal stairs quiet and quick. Behind us white smoke chokes the hallway and swirls thick above us as we hurry downwards.

Ground floor. We turn right, toward the rear of the warehouse.

I hear erratic flapping of wings, drawing my eyes up to see a pigeon erupt into flight – and one soldier standing on a rusted metal gangway overhead – as she looks down at Nikki and me. I fire first and tag her in the chest. She drops with livid ceremony causing her gangway to creak and slide, threatening to break free of the rusted network of catwalks. I take Nikki by the bicep and sprint away.

A soldier appears out of nowhere. I punch him in the face, shattering the plastic shield of his helmet and sending him to the floor in a bloodied heap.

We hurry over broken glass, chunky charred drywall, blackened splintered wood and blast-strewn paper, making a flash departure through the ugly new cavity in the side of the building. The perimeter of the cavity is still burning blue and enlarging. This is the signature damage from an ETU. It's a sonic unit and its initializing burst is what put Nikki and I on our ass minutes ago.

Nikki stays in step with me as we run from the building. I slow a step, and arm whip Nikki so that she's now running in front of me.

It's quiet, dare I say, serene. Sunny and cool with puffy cumulus clouds overhead. I hear birds. This feels weird, like an out of body experience. Yet this is Long Island, farmland or countryside, whatever you want to call it. I'm city. So if it's not concrete, glass and steel, it ain't right.

I glance back and see white and black smoke rolling from broken windows of the old warehouse. No soldiers in sight. Wait. Someone in a long black coat emerges from the left. Now two other men appear and stand next to the first. They watch as Nikki and I run away. A black mot comes to a quick stop behind the trio and hovers in wait.

We approach a chain-linked fence that is a few heads taller than me. Nikki scrambles over it with a hop and flip motion remnant of a dog-faced Marine. For me, it's a simple a two-meter hurdle.

We hop into my mot. I tap the green icon on the dashboard then slam my foot on the accelerator and we're racing off through farmland. I disengage the Bolt from the glove, remove both gloves and stash the unit in my coat pocket. We're less than a minute from the expressway. Once the mot is on the grid I can amp it up and get the hell away from here.

I check the rear view monitor as Nikki turns around in her seat and looks out the slender rear window; we do not see a pursuit vehicle. Yet I know they're back there and coming hard.

In the near distance, Manhattan radiates like a kaleidoscope, thanks to a bright midday sun striking massive panes of faceted crystal that adorn better than ninety percent of the city's skyscrapers. Coming up fast, the wide sleek expressway gleams with huge static holographic adverts that fold over and form a tunnel over the expressway. We fly through a black and white advert of Marilyn Monroe running down a snowy old Manhattan street, smiling and laughing, warmly clutched in the folds of her smoky black full-length

Thurby belted trench coat. London collection. *Thurby – Style Is*.

We hit the expressway and I accelerate to three hundred and sixty clicks.

"How fast can you go?" Nikki asks as she looks out the window at the blurred countryside. At this speed the motion adverts look like stutter-still shots. But you can still make out the logos.

"I reworked the guidance matrix, so I can rip up the road."

"Okay. You seem to be in control. We're not being followed are we?"

"Sure we are." I check the rear view monitor for the millionth time. Nikki studies the monitor as well.

Increasing to four hundred and eighty clicks.

"Where we going?" Nikki asks.

"Right now, toward the city. I figure we...."

In the rear view monitor I see something long and mean roaring up from the rear. I accelerate to six hundred clicks.

"Damn," Nikki states as she stares at the rear view monitor.

"It was just a matter of time. Sit still." I tell her.

We zoom down the expressway at better than eight hundred clicks, flowing around the lawful traffic like hot wind through wheat. Nikki is cool but I can see that her left hand clutches her seat, while the palm of her right hand rests flat on the dashboard. All bets are off on whether or not she's breathing. The long black mot is not gaining any ground; yet I have a feeling it's not for lack of want. My mot is bored out to plus eight. That's a beefier power block than official pursuit vehicles.

Passing midtown exits. "Going into lower Manhattan. We have a better chance of disappearing there," I inform Nikki.

I brake and pull the wheel hard right, now, sliding sideways along the expressway. Nikki and I pitch forward and to the left. Traffic passes over my mot like water flowing over a stone. I hold the wheel at pitch and accelerate. My arms are leaden. Such mean tension, fighting the flow. Those same forces also hold Nikki and me in check. It's like being hard set in a frozen mold. Zero movement.

Much too late, the trailing mot performs the same maneuver. The trajectory of my mot allows us to exit the expressway at ramp five. The other mot is forced to exit at ramp four or three. Sure, the other mot could back up, but the grid has buffers to limit all movement queer of the flow. It would take five times longer to back up than to exit down stream and work back via other avenues. Of course, the other mot will radio our exit to other units, but now I have a moment to think.

Or not. The mot once behind is now ahead of me. I watch a man in a leather jacket lean out of the window of the leading mot as it also performs a sideways sweep. The man in the leather jacket aims a weapon at us that I'm not familiar with and at the moment I'm not interested in learning what it is.

I set the wheel straight. My mot aligns with the grid. I disengage the collision buffers and punch the accelerator.

"Oh-no – are you crazy?"

"Yes," I reply as we slam into the tail end of the lead mot and mister leather coat lurches forward, nearly falling out of the window of the spinning mot. As we speed by, I see a pair of hands clutching his pants and leather coat, keeping his ass from a nasty fate, still, his weapon discharges, just missing to the right rear of my mot and so blowing a small crater in the macadam. Chucks of charred black road spray across the expressway. I hear and feel many small pops against the right side and rear of my mot – the right rear quarter window of my mot shatters, spitting glass shards into the cabin. Nikki flinches but doesn't yell. I accelerate and restore the safety functions. In the rear view monitor I see traffic continues uninterrupted, flowing neat and smooth over the large hole in the expressway. Seems no damage suffered by any other mot.

I see Mr. Leather Coat's blast-battered mot is at a complete stop. Nice.

"Yes!" Nikki pumps her fist as she studies the monitor.

We exit at ramp three and I set the mot to auto-drive. It's best to go on the grid while driving in the city. The gentle slope onto the turnaround of the Manhattan Bridge is a buffer zone, slowing my mot to a crawl for vehicle inspection. We face forward so the beams can perform an eye scan. Soft red beams sweep the exterior and interior of my mot. If we don't allow an eye scan, security measures will kick in and my mot will come to an immediate stop.

This is a big surprise, no seizure ensues and we keep rolling but I feel we're not clear. I'm sure Mr. Leather Coat reported our exit point so converging units should hit us in seconds.

Manhattan.

The fabled city of gold, realized.

The streets and sidewalks are unsoiled level planes. The massive glass skyscrapers are tall, clean, masculine, and gleam like diamonds during the day. This city is all business. Be it a restaurant or data recovery service, law practice or photography, you must be burning with brilliance or the death of your business will be immediate. No learning curve for debutantes. In this city stress is a basic food group, a base element with a better distribution system than air.

Canal Street, Chinatown, is wide and luminous and whirling with life. Bright banners in Chinese, Korean, Thai and dozens of other Asian languages, flashing colored neon, and frenetic adverts compete for what little space is left in your mind. The sidewalks and crossways are thick with beautiful young men dressed in either jeans, t-shirt and jacket with plain kicks, or tailored suits and patent leather shoes, and fabulous young women oscillating from classic demure in long dresses, pearl necklaces and slender heels to screaming metal bitch in micro mini-shirts, steel pierced flesh and thigh-high platform boots. I realize that it's lunchtime for those who lead a normal life. Every restaurant, curb waiter, short grill and noodle shop is deep with customers. Delicious smells roar across Canal. My stomach gives me a quiet pinch. I want something to eat.

"We have to ditch this mot," I state.

"Yeah…" Nikki studies the street signs. "Get us to the Lower East Side."

"What's the plan?"

"I have friends in low places. I know someone that deals in stolen mots. So I'll ask a favor and get us a new rig with a certified grid signature. It will also be a good place to collect our thoughts."

I look over at her. "I had you figured all wrong: thief,

hacker, arsonist, exotic dancer, black marketer, what's next? Grammy winning recording artist?"

Nikki smiles, laughs a little. "You knew the job was dangerous when you took it," she says. She pulls her phone from her bag.

The large advert on my left states that Commons Recycling is looking for qualified applicants in recollection sciences. *Work Proud. Work Earth.*

"Hi, Lover," Nikki says, speaking on her phone. I don't get upset. I know she calls everyone *Love* or *Lover*. I was her lover last night and will be in the future. "I'm hot and need your help," she states with no hint of desperation.

I check my rear and side monitors. For reasons I can't fathom, the authorities haven't stopped us. Not even the courtesy of an impolite tail. Aside from people and mots, the only thing I see is advertising. It's all the time and everywhere. Small, medium, large and oversized floaters saturate the city. Above me I see the fabulous pop singer Pana Ryni offering fresh bottled water courtesy of the Adirondack Cooperative. On my left, a large advert of veteran stage actor Winston, touting the virtues of Municipal Savings and Loan. At my right, the advert states that Son Vincent has the solutions to secure my financial future. I hate advertising.

"See you in a moment, Anton. Thanks again, Love," Nikki clicks off. "Turn left on Essex, then right on Grand," she instructs me.

I didn't see it coming and that's a shame. I'm trained to prevent this type of attack. I feel a spritz or two upon my neck, and right side of my face. I think it's also in my hair. I turn to see Nikki holding a small vial of *rage* by Sancóme. Smells of cinnamon. I want to protest but I must admit it's better than warehouse stink.

"Kinda potent," I say.

"Kinda necessary," she replies.

I nod in agreement. She studies the map displayed on her phone. I guess the blinking red dot is our destination. I check the monitors again. Expecting an ambush at any moment.

"There," Nikki points to a gap between the apartment buildings on the left, about a half block up the avenue.

I press the left turn button as I near the gap. Oncoming traffic compensates by humping over my intended path. A stop alert appears at the gap for pedestrians. The sensible wait while others rush across. And of course . . . I have to brake for the old lady.

Oncoming traffic flows over my mot without concern.

Waiting, I study the crowd. The sharp-dressed young Asian men at the right are in a gang called Sha'ner. The white-tipped canvas shoes are their mark. And now I see there are a few of them on the left as well. So are they guarding the alley? I'll find out in a moment. They all wear suits but of different cuts and colors. They're each engaged in separate personal pursuits like talking on the wire or listening to music, maybe playing games, so if it weren't for the trademark shoes, you'd never know they were a gang.

The old lady is clear and I rush into the narrow alley. Not even a glance from the kids on the wings. Interesting. As we roll down the tight passage, I realize this is not a short drive. I check the rearview monitor and no one is trailing us. Then the alley opens into a cavernous used mot lot with a large trailer and active garage at the far rear. I park my mot and we both make a fast exit from the vehicle as though it is on fire. Skyscraping residential apartments corral the mot lot, a near perfect circle of solitude beneath a small oval eye of cloudless blue.

The feel of the city is so faint it's near distracting.

This forces me to wonder, as I often do, what had possessed the city designers.

The Commons had elected Christina Muri-Hiorto as city planner for Manhattan. The diminutive waif and well-known party angel had stated her primary mandate was to redesign the city, adapting it to meet future needs and demands. During the years of development, Ms. Muri-Hiorto ushered dozens of architectural and constructions firm into a shared hell as they pressed to create the future. Four major architects, including Muri-Hiorto herself, went into self-imposed exile and either "fell off the grid" never to been heard from again, or died as a result of a bizarre natural event. All of their unpleasantness experienced before phase four – *Underground* – had been completed. Their stories are well documented. And a new documentary or Hollywood epic about the unearthly fall of the Muri-Hiorto architects appears every few years. Over the last century their madness has been awarded genius status. All buildings have green roofs. The architects had studied the sun's movement as it related only to Manhattan. The face of this city is all glass and those translucent panels are also solar machines fueling a lion's share of the city's power. The buildings are erected at odd geometric angles and severe staggered heights with faceted crystal panes set all about the city. This irrational design cuts the morning, afternoon, and evening sun into shards and ribbons of colors that vibrates cool across negative spaces and radically sings in hot bright areas. Looking to the west I see shattered thin bands of psychedelic colors in the narrow chasms between buildings. In a moment the hues will change.

We zigzag through the maze of vehicles. Some in pristine condition, others not so good, and those shabby mots are labeled with big red tags: *AS IS for specialized hobbyists.*

A few meters from the trailer, Nikki's friend steps out and rushes to greet her. They embrace, a tight warm hug then quickly, an all too familiar deep kiss. Miss Asian-Latina garage monkey with small and perky tits looks at me with a smile, a subtle laughing smile. She's a beautiful woman, tall and thin. Flat black hair with a punk cut. Yet, it's her shadow ice green eyes that put my mind on hold. Anton catches me staring at her eyes.

"Nikki, it's so good to see you again. God, I haven't seen you in so long. You look marvelous," says Anton. Her voice is lithesome, innocent and distracting with a Spanglish accent. Her eyes are on me as she steals another deep kiss from Nikki. I assume this is to illustrate that she and Nikki are playmates and way too cool for me.

And the pisser is, she has succeeded in making me feel less than stud.

"Anton, this is Apollo," Nikki makes the intro. Anton thrusts her hand out, assuming we'd shake but I take her fingers in mine as though catching porcelain, then place a tender kiss on the back of her tattooed hand. In effect, planting my lips on the forehead of Felix the Cat. Her fingers are strong and rough. Her nails have a clear sheen, and are cut close and neat. She's a workingwoman, and she works clean.

"Oh, a gentleman. Nice to meet you. Let's take care of your mot," Anton says. She raises her hand and points at my mot. On that signal, a short Mexican man wearing dirty overalls and large yellow earphones exits the garage and hurries for my mot.

"Yo boss!" The call comes from the garage. A tall kid with long blonde hair waves at Anton.

Anton nods toward the trailer. "Go on inside and get comfortable. This will only take a moment," she says. Anton walks toward the garage. Nikki and I head for the trailer.

The trailer interior is upcycled chic, accent on used mot parts. The centerpiece of the office is Anton's desk, a disc of polished textured steel. It's the hood of a classic Petty T Black-Flash. All six seats in the trailer are from different vehicles. The crushed red velvet love seat is from a Bowie DIG 40. It's beautiful. I make my way to the love seat. Nikki follows.

I sit and a moment later, vow never to leave the love seat; it embraces the contours of my bum and back and holds me in a soft mold. This is mother's womb comfort.

"Wow… this is nice," says Nikki. She snuggles into the crushed velvet.

I snuggle up to her. "This is the standard seat in the Langford coupé series," I inform her.

She nods, respecting the brand. "Everyone talks about the speed of a Langford. This is the thing to talk about." She pokes the love seat with her fingers.

Then she playfully pokes me in the chest. "I like that little black toy of yours."

We smile. And before I get too happy, I have to clarify. "Which one?"

"The one you flexed back at the warehouse with the cute little gloves. Can you get me one of those?"

"I'll work on it."

"You lie." She gives me a small kiss anyway.

We sit in silence. I study Nikki's profile. Soft worry lines spoil her fine complexion. Yet, she seems both at ease and focused. Nothing dangerous or tricky or erotic flits across her screen. Something drives this girl and it's more than just the thrill of the moment. And it's not money. She's on a mission but she has so many balls in the air that I can't target her true goal. Most people are easy to figure out; feelings, ideas and agendas exposed through speech and manners. I've spent a lot of time with Nikki and the best image I have of her is akin to a well-rendered blue pencil sketch. She likes the rain. She likes the sun. She likes to dance. And she can fight. She has a sense of humor and it's not politically correct. She likes sex. She likes drugs. She doesn't see herself as a survivalist or rebel, even though she excels at each quality. Over the years, I've come to see her as a mercenary with a purpose. Lord knows what that purpose is.

Nikki sets her canvas bag in my lap.

Right.

The *Files*. Could this be her raison d'être, or one more piece in the great and fancy royal scam?

She loosens the strap and removes a manila envelope from the inner pouch without lifting the outer flap. I clutch the bag beneath my arm as I lean in and study the folder.

A heartbeat before the soldiers had stormed the junk warehouse, we were looking at another folder. That folder contained pictures of the Glass Shore.

"My contact, Ezra, said this would blow my mind. It will change my world. He said it was my grail," Nikki says to me as she opens the thin folder. It appears to have no pictures, just text. The pages have a big blue stamp of the United States Air Command upon them. We read.

Day	Hour	Min	Sec	
00	00	12	52	GC: Confirm live bogey Jump One. Maintain course. Do not engage.
00	00	13	01	LTCR: Roger Ground Control.
00	00	13	10	LTCR: Jump One to Base.
00	00	13	15	BASE: Go Jump One.
00	00	13	18	LTCR: Confirm live bogey.
00	00	13	20	BASE: Confirm visual of live bogey Jump One.
00	00	13	24	LTCR: Roger.
00	00	13	36	LTM: Adam, you see that?
00	00	13	39	LTCR: Yeah, I see it.
00	00	13	41	LTM: What the hell Adam? That thing is not from our world. How does it fly?
00	00	13	43	LTCR: Easy Jimmy. Focus and prepare to intercept.
00	00	13	47	LTM: Roger.
00	00 [R]			
00	00	17	21	GC: Jump One, can you hear me?
00	00	17	22	LTCR: Roger Ground Control. Locked on bogey.
00	00	17	27	GC: Maintain course.
00	00	17	30	LTCR: Roger.
00	00	18	33	GC: Jump One. Radar indicates bogey has entered US air space at alarming speed. Execute.
00	00	18	40	LTCR: Repeat order Ground Control.
00	00	18	44	GC: EXECUTE BOGEY.
00	00	18	46	LTCR: Understood Ground Control.
00	00	18	49	LTM: A-one is locked, sir.
00	00	18	51	LTCR: Roger.
00	00	19	04	BASE: What the hell is going on up there? Nuke the damn thing!
00	00	19	07	LTCR: Doing my best Base. Bogey is evading.
00	00	19	10	LTCR: Target locked. Missile away.

-END TRANSMISSION-

Nikki stares at me and I stare back at her. She turns the page over and we find it blank.

"They fired a nuclear missile at a real alien spacecraft. That's what created the Glass Shore in Washington State. Not three terrorists." I say, somehow managing to keep my voice to a low roar.

"This is insane. Gliddin ordered the nuke strike," Nikki states as she pokes the document. "They shot down an alien spacecraft."

"This has got to be a lie."

We sit in silence, save for the background din of a working chop shop, the sharp hiss of acetylene torches cutting through hardened metals, the dull yet oft times high-end frequency strikes of flat head mallets against steel, and the short bursting whirls of power tools. We watch the guys work, through the large office window. I can see Anton standing at the far right of the shop, wearing goggles, doing that supervising thing. She then walks away from her crew and disappears from view.

Nikki says, "It was all a lie yet it all made so much sense. In retrospect, a terrorist attack was comforting. I remember that day. I was scared. I mean I was, like, just rocking on the couch in front of the TV, chain-smoking. If they had mentioned aliens I would have lost my mind."

"Right. A nuclear explosion on American soil was bad enough. We were mobilized within two seconds of the event and it was scramble like nothing imagined. It came down to just weapons and ammo. No supplies. I remember thinking everyone was gonna die. I remember thinking, this was the last day."

"You were in the marines, right?"

"Yep."

Nikki takes her pack of cigarettes from her bag. She pulls one free. Lights it and takes a long pull. "So how you feelin' about aliens?" she asks then exhales.

"I'll get back to you on that. We have company."

Ms. Swarthy, all one point eight meters of her, enters her office. We look up at Anton. She tosses her goggles onto her silver desk.

Nikki passes the file to me. I secure it as she stands to greet our host.

"Thanks again for this, Anton." Nikki says. She gives Anton a quick peck on the cheek.

"Please, it's my pleasure," says Anton. Then Anton shoots a quick glance at me as she sits down at her desk. She does not lose her smile as she looks me over, but for some reason, I don't feel the love.

Anton turns on the TV. "Here, have a look at this. Your vehicle is being sought yet the driver does not seem to be either of you. Isn't that strange?"

The thin face of a woman wearing rimless square cut glasses, with a coffee-with-cream complexion and fine blonde hair that brushes her shoulders materializes in the large office window, eclipsing the view of the chop shop. The word "ALERT" appears in shocking red letters to the left of the newscaster's lovely head. The *Telesur* logo appears in the lower right hand corner of the screen.

The pretty announcer displays her clean white teeth and says, "National Security officials issue this ALERT AND SEIZURE warrant for this vehicle and the occupants."

My mot replaces the newscaster's face. ALERT AND SEIZURE flashes on the screen next to my vehicle.

The face of a man in his mid-twenties with short brown hair and pleasant off-center smile, accented with sterling white teeth, appears on the screen. The newscaster says, "An ALERT AND CAPTURE warrant has been issued for this man. He is the owner and suspected driver of the vehicle. He is wanted for the murders of six officers and arson. He is accompanied by an unknown woman with dark hair."

"I thought you said you didn't kill them," Nikki whispers

to me.

"I didn't kill them. Bolt strikes don't kill. Perhaps they died in the fire that you set."

Nikki nods, asks, "So who's the guy with the bright white teeth driving your mot?"

"He's my cousin."

"He's cute," she says. I see Anton nod in agreement.

"Next time I see him, I'll let him know he's got fans," I reply. Truth is, it's not my cousin. It's my business associate in drag. She was nice enough to do it for me because I don't photograph well.

A picture of my mot displays at the right of the split screen. The faux picture of me appears below it. The blonde newscaster continues, "This is an open call to international recovery agents, as well as licensed Model Citizens of Manhattan and the EC Commonwealth. Reward yet to be determined but guaranteed. Be on the lookout for this man and this mot. A woman with dark hair may still be traveling with this man. Unknown if she is a hostage or an accomplice. Exercise caution with both individuals. Suspects are wanted for questioning. To collect reward, suspects must be delivered alive and in good health. Freelancers will face jail time and harsh penalties for undue harm and death to suspects. Freelancers do not interfere with police or recovery agents in the commission of arrest. You may qualify for partial compensation of reward if you can conclusively demonstrate you provided positive assistance before, or during the arrest."

Nikki turns away from me, and sashays over to the sexy, over-tanned and oily Anton. She asks, "So, Anton, how long before our new mot is ready?"

"Soon." Anton looks me in the eyes. "And yes, you can trust me not to screw you."

"Thanks for the assurance," I reply, calm, meeting her stare. I don't believe her.

The blonde newscaster continues, "Earlier today in midtown Manhattan, evangelical extremists toting homemade flame throwers attempted to burn Underground patrons. The police rapidly foiled the heinous scheme without injury. The treacherous act was attempted at six UG gates in the thirty-fourth street area. All terrorists have been captured. Authorities want to assure the public that the Underground is safe.

"In Middle East news, for the second time in the history of the Orthodox Church of Jerusalem, Rawhi Arafatti, a Palestinian, is elected as the head bishop, or more accurately, the Orthodox Patriarch of Jerusalem. Insiders note that the results of the election are due to the absence of Greek clergy in Jerusalem which can be traced back to Israel's reluctance to renew the visas of many of the Greek ordained. 'We are now ghosts in our own home,' stated Theophilus V.

"Today's financial highlight remains Mkeyinc. It closes at eight-point-six percent, for a gain of seventy-three cents. This is the forty-seventh straight day that Mkeyinc has averaged a seven percent increase. The high realized two weeks days ago at thirteen percent due to gossip that gold had been detected on One Ceres. This amazing rally buoys the markets to another single day record gain. Across the global boards nearly twelve billion shares changed hands. This is Telesur international news and I'm Maria de Vernala. We'll be back in thirty."

"Best insider stock tip I ever exercised. Space is the market," Anton says as she turns off the TV. The east wing of the chop shop returns to view. The sweaty crew works hard converting stolen vehicles into pre-owned luxury driving opportunities.

#

I hear a soft, dull ping. I see Anton tap her earpiece and nod. She turns to us as she taps her earpiece again. "We're good, kids," she says as she heads for the trailer door.

As we exit the trailer my nose is assaulted by the acrid scent of something akin to burnt hair and baked cat piss. Nikki's face tells me that the stink has hit her like a brick as well.

"What the hell?" Nikki utters as she raises her shirt up to cover her nose and mouth.

"Unfortunately, we work with a lot of gases. Cutting metal and such, it is a stinky business," Anton replies with a smirk and light shrug.

We walk in a straight line, through the thick of the renovated mots. I almost walk right by my mot. I've had it for better than five years and I didn't even notice it until I was right up on it. It is a sixty-four Ono-Wong Series Eight. A slim, all muscle two-seater with a massive trunk. It had been midnight blue. Now it was a neat silver-tone. And it was more than just a paint job, they modified the body with a touch of old school class.

"Anton – this is my mot, right?"

"Oh yeah. I thought you were going to walk right by. Good eye."

"I love the tail fins."

"Good, good. My touch. They're coming back in style."

"I know. Man – this is sweet. Nice job."

"Thank you. A satisfied customer is the sound I live for."

"So we're good?" I ask Nikki. I open the passenger side door for her.

"Yeah, I covered the cost," she says.

"Thanks again, Anton. Take care," Nikki says with a light wave.

"You too, Nikki. And don't be a stranger."

Nikki gets in the mot. I shut her door.

Anton unplugs the mot and sets the power jack into the catch.

I nod to Anton as I round the front of the mot. She nods back, turns and walks away.

Suddenly Nikki pops into view …

Anton whips around, as if on fire, her hands going up to her neck. Anton stares at me with eyes wide and blazing, her jaws shut tight. I can almost feel her teeth grinding. Her body is rigid and yet she trembles, as if her skeleton is set to vibrate and it has just received an incoming call. Then her eyes close and she drops to the ground like a stone.

I look to my left; Nikki is getting back into the vehicle.

I get into the mot.

I tap Go on the dashboard.

"What did you do to her?"

"I shot her with a gevva dart."

I look toward the garage. I see two bodies rushing out the

back door. No other movement.

Nikki follows my gaze. "Don't worry about the crew. No loyalty here. They were gone with their tools before Anton hit the ground."

Not entirely true, but true enough. I stare at Nikki with solid consideration. She is trustworthy but is also fucking problematic. "You scrambled her brain. Damn woman – how long were you planning this? Do you walk around with gevva darts out of habit?"

"Out of habit, no. I came prepared today."

"What, you got one of those planned for me as well?"

"Of course not. Relax."

We sit in silence for a moment. It's about an hour from sunset. I glance over at Nikki and say. "You know that smell that knocked you out back at Anton's place?"

Nikki nods. "Yeah, what was that?"

"River. She was running a drug lab as well as a chop shop."

"And you know about drug labs, how?"

"I'm a detective, Love. I also have friends in low places."

A minute later, I park the mot, about two clicks from Anton's chop shop.

I pull out my digital bug check. I open the mot's door and step out.

"What's that and where you going?" Nikki asks. She opens her door and gets out of the mot.

"It's a FIG. I'm looking for bugs. You know, tracking devices."

"You think Anton turned us out?"

"I trust her as much as you did."

She pulls out a cigarette pack from her coat pocket. Yet, it was no cigarette she ejects from the pack. Nikki lights the joint with relish. She offers it to me. I decline.

"That's right, you're working on keeping me alive. Not a good idea to have you trippin'. Silly girl." She takes another hit.

I have full bars on the FIG as I near the trunk. I open the trunk.

"Find something?"

"I think so." I sweep the empty trunk. A green light appears as I hold the FIG at the upper left of the trunk. I don't see anything. I run my hand over the fabric and feel a bump.

Nikki hands me a penknife. "You have the cleanest trunk I've ever seen." She takes a hit from her joint.

"I travel light. Can't say the same thing about you. Gevva darts, penknife, vial of kerosene." I cut through the fabric, exposing the small gray device. I remove it. I check the FIG. The trunk is clean. I give Nikki her knife back. I hold onto the bug.

Nikki and I get back in the mot and drive away.

I stop next to a parked delivery mot. "Would you do the honors?" I ask. I hand the bug to Nikki.

She takes the bug and steps out of my mot. The dashboard monitor captures Nikki as she attaches the bug to the underside the delivery mot's bumper. She returns to the mot.

We continue down the avenue as legion of *personals* scan us, then display items they know we want.

I pull out my flash drive and insert it into the port on the dashboard.

The menu pops up and I select address book, logistics, security and music. Then press add. I reclaim the flash drive a moment later, when the task is completed.

Nikki's seat swivels towards the rear of the cabin, she reaches for her backpack. She opens it and removes her chrome laptop.

The familiar, *ding*, as the computer awakens. Nikki's link to the world is ready to serve but a second later, "Damn, that's right, we're not on the grid," she says, annoyed.

"No. You'll have to pirate."

"Yeah, I'm on it."

"My I ask what you're doing?"

"Booking us a hotel room in the city. Unless you want to leave Manhattan."

"No. Let's stay in the city."

"I hope you're not averse to luxury."

"Bring it on."

"You got it. Five-stars comin' at ya. The Bombay Plaza on CP West."

"Nice. I could use a massage."

"Stone, Swedish, Shiatsu, tantric or other?" Nikki asks.

"What?"

"What type of massage?"

I think about. "Stone," I reply.

"Oh. What's that like?"

"Never had a stone massage before," I say. "I know it involves heated stones and deep muscle work."

"Well, you'll have to tell me about it. I'm going for the Pamper Me Well option. Three hours of bliss."

"That sounds dangerous," I reply with a smile.

Accept Destination pops up on the dashboard. I press the walking man icon. The countdown clock appears on the dashboard. "We'll be there in under four minutes," I advise Nikki.

"Good. Our room is ready now."

The phone beeps. It's Liz. I tap the talk icon. Liz's pretty face pops into view on the mot's windshield. "Hello Liz."

"Hi boss. So, you all right? I just turned on the TV and there's an alert and –"

"Seizure post for me and the mot. I know. I'm good. Got a new mot. And I'm using my last active matrix code so I need you to write a few new shadows for me."

"Will do. Anything else?" She looks calm.

"You good to talk?"

"Of course. I just got worried and all when I saw the report. No calls or visits from law enforcement as to your health and welfare."

"Good. Run a background check on one, Ezra ..."

I look to Nikki and without missing a beat she states, "Biconeer. Twelve forty-one Greene Street, Brooklyn.

I look at Liz and say, "We're very interested in his health and welfare."

"You got it." Then Liz asks, "Is there anything that our new client needs?" Liz smiles as she looks at Nikki.

"No, she's good."

"Very well." She hangs up and fades from view, replaced by the city.

"How long has she been with you?" Nikki asks.

"Close to three years. Liz is good people. And she's a great partner."

"So she knows who I am? I actually have a file? I'm a *client*." She made the word sound ugly.

"Easy. That's business. You know the drill."

She lights a cigarette.

I could use one of those right about now. I pull out my pack. Get a smoke and light it. I take a slow drag.

Nikki turns on the music. A preset program appears on the windshield.

"I'm talking about the loss of human rights. This is a real issue! How can..." Nikki turns the channel.

"No talk radio. Let's dance." Nikki dials in 990. I recognize the station logo. WBMB – The Bomb!

It's late afternoon so kids are rushing home from school. Adults are rushing home from work. Bars are packed with people who just want to unwind. The Bomb's motto is Blast Away the Day! The franchise is built around Fabulous Athena DJ. She is always live from some trendy bar. She just shows up unannounced and rocks the joint for a few hours.

"Hey dance whores! I'm Fabulous Athena DJ. And someone's knocking at my door! Why it's the loveable Kim Ace! Looks like Kim's in love. Her new one is called, 'Minute Mouse Wants Some Candy'. Stomp to this one, kiddies!" Fabulous Athena DJ commands her audience. And Nikki is her audience. The song is bubble gum break beats and slap candy guitar hooks with inane sugary haikus screeched from untrained vocal chords.

Nikki is bouncing in her seat, car dancing, and smoking her cigarette with purpose.

I think my ears are bleeding. Yet due to the hours of torture training issued by the marines, I can endure this manically musical assault.

We pull into the roundabout of the Bombay Plaza. Two valets approach my mot and open the doors for Nikki and I.

"I can't believe you like that dance crap," I say to Nikki.

"I like to dance, Apollo. I like being alive."

We stroll along the purple carpet walkway then stop dead in our tracks. We look up in awe at the renowned Swarovski crystal double doors. The brilliant entrance is a four point two meters by six meters wide dedication to magnificent craftsmanship. At this distance from the great entrance, the hidden spotlights highlight a three meters by three meters delicately etched impression of the Swarovski icon, the resting swan. After a moment, we take one step forward and the Swan icon is no longer visible. It remains undetectable to the naked eye as we pass through the slowly, auto-opening (don't touch the crystal!), double doors.

The lobby is a deep, quiet, sophisticated landscape. Seamless construction marry a wall of virgin white turquoise to gleaming floors of gold-veined black marble. The open room is well lit but the light source is not visible. On the south wall, a shelf juts out just off center, lower left frame. A single orchid rests within a thick glass vase. A single fat air bubble suspended lower left of center mars the vase. One Wenson-designed couch placed alone in the south quarter of the lobby. To my knowledge Wenson has only designed nine couches. I estimate that item's worth at about two millions dollars.

"This lobby is beautiful," Nikki says.

"Yeah." I reply. I point to the wall. "What's with the painting?"

Set high on the north wall is a large and infamous oil painting. A stark realized perspective of a pair of bloodied feet walking upon the restricted Glass Shore. The glass is cracked beneath the cut and bleeding feet as sea foam rushes over the crystallized ocean rim.

"I noticed that. I thought ownership of any rendition of that event, especially the video, would land you in jail. I'll ask the concierge when we check in."

I nod.

"Oh, I only booked one room." she states with a sexy pout of her full lips, as strands of thick hair rake her pixie face. She steps to the front desk.

"Karen Davenport," Nikki says to the smiling clerk behind the teak counter.

"Hello Ms. Davenport. One moment please," says the clerk as she consults her registry. She taps on her keypad.

Two keycards eject from a thin slot in the counter top.

"Thank you Ms. Davenport," the clerk says with a warm smile.

"What's with the painting?" Nikki asks. And since it's the only painting in the lobby, Nikki doesn't' have to point to it or say anything else.

The clerk looks at Nikki, never loses her smile or grace as she answers. "The management understands the Administration's views regarding that tragic event."

"And?" I say, waiting.

"There is nothing more to say, sir. Enjoy your stay at the Bombay."

"Thank you," Nikki and I say in off-unison.

"Creep," Nikki says as we walk to the elevators. "What the hell?"

"This hotel must be owned by a strong corporation. You pay for privacy when you buy a room here. I didn't know that about the Bombay."

"What do you mean?" Nikki says. A lift arrives. We step in. Nikki inserts her hotel key into the slot, then, removes the card. A moment later, the doors close and the lift ascends.

I say, "The management of this hotel displays that painting, to me, it states they are obvious opponents of Gliddin's party. So you can imagine they would get harassed all the time by federal agencies over any minor thing. So where other hotels buckle under the pressure of fines for failure to comply, I bet this business is reticent to allow their guests to be bugged. They can afford the fines."

She nods in agreement, then, says, "Twenty-seven hundred

a night for our room."

The car stops and we get off. Our room is about a dozen steps from the elevator.

Nikki waves the key card before the door. The door zips into the wall slot without so much as a whisper. The lights ease on.

"Welcome Karen Davenport and friend." Announces the warm female VOD. Nikki winks at me; then enters the suite.

"Hello VOD. Play dance program," Nikki says. A heartbeat later, drum and bass erupts from hidden speakers. Fabulous Athena DJ, the Dance Whore, blasts her way into our hotel room.

"Hallelujah" – it's raining men!" Nikki sings out. Then starts this frenetic, aerobic fit that hurts to watch. I sigh and enter the exclusive nightclub. The door shuts behind me.

"The door is now secure." VOD pleasantly states.

Next time, I book the room. I program the music. I bet she already ordered dinner.

"Room service awaits your attention." VOD announces with genuine cheer. "Shall I open the door?"

I turn to Nikki but she has lighted another joint and is busy kicking up the natty carpeted floor. I turn back to the door.

"Yeah, open up." I say.

"Thanks, friend." VOD replies.

The door opens. A young man stands holding a tub with ice and two Champagne bottles. "C'mon in." I say.

The steward walks over and sets the tub in a gold wire pedestal. He turns to me with a smile. "Will there be anything else, sir?" His PayBay hangs from a thin silver cord attached to his belt, and he is about to present it to me to swipe my Lifecard, but I hand him fifty in cash.

"Thank you sir," he says with a polite, fat smile. "Don't have to report this. Very cool. Let me know if you need anything at all. My name is Dave."

"My pleasure, Dave."

The young man leaves the suite with a bounce in his step. The door shuts with his departure. "The door is now secure," VOD states with pleasant assurance.

"Thank you, VOD."

"You're welcome."

I grab a Champagne bottle. It's a Dom Pérignon Rose 99. Ouch. This is pricey. I grab the other bottle, a Bollinger RD Brut – the blue label. Another colossal price tag. I can't help but smile as I hold a few grand in booze.

"Are my WHORES sweatin' yet?" screams Fabulous Athena DJ. "I'm gonna give you two seconds to find and finish your drinks. And girl in the blue dress, put your titties back in. Time's up! Get wild buckaroos!" The beat changes, still thumping bass but less chaotic chops. I take advantage of the moment.

"Oh dance whore – you wanna drink?" I hold up the champagne.

"Hell ya!"

I choose the '88 Brut. I pop the top and pour two glasses. I drop the bottle back in ice then walk over to a sweaty Nikki. She smiles at me and stops popping about like a manic cheerleader.

"VOD, play program Miles Davis, please." Nikki says, and just like that, Dance Whore is out and *'So What'* is on.

"Thank you," I say.

"You're welcome." VOD and Nikki say in unison.

Nikki and I laugh and then toast VOD.

Nikki collects her backpack and walks over to the mini office. She removes the files and sets them in a pile. She opens her laptop. Her fingers dance over the keypad. She grabs her phone and begins taking pictures of the files.

She pats the chair next to her. "Have a seat," she says.

I sit. Sip champagne.

"I'm scanning the docs."

"Yeah I got that." I pick up the manila file folder. As I shift the folder in hand, my fingers detect a ripple on the back of the folder. I inspect both sides of the back panel. Something is there. A disc? I tear at the back panel but can't find a way to free the thin disc.

"What's up?" Nikki asks.

"I believe it's a disc but I can't work it free."

Nikki looks on, then, "I know what you need." She stands up and walks across the room.

I continue to fiddle with the disc. I can't figure out how the damn thing is attached.

Nikki returns. She holds out her fist. I open my palm and she drops an ice cube in my waiting hand.

"Oh yeah?" I query as I study the ice cube, like it's my first encounter with ice.

"Yeah. Ezra liked science. Rub it over the area and you'll see." She has a modest sip of champagne.

I rub the ice cube over the disturbance in the folder. The cold and wet initiate a rapid change. The disc is visible within a few seconds. In no time, the disc peels away from the back panel of the folder.

"Voilà," Nikki says.

"Abracadabra right back at ya." I hold the clear disc up for inspection. "How was it secured to the folder?"

She shrugs her shoulders. "I have no clue but I know Ezra could tell you. I just remember that trick from a long time ago."

"Well didn't you ask him about it a long time ago?"

"Yeah, but every new thing I learn pushes something old out."

"Right. You know there are medications that would alleviate that problem."

"I'm sure there are," she replies as she inserts the disc into her laptop.

It takes a long time for her unit to recognize the disc.

Nikki lights a cigarette, then sits on my lap. We get cozy and watch the monitor.

The program starts. It's a chambered conference. The camera's POV is center, level, atop a dark and polished wooden table. Four men sit on the left side of the table, facing a bank of six wall monitors. Only two monitors are on and one of those monitors has the US presidential seal below it.

The running time stamp reads: 2062 – July 15th. 11:41 EST.

Neat white letters appear at the bottom frame of the monitor:

War Room-Pentagon. Washington D.C. In attendance via vidcom from the Oval Office, Theodore Cresthaven, President of the United States of America. In attendance, via vidcom, NADD

Commander Col. Paul Gliddin (former USAF). Live attendants: Defense Secretary, Ashton Greene; National Security Advisor, Admiral Gene Orison (USN); Security Council Pro-Chief, General P.G. Bradshaw (Army), C.G. Thorosen, Special Consultant to the President.

The text disappears, save the time stamp: 2062 – July 15th. 11:43 EST.

General Bradshaw smokes a cigar.

"What's our status?" asks the President.

"Well, Mr. President, I'd like to begin by stating that protocol for this type of event was followed to the letter. We are still in the process of ascertaining what happened," replies Orison. Admiral Orison is built like a fire hydrant, short, stout and hard. He has a simple face that supports his round, thick wire-rim glasses. He wears a thin mustache. His curly hair is cropped close. He sighs as he leans back in his chair.

"We fired a nuclear missile at a UFO," states an angry President. "Nuclear weapons are not protocol for engagement with extraterrestrials. Is that not the vid-clip I just watched? Is that not the fact, Colonel Gliddin?"

"Yes, sir, that is a fact," Gliddin replies. "But it was a small nuke, Mr. President. Not big enough to do this type of damage, sir."

"It was a nuke. What the hell is the difference between large and small?" counters the President.

General Bradshaw exhales a thick cloud of smoke then speaks, "Sir, with all due respect, there is a distinct functional application regarding nuclear weaponry and contact with advanced beings. The UFO had penetrated our air space. At that moment it became a prime threat. Nukes are approved for prime threats. The weapons we used in this incident were class double-c missiles, designed for this type of engagement." General Bradshaw states with raw certainty. He places his cigar in his mouth, rolling it about with his thin, dry lips. Bradshaw is a big and ugly man. I'm guessing he stands a few fists shy of two meters in height and his stocky frame probably weighs in at two hundred kilos. Much of his mass is tight and hard. Clean shaven head and face; his face is pitted and weathered like aged quarry granite. He has a flat, button nose and thick jowls and heavy baggage under the eyes. He takes a long pull from his cigar, then, exhales a long thin stream of smoke.

"We destroyed something obviously intent on doing us harm. Real Time records show the bogey radically altered its trajectory and made a beeline for North American airspace and soil," Bradshaw says.

Defense Secretary Greene speaks right on the heels of Bradshaw. "Sir, a little FYI concerning the blast site at Puget Sound, Bangor, Washington. We had the most advanced nuclear base in the world at that location. The reactors that power our naval and space fleet were built there. We also stored experimental weaponry as well as conventional ordinance at the Sound."

Silence. Greene looks at Orison. Orison sighs. They both look at Bradshaw.

General Bradshaw takes a long pull from his stogie. He seems more concerned with the state of his cigar than the state of emergency that convenes this Security Council.

Orison picks up his water glass and has a quick sip. He sets the glass back on the table with a nervous thud.

Hard silence as the President considers the facts.

"Give me the damage report, Greene," says President Cresthaven.

Defense Secretary Ashton Greene is a tall and slender man, and I would say, cut from wood. He sits rigid and straight, at a perfect ninety-degree angle. His entire body is made of acute angles. His ash blonde hair is neat. He fills his water glass with prim control. Greene has a calculated drink of water as he consults his computer. He speaks with a stern and direct voice.

"Aerial photography indicates a blast site of one hundred and sixty kilometers in circumference. No standing buildings or trees within the blast site. Floodwaters reach approximately twenty-four kilometers inland. Severe earth tremors reported in Alaska, California, Montana, Idaho, Oregon, Utah, Nevada and Western Canada." Greene lights a cigarette. He has a short drag from his smoke then continues his assessment.

"We're waiting for the Edge team to evaluate the situation. Once we're clear, we'll send in rescue squads and such." Greene taps the end of his pen on the tabletop as he reads the monitor.

"But, that won't be for another three or four days." Greene steals a short hit from his smoke as he looks at General Bradshaw.

Greene looks at C.G. Thorosen, perhaps for support or advice. Carroll Gaylord Thorosen is a tall man, built like a reed, perhaps devoid of bones. Thinning silver hair that suggests old age but his skin is tight with a healthy glow. It's clear he began taking advantage of rejuvenation therapy late in life.

"Mr. President, I suggest we work on a cover story to sell to the international community, as well as the home front," says Greene.

"Well no kidding. I'm not telling the world we fired on a UFO with nuclear missiles. The truth is not an option," the President states. "Is my Security Council withholding information from me?"

"No sir, we don't know what happened – but we're damn sure going to find out," says Bradshaw firmly. He stares at Thorosen.

"We're forgetting a very important event that coincides with this disaster." Thorosen says with a flat voice.

"Which is?" Bradshaw asks for the group. And I have a feeling he knows what Thorosen is about to say.

"The maiden voyage of Mkeyinc's commercial space flight. The *Apricot Wind* is a nuclear powered vessel, carrying forty-five passengers and eleven crewmembers. I just checked NAAD's log and its signature has gone."

Silence.

"Jesus." The president hisses. "Dale was on that flight! Ah hell!" Then, confused and angry, "Is that what you thought was a UFO?" he asks.

"No sir," replies Greene. "We were just so caught up with the ground disaster that we forgot about the space flight."

"Satellites do in fact confirm three flight signatures in the strike zone. Other countries also have this data as well. If they don't know already, everyone will soon realize that we sent an interceptor to investigate an errant signature in the atmosphere. What we call a UFO," Colonel Glidden says.

"Most believable scenario for us to present at this time is that a meteor struck the Apricot Wind, and our interceptor, then struck the sensitive military installation on the ground," Greene offers.

The President speaks with concentrated anger. "I'm not going to say anything that half-ass. A cosmic eight ball shot into the corner pocket. C'mon Ashton – we can do better than that."

Greene shrinks into his leather chair after the harsh chafing from Cresthaven.

Thorosen, the silver-haired sage, speaks with solid resolution. "Terrorists hijacked the Apricot Wind and aimed the commercial spacecraft directly at the base at Puget Sound. We sent Jump One to intercept the spacecraft with the intent to shoot down the Apricot Wind but that was unsuccessful. God called a few more heroes home today. You can sell that Mr. President." Thorosen lights a cigarette then exhales a wisp of smoke.

"How are you going to account for the third signature in the atmosphere?" Greene asks.

"Give my staff time to gather information and we'll provide the truth," Thorosen replies with a curt clip.

"Make it a simple story." Cresthaven instructs Thorosen. "Don't make it too involved. Brief and informative. We can amend it in time with new information. The press conference is in ten minutes. I need copy in five minutes so I can prepare. Goddamn, my vice-president is dead."

The President glances down and away from the vid-com. Perhaps he is studying at his notes. Perhaps he's just staring at the wood grain of his table.

Then he looks directly into the vid-com and says, "I'll also need the latest damage reports including projected death count and economic loss. Detail the environmental destruction with special care to future restoration. Cresthaven out."

The presidential monitor goes black. Even though Cresthaven had not physically been in the room, his presence had not been diminished by distance; his exit creates a cold emptiness in the chamber. The four live men (and Gliddin on a monitor) sit in silence and do not look at one another.

"After a respectful moment, Gliddin looks straight ahead and says, "Thanks C.G. I told Claire to send Allison all the details."

"Yeah, Allison just pinged me. Well, all said and done, that went better than expected," says Thorosen with a loose smirk. He opens his laptop and begins to type…

Nikki's monitor blinks. The screen goes black and the laptop spits out the disc. Nikki grabs the disc the immediately secures the disc in her bag.

"Of course at the time, fourteen years ago, Gliddin had been the Principal Share Owner of NAAD," she says.

"He still is PSO of NAAD," I remind her.

"Yeah I know. And now he's the President and his entire Security Council is made up of his defense contractor cronies and a few banker buddies."

Silence. Nikki and I study the floor, the walls, each other, as we try to make the tiny marbles fit into the tiny holes. The thought jumps upon me like a hungry animal. I try to evade but it's faster than I can counter.

"Dollars and cents," I say to Nikki. "NAAD is a defense contractor, a subsidiary of Mkeyinc. The truth is a PR nightmare for the parent company. So retool the truth with fear and logic and we get terrorists hijacking a Twilight Jet, a spacecraft utilizing nuclear thermal propulsion, and using that vehicle as a weapon. This story clears the government and NAAD of fault and makes Mkeyinc a business martyr. The story is so tight that to question it is unthinkable. The government then offers a form of disaster relief to Mkeyinc, granting exclusive no bid contracts to rebuild, reforest, to re-construct the devastated property."

Nikki looks at me, waiting. Stress lines scratch her brow.

"Mkeyinc holds charters of incorporation for hundreds of cities," I say. "They provide security for the whole of the Pacific Northwest especially the Glass Shore. The company sets and regulates the standards for the industries of removal and storage of radioactive debris, soil decontamination, water cleansing and reforestation. It's been going great for Mkeyinc."

Nikki finds her cigarettes. She lights one real quick and takes a short pull. "Are you thinking Mkeyinc *created* the UFO? The company *created* the situation?" she asks.

I nod. "You know as well as I that aliens are BS. Most space stations operate as research and training centers, as well as commercial construction facilities. Build separate units of the *UFO* at separate facilities. Join those parts at another facility and launch."

She looks at me. Speechless. That lasts for a moment. "This is fucked up," she mutters.

"What the hell are you going to do with this information?".

"I have no clue," she responds to the wall. Her voice is tiny.

"Blackmail Gliddin? What would you ask for?"

She ignores my question then asks, "Who the hell is Thorosen? I want to find out about this guy. He's the one that creates the *terrorists*."

"Like you said at Anton's, terrorists were comforting. Something you could understand. I think that had to be the cover story from the start. Mkeyinc owned the Apricot Wind and NADD also belongs to them. Yet it feels that the situation got out of control. Gliddin shouldn't have used the nukes."

Nikki smokes her cigarette. At length, she says, "That disc will open the door to a massive investigation. Yet everyone will concentrate on the UFO. That will blind the conversation. The flightlog is evidence that Jump One acted on orders. The disc proves that NADD acted in the best interest of the country," she looks at me. "We have to prove that Mkeyinc constructed and launched the UFO."

I knew she was going to say that.

"I feel like a shower," she says with a devious smile. Nikki heads for the bathroom.

"Yeah, I'm feelin' dirty too."

I grab the champagne bottle.

We laugh and giggle and tickle our way to the bedroom. The grandeur of the bedroom causes our play to pause. The bed is huge, rectangular and from the looks of it, comfortable as hell. The floor is covered in a plush, white carpet. We kick off our shoes and wiggle our toes in the luxurious shagpile carpet. I walk over to the mirrored (*Twinkle*) wall and push the down arrow on the control panel to decrease the window tint until the Hudson River and New Jersey cliffs beyond come into the view. River traffic is heavy, as usual. I finish my drink. As I refill my glass, I stare at our reflections in the mirrored closet door. In the reflection, I see Nikki waving her free hand at me as she downs her champagne. She then raises her empty glass. I walk over and fill it up.

#

I slip my socks off. Shed my pants and shorts and shirt with urgency.

I step into the bathroom and find Nikki pin-up-posing by the shower, wearing a black lace bra and black panties.

She turns the shower on. I float over and beg for a kiss. And being a good doggie, I get a tiny peck on the lips. It's a touch of a fluffy cloud, a nectar tease.

Nikki slips off her bra. I kiss her nipple, and then she shimmies out of her panties. We step into the deep tub and stand beneath real falling water. I grab her thighs and lift her off the floor, her back pressed against the wall. Our breathing is shallow, speeding hearts with a perfect sense of harmony. A soft kiss turns into a hard kiss and then she bites my lower lip. That deserves payback so I enter hard and drive into her. Nikki grunts and squeezes and I continue to pound her flesh as the water rains over us, warm and clear and blessed like the rivers of Babylon.

"C'mon boy," she says in a hushed voice.

And that voice almost sets me off. I fight not to enjoy this moment and it's like a razor slashing the psyche. Denial is unbearable, vicious, and I drink in the resistance. I steal a kiss. Then say, "You're so damn beautiful."

We hold tight and kiss light.

She tastes of fruit. It's like having a perfect red apple melt in your mouth. I press for more.

"Your personal consignor is at the door," VOD states.

We both laugh and Nikki says, "Take a message."

"Security override. Personal consignor entering," VOD, says.

"What?" I stammer. Start to think and that just screws up the entire game.

Nikki looks at me ... inelegance turns to irritation, which twists into anger. We disengage.

I turn off the shower and slide the glass door aside to find our personal consignor standing there.

"Hello Dave," I say and note the worry on his face. "What's up?"

"Yeah... sorry..."

"Get on with it," I command.

"Right. I was advised, indirectly from management, that there's some interest from law enforcement regarding this room. I suggest you use the stairs when you leave. Just go down one level. Then take elevator four. That will take you to the garage. I also took the liberty of securing your mot key." Dave sets the key on the countertop.

"Why are you helping us?" Nikki speaks at Dave through a thin sheet of opaque glass. Dave does his best to address me but his eyes keep wandering to her silhouette.

"It is the policy of management that the customer comes first. I suggest you get going. Peace."

He leaves.

"How do you think they tracked us here?" Nikki asks. "Are you sure you found all the bugs?"

"Yeah, the mot is clean," I reply and step out of the shower. I grab the towels and hand one to Nikki.

Dry as we'll ever be, we rush into the bedroom. We speed dress.

"What if Anton gave us up before I scrambled her brain?"

"Possible. Of course, that means they know what we're driving. The mot is useless to us now."

Nikki gathers up the files. She secures her bag.

We hit the hallway hot and ready to mess up someone's day. I like sex. Nikki likes sex. We both want to meet some opposition right about now so we can express our dissatisfaction.

We reach the stairwell without incident. There are cameras in the stairwell. I see the red light wink out.

"Nikki, they turned off the cameras."

"How do you know?"

"I saw the red light turn off."

"The damn place is worth every penny. But I was really looking forward to that Pamper Me deal."

"I promise I'll pet and pamper you later."

"I'll hold you to it."

The security door opens on the lower level. We enter and head fast for the elevators.

We enter car four. Remain silent for the duration of the short ride.

We reach the garage floor. The door slides open and we enter a quiet, bright and expansive parking lot.

"Let's take our chances with the mot," I say.

Nikki doesn't argue with me. Nor does she have a hard time keeping pace with me as we run for the mot.

I pull the key from my pocket and point it at the mot. The doors open as the engine hums to life.

Nikki rounds the rear of the mot, heading for the passenger door. I hook a fast left and nearly step into the driver's seat when I feel something akin to a red-hot sledgehammer slam into my back. I pitch forward; my head bounces off the roof of the mot. It's a mighty blow but not crippling. It would have been more severe to a normal man. I spin around and thus catch my assailant by surprise. He stops in his tracks, jaw slack, fear racing in his wide black eyes. He studies his weapon, a Strummer V, and resets it for another strike. He looks up, raising his weapon.

I plant my fist into his nose, crushing cartilage, bone and tooth. He hits the clean concrete deck cold and bloody. I look around and see the only person watching me is Nikki with gun in hand.

"Put that away," I say.

She puts her gun away and gets into the mot.

I grab the motionless assailant by the hair and drag him to the rear of the mot. I open the trunk then think, do I want to question him?

I check his pockets. Find his ID in the left pocket on his suit vest.

Barry Clouts. Licensed Recovery Agent for Commons Territory. No, don't need to talk to this asshole. I drop his skinny ass.

I walk over and pick up the Strummer V. I disengage the trigger then kick aside the spent three-ounce pellet. Going back to my mot. I toss the Strummer V on Nikki's lap. I get into the mot stiff and mad.

We hover out of the parking space. I see Nikki looking out of the window, probably at Barry the recovery agent. I study the monitors, expecting another hit at any moment.

"Is he dead?" she asks.

"No... at least I don't think so."

"So he could wake up and tell the police about us?"

I stop the mot. I reverse the vehicle.

I get out of the mot. I open the trunk. I pick up Barry and put him inside. I get back into the mot.

We drive on.

Holding the Strummer she asks, "How do I use this?"

"The orange button on the right side of the grip activates the pulse. It takes a second to go green. The trigger will literally become green in color. Then just pull the trigger. It fires a three-ounce pellet that can put a normal man on the ground like spilled milk."

"But you're not normal."

"I'm not normal."

"Excellent."

Still, the damned pellet stung like hell. But of course I don't complain. Why break my client's belief that I'm nigh on invincible.

We exit the parking lot without incident. Turn left and ease into the north flow of CPW. I see three police units parked outside of the Bombay Plaza and two units hovering above at twelve meters. The cops don't mark my passage as a big event and I don't give them any reason too.

"So who used to own this and what's it called? Nikki asks as she studies the weapon.

"The weapon is a Strummer V, courtesy of a recovery agent named Barry Clouts. Here's how I figure it. Anton tips Barry to us for a cut of the reward. The guy doesn't want to confront us directly, so he follows our mot. He put the cops on us. Yet, I don't believe he told them about the mot. That was his ace in the hole in case, as we did, we elude the cops at the Plaza. So he stakes out the mot in the garage. And thought he could take us down."

"So with Anton's brain scrambled and this guy in the trunk, we should be free of tags." Nikki says.

I ran it through my mind for a moment, checking the rearview monitor all the time. "Yeah. We should be clear."

"So where we going now?"

"Don't know."

The cops didn't cover the stairs or the garage. Why? I take a right on the next avenue, heading for the outer loop.

"We're going to Brooklyn. I know someone we can trust."

"Good by me." Nikki lights a cigarette. "Who is it?"

"Lynch Alstor, retired military like me. We served together in another lifetime. These days he's a bodyguard for Malcolm Space. Yeah, the one and the same multi-billionaire."

"Nice." She takes a long pull of her cigarette.

Silence: each in our own world as we look at the city.

I call up my address book and drag Lynch's address into the travel bin. I press the walking man icon. *Destination accepted* flashes on the dashboard then blinks away.

Nikki turns on the radio. A pulsing bass and drum riff fills the cabin as a mechanized horn sits on the rhythm as the girls sing, "You're the love rockin' me," over and over, their vocals out-fitted with numerous filters and enhancements.

10

We stare at the Statue of Liberty as we zip over the Brooklyn Bridge. Brooklyn has no mammoth mega-structures of glass and metal like the city. Brooklyn is the headquarters of the mighty-mighty rich. The borough is home for one hundred and six families, the most powerful families on Earth. These people with true, hard money maintain a watchful eye on their brilliant investment, the city of Manhattan.

My mot slows as we approach the checkpoint. Nikki and I look straight ahead. We see the scanner's red eye glow bright then dim and we receive a green light. Beneath the green light, the greeting: Welcome to Brooklyn – Home of the Strong. The mot regains speed as we glide down Cadman Plaza loop.

"I have contacts. How are you cheating the eye scans?" Nikki asks.

"Military enhancements,"

I punch up Lynch's number then tap the talk icon on the dashboard. The phone rings twice before I catch his answering machine.

"This is Lynch. Leave a message."

"Lynch. Apollo."

Suddenly Lynch's face appears on the windshield. "Yo, Apollo. Long time, bro. Talk to me."

"In the neighborhood and thought I'd drop by. Got a friend with me."

"Yeah I see … good. Good. I could use the company."

"I'll be there in five."

"Right."

He hangs up.

"That was a weird conversation." Nikki says.

"Yeah, he's distracted." I say. And, thinking about it, Lynch's demeanor distracts me.

"You still think it's safe over there?"

"Reading minds isn't polite." I say. "I don't believe we're

his problem. We're not the only fugitives in the city. There's no reason for him to suspect us of anything."

"When was the last time you called him?"

"It's been awhile."

"And you don't think he finds a call out of the blue a bit … intriguing?"

"Yeah, I'm sure he does."

"So what's our story?"

"Damn woman, slow down." Sometimes being with Nikki is like hanging out with the business end of a chainsaw.

It takes a moment before a cover story comes to mind. It's a true case that continues to pay for my smooth lifestyle. "We tell him you're hiding from your mob husband."

"Okay, I can easily relate to that."

"Oh yeah?" I look into her beautiful brown eyes.

She doesn't blink. "Yeah, but this is your story, not mine. So please continue."

I nod. "You have proof of his disturbing fetishes. The proof is a thirty-four minute disc, but this disc was culled from hours of footage."

"I like this, keep going."

"You told your gangster husband that you wanted a divorce and not to fight you on it. You took both houses, and you want to get paid without a fuss or the sick disc comes out."

"Do detail the fetishes," Nikki says with a fat smile.

"I'll give you subjects and you fill in the blanks. Black dog. Potbelly pig. Tools."

"Tools?"

"Your mob husband would jerk off using pliers, barbecue tongs, forceps, shall I continue?"

"Who made this disc? Who held the camera is the question?"

"Me. I followed his ass around for about three weeks."

Nikki shakes her head and laughs with glee.

"Of course the gangster husband said he would kill you," I continue. "That's when you tell him you hired someone that's keeping the disc safe. Now my story is, I'm coming to Lynch for a bit of shop talk about this case."

"I like this story. How'd you come up with it so quickly?"

"It's inspired from true events. No names: client

confidentiality and all that jazz."

"Can you tell me if the mob wife is still alive?"

"Yep. Alive and kicking."

"And the husband?"

"He died of natural causes before the divorce was even an issue."

"Right. And you had nothing to do with that."

"Not a thing. Not at all."

She nods, believing me. "I guess the fetish disc is useless."

"No sweetheart, the disc is very vital. Family pride. People love to talk about the dead. The gangster guy and the wife were married for fourteen years and never had children, so now you understand her vitriol. And this mobster has seven brothers. His parents are still alive. His grandparents are still breathing. Memory is all that you leave behind. At lot of wrongs are often forgiven but sexual deviance never is. Once stained, forever marked and the family has to shoulder that burden. People will kill to preserve their image. And the image of a man of honor, influence and strength, a man that made his family's name synonymous with power is worth any price to keep intact."

Nikki nods. "So the ex-wife is still holding the secret over the mobster family. Still getting paid to stay quiet."

"Yep. But only one brother knows the secret, you know more than the family. And I receive a monthly check to keep the disc locked away. To be released if any suspicious harm comes to the ex-wife."

"Such drama."

"Easy money as far as I'm concerned."

#

The neighborhood is quiet. I park under a tall elm tree.

We step out of the mot and into a brisk wind. The sky is soft blue, cloudless and alive with silent traffic. We walk down the sidewalk without being molested by *personals*. I feel a great peace of mind, now free of advertising.

We stop and stand before an outsized red brick townhouse, looking up at the towering French doors made of, I believe, Spanish cedar, with small onyx window and trim. We step up the clean marble steps. Standing on the top landing, Nikki runs her hand along the trim of the doors, enjoying the feel of the wood.

"Real wood. Impressive," she says.

"I understand this home is a job perk."

"Some people…"

I push a small black marbled button inset in the red brick.

Lynch opens the door before I return my hand to my coat pocket. I had forgotten how big a man Lynch is. He is a tall brother, better than two meters, and thick like a slice of mountain. He has short-cropped hair, a smooth cut face and stern lips. No tattoos, body mods or jewelry. He appears calm but his eyes betray a frantic mindset. Something is out of square with Lynch Alstor; that's for damn sure. He invites us into his home with little more than a polite smile and distracted greeting. Still, I step back, open right palm, our hands come together in a semi-grasp, release, then knuckles-to-knuckles, fists to chests. Lynch performs the ceremony as habit, with no emotion. Yet, he isn't quite dead, he smiles as Nikki's ass moves into the next room. She's got a sweet ass.

"So what's up, Lynch?" I ask.

"What's up with you?" he counters. "It's been a long time. What suddenly brings you to the neighborhood?"

"Need a safe house while we figure things out," I say workman-like.

"Yeah?"

"Yeah."

"So what's her story?" Lynch says with a hush as he nods toward Nikki.

"She's under my protection. Her husband is connected and has threatened her life."

"Damn. No matter how pretty they are, somebody is tired of them."

"True enough."

We exit the large foyer and enter the living room. The room has blonde hardwood floors and high ceilings. Expansive bay windows offer an opulent view of the bustling East river, the hectic Kid's Island play park, former Governor's Island. The Statue of Liberty is dwarfed, ant-like, by the massive energized city of glass. Nikki absently sets her messenger bag on the large black sofa as she walks over to the windows. She stands still, looking at Manhattan. Even from here, way across the room, I can see brilliant rainbows and colored flecks flutter and dance about the twin faceted crystal spires of lower Manhattan. The memorial is amongst the tallest structures in the city and the refractive sunlight off the clean crystal sprinkles colors over the city. Unlike the view from within the city, this very handsome panoramic phenomenon is courtesy of not only the density and irregular angles of the glass structures, but also the constant condensation from old hydrogen fuel cells, and the bright blast of the late afternoon sun.

"This is very tony, Lynch. Love the view," I say.

"So do I," he replies.

"It's nice, real nice," Nikki says without looking at us.

The furnishings inside Lynch's home are sparse and efficient, all wood items of retro euro-mod design. On a table by the entry to the kitchen I see his laptop is open. He's checking a personals page.

The sound is near muted but I can still hear the amazing speaking voice of John Terry. His baritone elegance is easy on the ears yet commands your attention. His voice flows from small monitor above the petite yet well-stocked wet bar as he narrates the infamous ninety-four second vid of Thomas Forrestt, the first and only man to walk on the Glass Shore.

"Puget Sound. July fifteenth, two thousand and sixty-two, the murderous bullwhip crack shattered the sound barrier. In that instant planes, birds, trees, flesh, bone, rock, fish, metal, concrete, dirt, candy and love – all things had become undone. In that instant sand was pounded and melted to perfection. Vitrified. Super-cooled. In that instant sand was turned to miles of solid, smooth crystal shoreline."

Upon the monitor is a barefooted man walking over a sheet of smooth virgin glass. Each crunchy step of the walking man cracks the blue-green glass in a spider web pattern beneath his feet. His feet are cut with each step he takes. Bloody footprints upon the cracked glass stretch into the distance. The sea rushes in and away as glass splinters under the feet of purpose, the feet that seem oblivious to pain. A faint and familiar hum rises in the background, slow and swelling into the roar of helicopter rotors. The scene becomes frantic, as bloody feet smash upon the wet and pristine crystal shore. Then all is black.

The scene replays, obviously on a loop. This video has been declared illegal and possession carries a heavy fine, but only in America. The rest of the world has no problem with the video. It's on permanent display in the Louvre. Thomas Forrestt, who is a very old man these days, continues to elude American authorities.

Art is anything you can get away with.

Lynch walks over to a white stone pedestal and opens a small drawer. He then pulls out a pack of cigarettes. He offers one to Nikki. She accepts the smoke. He lights her cigarette then his own.

"I like what you've done with the place," Nikki says.

"Danke."

I take the window of opportunity offered.

"Say Lynch, is your garage free? I need to check out my mot."

"Yeah. It's roomy and clean. Your mot got a knock in the trunk or engine? I ain't got no tools for engine troubles."

"Problem's in the trunk."

"Need help?"

"No. I'm solid."

"Tools for trunk problems are in the bottom drawer of the red cabinet. I'll open the garage door for ya."

"Thanks."

Lynch shows me to the garage entrance. He pushes a small silver button on the wall.

11

I enter the garage and watch the large metal door slide into its housing. On my right, neat rats scurry in a well-kept glass enclosure. Lynch has pet rats. Learn something new every day.

I stand next to Lynch's mot. He owns a brand new, low profile, iridescent maroon Cadillac named, The City. It's a sweet mot. It's even got tail fins.

I tap the yellow button on my car remote. A moment later my mot hovers into the garage and comes to rest next to Lynch's Cadillac.

The garage door zips closed.

I walk toward the rear of my mot and pop the trunk with the remote. I ready myself for Barry to make his move but no sudden attack, or lunge to escape. No shouts, screams or moans. Just silence. I look into the trunk with more than mere concern. Had I killed the man when I punched him in the face? Sometimes I forget my own strength. There's a lot of blood in the trunk. The recovery agent's face is busted and bloody. His nose is broken and his right cheek is a breath away from a sloppy collapse, so much so that his right eye does not set right in the socket. His upper right lip is ripped back, exposing smashed gum and broken teeth. Blood and snot bubbles dot the human face that is now a bad Dali landscape.

I study the movement of his chest, he's breathing. I look around the garage. I don't know what I'm looking for. I guess I'm looking for something that will fix this.

"Damn!" I say as I slap the side of my mot.

A heartbeat later Lynch and Nikki rush into the garage.

"Yo! What up, Apollo? What was that noise? Everything cool? " Lynch says as he takes three big steps to me.

"No, not cool. Looks like I don't have to worry about that knock in my trunk no more," I reply.

Lynch and Nikki look into the trunk. Nikki turns away.

Lynch just nods, inspecting my work with understanding.

"Never strike in anger." Lynch states. "At least he's still alive."

"Yeah." I say like a dummy.

Nikki torches a cigarette. "So you did that with one punch?" she asks between puffs.

I meet her eyes. "Yeah."

"What did he do?" Lynch asks.

"He hit me with a Strummer V."

"So," Lynch replies.

"So the damn thing hurt and it pissed me off so I broke his face."

"Never strike in anger."

"I know the first rule, Lynch."

"You guys have rules?" asks Nikki the snark.

"Yeah, and right about now I'm holding tight to rule one. You read me," I hiss.

She gives me the finger and smokes.

I send her an air kiss.

Lynch runs his forefinger along the bounty hunter's right forearm, his finger stops midway. We can see the pellet.

"That is linked to local and federal authorities." I inform Nikki, answering the question before it's asked. "It's a tracking unit. It will signal the cops the moment he dies."

"Well, we can remove the pellet and insert the seed into one of my rats. Then release that rat in the city," Lynch offers.

"So that's what they're for," I say.

"Okay, that's freaking me out. You've done this type of thing a lot?" Nikki asks.

"Yes," Lynch answers with flat sigh.

"What happens to the rest of the body?" she presses.

"It's disposed of," he says.

"How?"

"It surgical and messy. You don't want details," Lynch ends the conversation.

Nikki shakes her head with clear understanding. She smokes her cigarette and paces about the garage.

"It's an option," I say. Yet, I'm thinking that if I leave now I can dump the body in the boondocks while it's still alive.

"Is this a dolly?" Nikki asks as she points to a flat platform hanging on the near wall of the garage.

"Yeah. I use it to move plants and stuff."

"We're gonna use it now for this problem," she states and removes it from the hook. She walks into open space and sets the thin platform on the floor. She inspects the handle and finds a recessed latch.

"Need a thin blade," she says. "My bag is in the main room."

Lynch walks over to the red metal tool cabinet. He returns a moment later with a slender silver probe, about the size of her forefinger.

Nikki inspects the tool, smiles and says, "Thanks." She looks at me. "Apollo, I need my computer."

"I'm on it." I leave the garage.

I walk into the living room and see Nikki's bag on the black leather sofa. I glance at the TV as I walk over to the sofa and the news story stops me cold. *Breaking News* is in big bold letters at the bottom of the screen. The top right corner of the TV displays a still shot of a hotel door A4T. The title below the door reads *Bombay Plaza, New York*. The very room Nikki and I had scrambled from about thirty minutes ago. The dove white face of a thin woman with perfect fluffy blonde hair occupies the rest of the TV screen. She speaks with a generous mouth full of bright white teeth. "I'm Anne Cannon and you're watching INN. Real news for a real world. This smashing news story, Fury Randell is dead. Her bloody body discovered less than an hour ago in a posh room of the luxurious Bombay Plaza hotel. Ms. Randell's death comes as a shock to the world. Her father, former US president Denson Weller Randell, has offered a twenty million dollar reward for the capture, leading to conviction, for Fury's killer. Unconfirmed sources state that the twenty-four year old *fashionista* was strangled to death. The police are known to be in the process of questioning male model and budding actor, Bobby Grant. He was last seen entering the Bombay Plaza last night accompanied by Fury Randell."

I stare at the TV and realize that Fury's corpse had been in the room while we were there. The cops were not there for Nikki and me, but to check out the room because Fury had been traced there.

Fury Randell was a faux-pretty socialite. She had an ultra thin and shapeless physique complete with an unformed brain. Her father had been an amazing President. He led the charge for space exploration. He increased spending on education. The manufacturing sectors and small businesses returned with vigor on his watch. America was built anew during his eight-year term. He also survived four assassination attempts.

I grab Nikki's bag and return to the garage.

#

I enter the garage and see Lynch looking down at Nikki.

They both turn to look at me as I approach. Nikki has the handle off, exposing the brain of the platform. I pass the canvas bag to her.

"Thank you," she says as she takes the bag from me.

I decide to stay quiet until this task is over.

She pulls her computer from her bag and opens the unit. As it awakens, she fishes around in her bag and pulls out about a half dozen wires with male jacks at each end. Finding the wire with a compatible jack for the platform, she plugs one end of the wire into her computer and the other end into the tiny port on the platform.

"I see you've done this type of thing before," Lynch says.

"Yeah," replies Nikki with a flat sigh and a smile.

Nikki's computer monitor displays the platform's schematic. Nikki types on the keypad. Then the owner information appears on the monitor. Nikki opens a few folders, then deletes the platform's work history and erases Lynch's ID code. She makes St. Mary's General Hospital the owner of the platform and rigs the travel log to show that the platform has always been on site. Then she closes the system.

She disconnects the plugs.

She secures her computer.

Nikki fits the cover back in place on the platform's handle. She engages the platform, setting its dimensions to normal. Which is big enough to support a body.

I get it. I walk over and pick up Barry. I place him on the

platform.

Lynch offers me a thick blanket. I lay the blanket over the recovery agent.

Lynch grabs a clear spray bottle from his workbench. With blue rag in hand, he sprays and wipes clean the exposed metal of the platform. Then he walks over to the far wall and opens the garage door.

Nikki sends Barry to the hospital. The platform exits the garage and turns right on the avenue.

Lynch closes the garage.

"Pretty smart for a mob girl," Lynch says as he places the spray bottle back and rag on the shelf.

"Yeah, who do you think keeps my husband out of jail?" Nikki replies with confidence.

Lynch nods his approval. "Now let's take care of your trunk," he says to me.

We tear out the blood-saturated fabric that lines the trunk.

Lynch wraps the thin bloody carpet in plastic. Then he dumps his messy plastic smock in the same plastic bag as the red stained carpet.

Nikki leans against Lynch's workbench as she smokes a cigarette and watches us work.

Lynch eases up next to Nikki, they share a smile, and he reaches up and grabs the clear spray bottle from a shelf above his workbench. He hands me the spray bottle and I see *Disinfectant* written in black marker upon on it. The plastic bottle feels cool. He tosses a blue rag at me.

I spray the bare metal and find the disinfectant odorless. I wipe away the blood and note it doesn't smear or spread. Even the cleaning rag has only minute traces of blood. I assume the cleanser has tek-mites that consume blood.

Done with the trunk, I set the spray bottle and rag on his workbench. I remove my plastic smock and stuff it into the same plastic bag.

"I'll burn this junk," Lynch states as he secures the plastic bag.

"Let's go get drunk," Nikki says.

"Damn straight," I reply like a shotgun.

"Right, party's on me, but first, I gotta talk to you about something. I got a problem. At first, I thought you were part of the deal. I mean a phone call out of the blue after two years? I found the worst-case scenarios very easy to be true. Yet, this whole thing suggests you have your own problems and I was a last resort."

I nod. Well, I had thought something was wrong with Lynch since that phone call. And here it is.

Lynch pulls out a pack of cigarettes, snaps one free and sparks up.

He exhales then says, "I gotta find a flash drive."

"Oh yeah? You lost it or you want to acquire it?" I ask.

"I lost it."

"I'm with you."

He takes a long drag off his smoke. "I think I know where it is, but getting it back may prove tricky and I can't afford to get dirty on this one."

"Can't negotiate in good faith?" I ask.

"No. If he doesn't know what he has, then ignorance is bliss. But to accuse him of possession would lead to confrontation. I would have to search him, his mot, and apartment. That would not set well with this person. And a heated conversation with this person may force me, as you had earlier, to strike in anger. And you know what happens after that." He rests his hand atop the metal workbench.

Yeah, I got it. I can see that Nikki's up to speed. She's quiet, just smokes and studies us.

"I take it this is a public figure. Well placed and private but would have no problem getting vocal," I say.

He takes a long time with his reply; he smokes, looks me in the eyes.

"He's a well known male model, and he just signed a big movie deal. It behooves him to stay in the closet. The trouble is, his brother is a lawyer and knows of our relationship."

Now I'm the one taking a long time to speak. All I can say is, "Shit."

"Yeah, a big fat-river of it. We were together last night. After playtime, I showered. When I came out, he was gone. I thought nothing of it because that's our usual thing. Then, for some reason, I checked my stuff and that's when I found the flash drive wasn't there. The flash drive is yellow with a metal band. It's very distinctive and one of a kind. The damn thing belongs to my boss. And I'm short on time. Space expects me to give him that flash drive tonight."

"So where does this guy live?"

"Ernest Landing complex on the West Side. End of one hundred and Seventy-fifth Street, apartment six-C."

I know the area. "What if he's not there? Where does he hang out?"

"He likes a bar called *The Hump*. It's at Seventy-second and Mankin."

I let the obvious smart-ass remark go by the wayside. "Let's go have that drink," I say.

We leave the garage with Lynch in the lead.

Nikki pinches my arm behind Lynch's back. I glance at her and receive a wide-eyed 'Holy Jumping Jesus' face.

I respond with raised eyebrows and a half head tilt.

12

We head straight for the small wet bar. I glance up at the monitor above the bar and watch bloodied feet pound upon sea and glass.

In the living room, the TV volume is low but audible and this news is not going away so I don't have to tell Nikki about why the cops were coming to visit us at the Bombay Plaza. The same thin dove-white-faced woman with perfect fluffy blonde hair and a generous mouth full of bright white teeth speaks. "Repeating our top story, Fury Randell is dead. The lifeless body of the daughter of former US President Denson Weller Randell was discovered earlier today at the posh Bombay Plaza hotel. Her father has offered a twenty million-dollar reward for the capture, leading to conviction, of Fury's killer. The police are known to be in the process of questioning male model and budding actor, Bobby Grant. He was last seen entering the Bombay Plaza last night accompanied by Ms. Randell. It is believed they shared the room where her severely beaten and bloodied corpse was found. Ms. Randell was twenty-four." The TV displays a still shot of the door of the murder scene. Room A4T.

Nikki looks at me with an off smile. I nod in return. Okay, she's on track.

I look over to Lynch and see that he's in the grip of a mild panic attack. He doesn't blink and I don't think he's even breathing.

Nikki notes that something is amiss. I see her eyes narrow and her head tilt just a touch. She looks to me with her forefingers interlocked then her eyes dart to Lynch then to the TV.

I confirm her suspicions with a slight nod: Bobby Grant and Lynch are very friendly.

We listen to the newscaster talk about a protest over the removal of the Origin of Man exhibit at the National Museum in DC.

"How you doing, Lynch?" I ask.

"Simply peachy," is his snap fire reply.

At least he's breathing.

Then he asks us, "You two seem to have just shared something. Want to cut me in on the joke?"

"Just a big Fury fan." Nikki says as she lights a smoke. "I envied her shoe collection."

"Yeah. Okay." Lynch replies with a hooked grin. He looks at me. "You got a shoe fetish too?"

"Truth tells, yes. Tall stiletto heels get my dick hard every time."

"I'll remember that," says Nikki with a sharp smile.

"Comedians," Lynch says. He lights a cigarette.

"I'm not joking. Fishnet stockings and high heels and it's a party."

"Buy me a pair of Christian Louboutin's and I'll fuck up your mind," Nikki coos.

"Both of you shut up!" Lynch spits the words at us. He grabs a bottle of whiskey from the rack and spins off the cap. He takes a long swig of the brown liquid.

I reach for the whiskey bottle and Lynch passes it to me. I look at him square as I hit the bottle.

And then it hits me. Bobby Grant is the lover with the flash drive I've been asked to collect. The same Bobby the cops are looking to talk to about Fury's death.

Lynch stares at me. I guess a light bulb is shining above my head. He knows I know that Bobby is his boy. He then glances over Nikki.

Nikki looks at Lynch. Her eyes pull away from him and come to rest on me. Then she searches both our faces. "What'd I do?" she asks.

"Nothing. This is still about the Fury Randell story," I say. I look at Lynch.

"Okay, we lied to you with the 'Damsel in Distress' tale. Just under an hour ago, Nikki and I were in that very room. The room where they found Fury's body."

"And my question is where was her body?" Nikki interjects.

"Well, the rooms are supposed to be cleaned after check out. And they wouldn't have given us the room if someone else had booked it." I say. I take another swig of whiskey and pass the bottle back to Lynch. I don't offer the bottle to Nikki because she's refilling her glass with vodka, straight, no ice or chaser.

"So where was the body hidden that a maid couldn't find it?" I ask.

"The bed was huge," Nikki states. "She could have been under it."

I nod and pushing my point home, I say, "So it comes down to a sloppy housekeeping. It would seem that no one cleaned under the bed or maybe even checked the closets."

I hear an audible beep. I look at Lynch.

He glances at me as she walks away from the bar. "Only one person has this number."

"Space," I state.

He nods. "And I ain't getting none."

Over my shoulder I see Lynch tap the unit in his ear.

Nikki speaks clear and strong. Her breath is sweet. Then I notice her vodka is strawberry-infused. "It's only a matter of time before they place us in the room," she says. "And when they check the garage vids they'll see you take down that recovery agent. We're going to be high on their catch list."

"Your logic is solid but for two things. One, since they turned the cameras off in the stairwell, we can assume the cameras were off in the garage as well. If not, well, they'll only going to have your image on playback. I am a ghost." I say and watch her eyes twitch.

She takes a long minute then says, "Explain."

"Call it a gift from your Uncle Sam. Skin grafts allow me to blend into black or induce white noise."

She studies me for a moment. "So you're a blur in photos and live," she concludes.

I nod.

She hits her smoke. "I read about that somewhere but I didn't believe it. Yet, won't they then realize that the blur is a military unit?"

"Not necessarily. Skin suits with the same properties can be had on the black market."

"Of course, so it's only my ass on the line. Great. So what's the second thing?"

"Since the hotel went out of their way to get us out of the room, they've probably erased your log-in. Check your bank account. I bet you got your money back."

She picks up her bag and retrieves her phone. She punches a few digits. A moment later she looks at me, nods and says, "Like it never happened."

I nod and say, "Gotta love free champagne."

Smiling, she puts her phone away and says, "I was loving the warm shower."

"So was I. Can you imagine if we had been on the bed?"

"Ow, that's sick," she says, and then punches my bicep.

We look over at Lynch, who is engaged in a spirited conversation, albeit in hushed tones.

"So what else am I missing?" she asks, then sips her strawberry vodka.

"Bobby Grant is Lynch's boy-toy. He's the one with Space's flash drive."

She shakes her head and lets a soft laugh escape. "'This is a safe place,' you said. 'Let's go hang out and relax,' you said."

"How was I supposed to know that my old buddy was sleeping with pretty boys with sticky fingers?"

Nikki smiles. Takes a hit off her cigarette.

I continue to drink and watch glass spider-crack beneath a pair of bloody feet as off-blue water swirls in and away.

"What's our next play?" she asks.

"Working on it," I reply. Then take another swig of whiskey.

"By the by, I know we went over this before but did you say you thought the recovery agent was there solo, working without police?" she asks, swirling the liquid around in her glass.

"I think so." I reply. I can't take my mind off Lynch. His body language suggests he's way over his head, and he can't see a way clear.

"Big trouble with the boss." Nikki states, casting a quick eye at Lynch.

"Oh hell yeah." I reply.

"So we gotta find a flash drive, right?"

"Yep. Basically the same job you hired me for. 'Apollo,'

you said, 'I need a favor. I need you to help me find something.'"

"Yes I did. And thank you for helping me find it."

"You're welcome."

13

Lynch taps the unit in his ear.

He roars over to the bar. I hand him the bottle. He kills the remaining four fingers of whiskey without pause. He grabs another bottle of whiskey from the rack and cracks it open. He has generous swig then passes the bottle to me.

Lynch reaches beneath the bar then produces a large square mirror and a rock of coke. He sets the mirror on the bar.

"It's gonna be one of those nights?" I say.

"Long before you got here," he replies.

"I like these nights," Nikki states.

"You still need me to find the flash drive?"

He nods. "I need that flash drive. You want me to have that flash drive. You hit the city. I'll dispose of that stuff in the garage. I'll call you when I'm city bound."

"So you want me to crack him open?"

"I need the drive more than I need his love," he states. "But if I tried to muscle him, he'd clam up until I'd be forced to kill him. He'd do it as a challenge at first, then out of spite until the bitter end. He's a little bitch but god can he suck dick."

Lynch sets up a fat pinky line and, nose to glass, whiffs it in one rail. No straw or rolled bill for this maniac.

"Dammit Bobby," Lynch sighs, a sour look screwed on his face. He sets up another fat line and passes it to Nikki. Nikki accepts the coke without a hint of hesitation. She also performs the task sans paraphernalia. It's all about focus and strong lungs.

"Oh, this is nice," Nikki says. She wrinkles her face. Performs the ritual of fingers to nose – *sniff*.

"Were you with him last night? Will he use you as his alibi?" Nikki asks Lynch the questions like an old friend. "What, is he a kleptomaniac? Did he just steal it outright?"

Lynch looks at me for help. I smile and with an easy wave of my hand, invite him to address the lady. He lines up another rail then slides the mirror my way. I decline.

"He's my bodyguard. I prefer he stay somewhat sober," Nikki says.

Lynch laughs. "Yeah, right." He rubs his eyes. Then, in a very relaxed fashion, takes a deep breath. I can see that the day, the drink and the drugs are collecting their due from Lynch.

"So did you argue or something? Maybe it was an act of spite." Nikki presses. "Maybe all you have to do is apologize."

"No, we didn't argue. I know it was in my wallet. He just stole it. He doesn't even know what he has. He doesn't own anything that can read it."

"What type of mot does Bobby have?" I ask.

"A blue Mariah. He parks in the garage, under the apartment building."

I nod. "I'll put the squeeze on him and get the drive."

"Like I said before, it's yellow with a silver band. Its razor thin and ultra light and damn near indestructible. And don't go thinking about copying it. It's got a program that produces a feedback spike. The spike will shut down an unauthorized reader. And Space has the only authorized reader."

I nod. "I understand."

"C'mon little girl, let's finish this," Lynch says to Nikki. He bends over and snorts up half the line, then pushes the mirror to Nikki. She cleans the mirror with easy grace.

Now, they both light cigarettes from Lynch's plain silver Zippo.

"One more question," Nikki says to Lynch.

"Sure."

"What's with the vid?" She nods at the Thomas Forrestt piece.

"Because it's beautiful. Look at that. And look where we're at now. The Event should have been the precursor to global war. But it didn't happen. It's insane. And I always wondered what that sounded like, when the sand turned to glass. Was it a hiss and crackle then ear splitting pop or a slow fusing burning whisper?"

"Interesting," says Nikki. We all watch the vid.

"You probably couldn't hear anything over the explosion,"

I say.

Lynch and Nikki nod in agreement.

"Okay, let's roll, Love," I say to Nikki. I look over to Lynch. "See you in the city."

Lynch nods and smokes his cigarette.

14

We exit the house and step into the garage.

I press the green button my remote and the doors of my mot swing open as the engine hums to life. I watch Nikki stare down the rats as she gets into the mot. I slide in and shut the doors.

Lynch opens the garage door. I pull out.

In the street and ready to go, I wave him off. Lynch nods and closes his garage. We hover down the avenue. I enter *Ernest Landing* then press the walking man icon. A nine-minute countdown clock appears on the dash.

"So talk to me," Nikki says as she turns in her seat.

"Still turning it all around in my head." I reply. "A multitude of conspiracies contend in the night."

"Now you're getting philosophical on me. I'm stoned, Apollo. Baby steps man, baby steps."

"What's on this flash drive that I'm going to retrieve?" I ask.

Nikki is silent. She smokes her cigarette. In time she offers, "Something very bad for Space. Like your earlier story, he's performing some sick sex."

"Possible." I say. "But I'm thinking murder. I'm more of a mind that it has something to do with Fury's death. Bobby knows exactly what he has. I bet his play is to blackmail Space."

Nikki studies my face, then, says. "You're saying Bobby was screwing Fury and, Lynch killed Fury in a jealous rage? Why would Space pay anyone to keep an employee out of jail?" Nikki winces as she realizes the answer to that question.

"Because the employee knows a lot about his employer," I say.

Nikki nods. Then says, "Who held the camera and caught the murder on film? Did Bobby film the murder or is there another player in this game?"

"Good questions,"

We ride in silence, but my thoughts are noisy. And the thought making the most noise is why the hell did I go to Lynch's place? I could have avoided all this crap if I hadn't chosen his place for a hideout.

Nikki plays dance music. The mot swells with pulsing bass and snap dance breaks. She rocks and gyrates in her seat. I sit back and watch her tits bounce. She looks at me watching her. We kiss. She pulls away and rubs my crotch. I take a deep breath and let the fire race over me. I love the feel of my dick straining hard against the fabric of my pants. And so does Nikki. She massages and caresses my cock and my chest and my hair. We kiss – no, we tongue wrestle. She tastes so sweet. She pulls away and I feel disconnected. Her heat is magnetizing and I fall forward, gripping her neck with my lips. This is what I want. Her flesh is taste of victory. And just as I seize her lips with mine she spins and plants her butt on my crotch.

"Okay, easy…. don't want to stain my pants."

"Your call, cowboy. I'm riding the wild with or without you." She rocks on me. She grabs my hand and uses my fingers for toys.

I love being used.

And so I go monk-like, discipline and denial. I check the slow, black pressure of growing release. It's maddening and one kiss will set me off into a roaring orgasm.

Just one kiss.

"I want inside."

"Of course you do." Nikki lifts up. She works her panties down until they bunch at her knees.

I open my pants and free myself. Nikki grabs me, escorts me to the gate and slides down.

"Feel good?" she asks with a laugh. She slaps my cheek.

I bury my face in her hair and breathe Nikki's scent. Again my lips find her neck and I savor her hot and taut flesh. I wrap my arms around her, crushing her into my chest, and then I dance with her.

15

We arrive at Ernest Landing. We get out of the mot. I press AP on the remote. The mot hovers away to park itself.

Standing on the corner, looking around for anything unusual. The city rushes about me as a whisper. The wind is warm and slight and I smell fresh baked bread.

No law enforcement vehicles about. If they were interested in searching Bobby's apartment, they'd be here.

"The cops aren't here," Nikki states.

"You're reading minds again. It's annoying." I say.

She shrugs her shoulders.

I shake my head and start walking down the sidewalk.

A bright yellow Peace Officer Drone emerges from around a corner of a building.

The small oval drone floats over and scans my eyes. Then it checks Nikki. Assured we are not wanted, the POD flies away.

"I hate those things," Nikki hisses as we cross the street.

"They're easy to beat. I don't pay 'em any mind," I reply. We walk into the lobby of the Ernest Landing complex.

I find Bobby's name on the apartment registry. Room 6-C.

"I guess I'll just push any button to get someone to let us in."

"Why not push Bobby's button?" Nikki asks.

"Well, I doubt he's home from his date with the cops."

"He might have a roommate."

"Lynch didn't mention a roommate."

"Maybe Lynch doesn't know about a roommate."

I nod. I push the button for 6-C. I step out of the camera's view.

Nikki opens her bag. She pulls out a messenger ID card with animated CMS (Commons Messenger Service) logo on it.

"Hello." The voice is strong and curt.

Nikki looks into the camera and presents the ID card for

inspection. "Hello. I've got a registered letter for Bobby Grant from Jet Allen."

"C'mon." The buzzer is shrill static. Nikki enters and I creep in behind her.

"The old standards." I say.

"Work every time." she confirms.

We ride the elevator to the sixth floor. It's a very clean lift with hardwood walls, a carpeted floor, and soft lighting. I wonder what the rent is like here.

Out of elevator and left down the hallway.

Nikki knocks on the door.

"Just slip it under the door," says the voice from inside.

"No good. You gotta sign for it." Nikki replies.

"Christ… Fine," replies the agitated voice behind the door.

The door slides open – I jam my fingers into that slender gap, grab the door and force it open. Nikki rushes in with her gun drawn. I follow her into the room and shut the door.

The agitated voice belongs to a naked guy who is on his back on the floor. Nikki has the barrel of her gun pressed tight against the naked guy's cheekbone. Naked guy isn't Bobby Grant.

Looking down and over Nikki's shoulder, I ask the very scared naked guy, "So where's Bobby?"

"I-I guess he's still with the cops. He hasn't called or anything," he replies fast and shaky.

"And who are you?" I ask.

"Tommy. I'm Tommy."

"Hello, Tommy. Anybody else here with you?"

"No."

"That's nice. Tell me, Tommy, have you seen a yellow flash drive with a metal band?"

His eyes grow wide. Nikki presses the gun further into his flesh. Her finger is off the trigger but Tommy can't see that.

Then the little punk pisses a straight hot stream at Nikki. We jump away from Tommy. I've never been pissed on and today will not be that day.

"He almost pissed on me!" Nikki shouts at me. And I see her finger slip to the trigger.

"Easy. Yes, he deserves to be shot but not now," I tell her.

The pissy little bitch on the floor starts crying.

"This is pathetic! You're pathetic!" Nikki shouts at the kid so hard that spittle flies from her mouth and lands on Tommy's lips. She keeps easing left to avoid the growing clear puddle of urine on the floor.

"Where's the flash drive!" She traces the barrel of her gun against his lips, teasing to thrust the gun into his mouth.

"In the bedroom…. on the bureau," gasps Tommy with red watery eyes.

I walk into the bedroom and, easy as pie, I spot the flash drive resting atop a small oval vanity mirror, which sits on a vanity counter littered with cosmetics. The vanity's hot lights are on, vivid brilliance radiates from the polished tri-mirrors like a siren's call.

I slide the flash drive into an insignificant compartment of my wallet.

I glance about the room; it's very clean, all white walls. A single, framed picture is set on the north wall. It's a black and white movie still of a dirty prostitute smoking a cigarette and on the verge of crying as she stands on a muddy and foul thoroughfare of an American old west settlement.

I walk over and stare into the large walk-in closet. The overhead light is dim but I can see expensive wardrobes for both men and women hanging on the left and right. A large yet tidy shoe rack composes the third wall of the closet.

I study the shoes.

"Did you find it?" Nikki asks from the other room.

"Yeah I got it," I reply. I exit the closet then leave the bedroom.

"So who dresses as a woman?" I ask Tommy.

"We both do." Tommy says drying his tears with the back of his hand. He seems to be comfortable sitting in his own piss.

"Both you and Bobby?" I ask, just to be sure.

"Yeah."

"For fun or profit?" I ask.

"Both," he says. "We dress as girls for all of our customers. We wear men's suits for the model gigs."

"Why did Bobby take the flash drive?" Nikki asks.

Tommy shakes his head and says, "Bobby didn't *take* the flash drive. It's his."

"Explain," I demand.

"The flash drive fits in a special camera. Bobby got the special camera from a regular."

"Who's the regular?" Nikki asks.

"I don't know. It's Bobby's gig."

I don't believe him – neither does Nikki. She grabs Tommy by the hair and puts the gun in his ear. "Tell the truth," she sneers.

"Okay I've met him." Tommy gushes with eyes wide open and a gun in his ear.

"More than just met him. Did you and Bobby entertain him together?"

Tommy nods. "He came here a few times and we partied like that, but Bobby is his girl."

I nod.

Nikki shoves Tommy to the floor and asks without pause, "So what's his name?"

"Lynch," he answers shying away from Nikki.

"Just Lynch?" I ask.

"Yeah, that's how I know him. Big black dude. All muscle. All rock."

So Lynch lied. Bobby filmed something using a camera he could have only gotten through Lynch. So what did he film? Fury's murder returns to mind.

"What's on the flash drive?" I ask the naked putz.

"Don't know. We don't have anything that can play it. And the camera doesn't have playback option"

I believe that. "Didn't Bobby tell you?"

"No. He was really screwed up when he came home. You know, not stoned or drunk, more scared. He told me the flash drive was insurance. He said it was the kind of thing that would take care of us for life."

"Us, meaning you and Bobby," I state.

Tommy nods and continues his tale of woe. "Then the cops came for him.... I called his brother – he's a high-powered lawyer. No one has said a word to me since."

Damn... I believe him. Don't know why but I do.

Nikki points the gun to Tommy's head and asks, "Can I kill him now?"

"Oh God – why? I've told you the truth!"

I smile and wink at her.

I bend down and say to Tommy, "Tell anybody we were here and I will stomp you into the ground. Do you understand?"

Tommy nods like a broken bobble head doll.

"Let's go," I say to Nikki.

16

We leave the apartment. Turn left for the elevators.

"Lynch lied," Nikki says. "He never had the flash drive, he wanted us to get it."

"You believe Tommy too? Yeah, so do I."

"Your friend is getting much more interesting." Nikki says with a smile. She lights a cigarette.

"Yes he is. I like the way you handled yourself back there. You're a little ball-buster," I say and I'm a breath away from a full out laugh.

Her grin is fat as she takes a drag from her smoke. "Can you believe he pissed? What was that about?" She laughs. I laugh with her.

"That was sick," I say.

"What a little punk," she replies. Then, "I can't wait to see that flash drive."

"How you gonna read it? Remember what Lynch said about its security. It'll crash your computer."

"Yeah, we'll see about that."

The elevator is still on our floor so we hop in. I press L.

"Let me see it," she asks with hand out.

I look at her. "Wait till we get back in the mot."

She rolls her eyes and says, "What am I gonna lose it between here and there?"

We step out of the elevator and walk fast across the lobby. I pull out my remote and press the green button. The digital readout indicates the car is fourteen seconds away.

We exit the building. No cops in sight. Man, this feels so strange. Too damn easy.

I see it coming but what can I do? The mot is ten seconds away. So I suck it up and deal with it. A large *personal* advert assaults me on my left. It's a live feed from 1 Ceres. Space miners under intense spotlights extract zinc, nickel and silver from that cold and distant asteroid. The tag line below the space miners reads: *Mkeyinc – Truly Stellar Investments.*

Truly Stellar Performance.

"I can't believe it's this easy," she says.

I nod. "This is indeed too easy. Almost tailor-made."

I continue to check for police presence as my mot approaches.

A tall thin *personal* sidles up at my right. The scene is a lovely farm populated with happy, contented animals. The tag line, Friends Farms, appears over the scene. A soft voice says, "Friends Farms, famous for our nutritious and true-to-taste beef, chicken and fish. Friends Farms is solely machine-operated. No humans are harmed in the production of our products. Friends Farms. People Friendly. Animal kind."

My mot stops where we had discharged earlier. The doors open. Nikki and I step into the vehicle. I press GO. We hover down the avenue. I check the rear view monitor for a tail. We seem to be clean and clear.

Nikki pulls her laptop from her bag. She opens her computer then snaps her fingers at me.

"Let me have the drive."

I open my wallet. "I know you love that unit. Are you sure you want to risk this?"

"I'm not worried. My laptop was designed by Proto."

"Proto? The hacker?" I ask.

"The Shut Down god," she states with pride.

I'm impressed. Proto's been screwing with planet economics for decades. From stock markets to rock concerts. He has crashed every major and minor event the world has hosted. Proto is just plain evil. Which calls to mind the question.

"Is Proto a man or a woman?" I ask.

"A very old man. No body regen or enhancements. Keeps himself in good shape though. Rides his bike all over the place. He lives here in the city."

"Interesting. How do you know him?"

"He's a client," she replies with a smile.

I give her the drive. She studies it the same way a pitcher tends to a baseball.

She plugs it into her laptop.

The tiny clock icon spins on the monitor.

And continues to spin.

"I guess it can't be read," she says without a hint of defeat. She removes the drive from her laptop and the monitor goes black. She presses the power button and the unit reboots.

"Well, at least it didn't crash my laptop." She says at length and returns her scrutiny to the yellow drive.

"What are you looking for?" I ask.

"I haven't got a clue." She shrugs her shoulders, then, hands the drive back to me.

I call Lynch.

Five rings then VM switches on. "All Good. Ping me." I say, then hang up.

"That's strange." Nikki says.

I nod in agreement. "Where is he?"

Nikki's cell pings. She answers by the third ping. "Talk to me." She turns to me scared, shocked, and looking at me with sober-wide eyes, "Ezra! Where are you?"

Now my phone sounds off. I want to stay with Nikki's drama but I have to answer this call. "Yo, Lynch?"

"No. I am Malcolm Space. Is this Apollo?"

"Yes. Hello Mr. Space."

"I believe you have something for me."

"Yes."

"Very good. Come immediately to my office at four-forty Madison. Someone will wait for you in the lobby."

"Be there in less than ten minutes."

"Thank you." Space hangs up. So does Nikki.

"We have to get to Ezra now!" she says.

"Damn. Look...."

"I heard what Space said," she says, "I want to know what's on the drive. Let's keep it until Ezra's has had a chance to look at it. I'd like his opinion on it."

"What?"

"C'mon, what can it hurt?"

A deep sigh rolls from my chest. Thinking about it... "Alright, so where is your boyfriend?"

"Lower east side. Seventh and Avenue A. Bar called Niagara."

"I know where that's at. I used to date a bartender that worked there."

"Oh yeah, tell me about her."

"No. You already know more about me than my mother."
"You should call your mother more."
"Yeah, I'll do that."
Nikki snubs out her cigarette in the ashtray.
I punch up Liz's. After three rings, the VM requests my name and number.
"Apollo here, where you at? Call me back. Out." I hang up.
"Where the hell is everyone?" I say.

17

We hover past the bar. I want to get a feel for the scene.

I don't like the feeling I'm getting.

"This ain't right." I tell Nikki. "Feels all wrong. Feels like a setup."

Before she can answer, her cell pings.

"Don't answer that," I command.

"Why? It's Ezra."

"Cells are the best way to track and locate. Once you pick up, they'll know where you are."

"So what do we do?"

"You got any pictures of Ezra?"

"You're gonna walk into the bar and look for him? You look like a cop that would sacrifice his next of kin for information. If it's a trap, they'll cue up on you like flies on dog crap."

"That sums up a normal working day. So we're in agreement, you stay in the mot while I look for Ezra."

She sits, a silent twisted laugh on her lips as she works on legitimate reasons why she should go with me or alone. She opens her computer.

I park the mot about fifty meters east of the bar.

I smell curry.

Three, super thin, milk-white-skinned women, all with jet-black hair – Betty Page cut – and clad in black leather pants and jackets walk across the street. The dark dolls pass before my parked mot, then on the sidewalk, they turn east.

"Maybe you'll meet them in the bar," Nikki says. She points to the monitor on her laptop. "Here's a picture of Ezra."

"That milk-white skin is a full body tattoo." I say to no one. "I like it better than the perfect tan."

I look over at her laptop. Ezra seems like a very concerned man, with a thin face that is cut hard with worry lines from years of learning too much crap about humans. He has deep, heavy folds of flesh beneath his eyes.

"Damn, no regeneration therapy here," I state the obvious.

"He didn't like that idea. Told me he wanted evidence that he'd been alive."

Before I can reply, the phone rings. It's Malcolm Space. I think about it. Then let it ring. After three rings, the VM kicks in. Nikki and I listen to the message.

"Apollo, it is regrettable that you are not at my Broadway office. I note that you are currently in the lower East Side. Either come to me immediately – or I will come to you." The VM ends.

Nikki and I look at each other. I grab the flash drive. "Tracking device implanted on the drive." I say.

"How do we beat that?" she asks.

We both study the yellow unit with a metal band. In time, we both shake our heads in dismay.

I look out and around. The park across the way is quiet. I get another wonderful whiff of curry.

"Damn government – they are terrorists. Terrorist that control your life! Do not be terrorized!"

In the rear view-monitor I see a few people on the sidewalk, standing before a small convenience store, looking at a different kind of man walking in a circle. The circle walking man wears a hat made of folded aluminum foil with small pieces of mirror tacked on it. He is taking big strides in his tiny circle. He carries an antique, a boom box. Yet, it couldn't be a real one because those old things ran on batteries. This one must have been converted to run on depcells. He stops short, close to the rear of my mot and begins to swear to the sky. I roll down my window to better hear his rant, and to make sure my mot wouldn't receive the brunt of any delusional aggression.

"What's up?" Nikki asks.

"Local entertainment." I reply.

"I like the music he's playing." she says as she leans over and looks back.

"It's 'Curly Locks' by Lee Scratch Perry."

"Never heard of him but I like it."

The man with the hat of foil and mirrors holds the attention of the sidewalk crowd, as well as a few people who look down with dreary ennui from the safety of their apartment windows. The man with the hat of foil and mirrors is really picking up a head of steam as he shouts at the sky.

"It may be that the independent functional principle is functionally equivalent and parallel to an important distinction in mind control. We need not assume that you don't know where my asshole is at because it is being continually tracked with a GPS. Thank you sky mother. In and of additional mission constraints may remedy and, at the same time, eliminate all deeper conceptualization. Summarizing, then, this aluminum hat keeps you mothersuckers out of my independent structuralistic concept. Furthermore and compounded, and taking into account the management-by-contention principal, the mirrors reflect it back at you! So to hell with you! Goddamn philistines!" He spits on the ground, then, hurries down the sidewalk with big strong strides.

And with that, the crowd disperses.

"What the hell was that all about?" Nikki says.

"Mind control."

"See what paranoia will do to you. As a great poet once said, 'Paranoia will destroy ya.' There's your proof." Nikki eases back into her seat. "So what about Ezra?"

I sit in silence. What about Ezra? What about Space? What about Lynch? What about Bobby Grant and Lynch? What about Bobby Grant and Fury Randall? What about the Glass Shore disc and file? What on the flash drive? What about Liz? And hell, what about Nikki? This isn't the girl I used to know. The domino effect is in play and it's a real trick to figure out how to dodge the falling tiles.

Mind control.

One thing at a time.

Control.

Pick a problem.

The flash drive. Yellow with a metal band. What's the metal band for?

I set my front tooth against the metal band and grind upward firm and severe.

A moment later metal ejects onto to back of my tongue and throat. I cough and spit up the metal into my palm.

"Who's your dentist? That's insane," says Nikki.

"Government issue. Every inch of me." I say as I inspect the drive. The band is off. Now comes the point when theory meets proof. I slip the altered drive back into my wallet. I'll pitch the bent metal down a sewer grate first chance I get.

"Looks like you're coming along after all. I want you with me."

Nikki secures her computer in her bag. "Let's go," she says as she loops the strap of the bag over her head.

I hurry down the sidewalk. Nikki catches up and keeps pace. We pass a hot dog and pretzel vendor, pass some guy selling cloth finger puppets, and pass a blind woman whose sign promises accurate tarot fortune reading in one minute.

I see a sewer grate and I drop the bent metal into it.

"You know, it just dawned on me." Nikki starts.

"Yeah, what's that?"

"Why it's not your picture on your driver's license or vehicle registration. Because of your military condition, you can't be photographed. So who pretended to be you?"

"Inquisitive little bitch, aren't you?"

"Enough compliments, just tell."

"It's Liz in drag." I say.

Nikki stops walking and looks at me at though I have been struck by lightning.

"Well c'mon. We haven't got much time," I say.

I tug on her arm and we continue down the sidewalk in silence. I can feel her mind working, formulating, but so far no verbal offering.

A pair of guys in dark suits and sporting thin dark glasses rush by us and continue down the street. Nikki and I hang out and watch the men come to a stop near the sewer grate where I had dumped the bent metal band.

They stand, frustrated, and study the parked mots and storefronts.

Space is serious about his drive. Yet his hired muscle doesn't know what I look like. It's not like Lynch could show him a picture. The only picture they could have of me is from the arrest warrant. Space is going to have to be patient and wait for me.

I open the bar door for Nikki.

"Remember, don't strike in anger," she says.

"Be quiet." I reply.

We stand in the vestibule while we're scanned.

I feel a slow and lazy bass pulse from the main room. A moment later we get the green light and we enter the bar on the downbeat. The band is parked right next to entrance so we're slammed with mean blues guitar before we can get a breath. We scout around for Ezra. I also look for anyone looking at me. I see the dark doll triplets are tending bar.

Nikki grabs my arm and we work our way to the bar. I spot the floorshow and I pull Nikki to a stop. Nikki looks at the performer – a topless skinny geek – shakes her head and says, "I can do without this. I'll see you at the bar."

I, along with others, watch the topless skinny geek sitting on the floor. Blood wets her hands and spots the floor about her. Her tiny breasts and near-absent abdomen are painstakingly ascribed with henna designs. She lifts the sword above her as she tilts her head back. A live and squirming green frog, a live and wriggly red snake and a live and writhing black mouse are skewered upon the sword, a thick river of the victims' blood streams from the tip of the sword and into the geek's lipless mouth. The amphibian, reptile and rodent writhe, squirm and twitch. The geek opens her mouth wider … swallows the sword …

Her throat muscles perform queasy and confusing divisions.

A moment later she withdraws the sword, clean of frog, snake and mouse.

The loud applause she receives shuts out the band.

She bows with a sleepy gentle motion.

The show is over.

"Wow. That was insane. It must be illegal," says the blonde girl next to me.

"What's illegal?" I ask her.

"Well, killing animals – especially like that."

"They could be cloned," I say.

She nods. "Yeah, probably."

I add, "Plus, she ate them."

The girl gives me a confused look.

"There's no law against eating raw meat," I state.

"I'm going over here," she says, a touch of fear in her eyes.

"I'm going this way," I reply. I walk away from the girl and toward the bar. Nikki waits with drink in hand and another before her. I can see the guy behind her is thinking about talking to her. Then I step up and he jerks away as though bitten by a snake.

I reach for the shot on the bar: it rests next to the *Live*, a rotating display of the bar band that stands about as tall as a pint glass. For a moment, it looks like the lead singer is pissing into my shot glass. I grab my drink.

"Ezra is standing against the wall by the ladies' room, under the large painting of Groundskeeper Willie." Nikki says. "We made eye contact twice and he didn't recognize me. But, I have changed my hair color since last he saw me. Yet, that shouldn't throw him off. Maybe he doesn't want to acknowledge me."

"Two more of these." I say to the dark doll with a well-coifed, windswept hairdo and a brown rat resting on her slender shoulder.

"Just tell her you want to screw her and get it over with." Nikki says.

"In time." I take the shot. "So you say Ezra can't recognize you, I can relate. You've changed on me so many times today, I don't know who the hell I'm looking at."

"Adaptation is the key to survival."

The drinks arrive. The bartender holds her scan pen, ready to read my card, tattoo or implant. I place a twenty on the bar. The dark doll smiles and nods at me. She tucks the bill into her bra and floats to the next guy who wants a drink.

Nikki nods at a space across the room. We move away from the bar. I cut through the crowd with ease. We take up residence in a small recess. I stand, my back against the wall. Nikki stands across from me. Between us, on the wall, is a small black and white photo of a sad Norma Jean wearing a fuzzy white sweater. We can see Ezra.

I say, "You see the couple standing in front of the picture of Neo?"

Nikki sips her drink. "Yeah."

"I think they're watching Ezra."

The band kicks in with a hard bass line riding atop a

naughty kick and trap. Then a steel guitar whines over the steamroller rhythm and the singer issues a guttural hum…

I sip my drink. "They're watching us as well."

Nikki reaches over and gives me a long kiss on the lips. Her soft lips tug on my greedy lips as she pulls away. Now, just inches from my face, she looks at me with pixie dust eyes and I'm damn happy to be me.

"What was that for?" I ask.

"Fun."

I smile, raise my glass to my mouth, glance over at the couple, and it seems that they are no longer interested in me. Nikki's fun kiss just made me another dude in a bar.

I sip my scotch.

A couple, a few tables away, are having a discussion. The woman swipes her palm across the tabletop, closing the *Live*. Now she has his attention.

A dark doll carrying a tray of dirty, used glasses stacked with chaotic calm makes her way through the thick wave of patrons. I glance back at the bar and see that three dark dolls dispense liquor. I scan the room and note seven girls with milky-white skin tattoos. Yeah, I could do seven. That's a nice number.

"We're going to have to do this quick and hard," I advise Nikki.

"Just lay it down and I'll stay out of the way."

"Smart girl."

I ease away from the booth; another dark doll – number five I believe – passes before me with a tray of drinks. She was the calm before the storm because the band has turned the crowd into dancing fools. I move through the mass as though I'm swimming in mud with a heavy granite stone tied to my waist. I can't see Ezra.

Through the crush of dancing bodies I catch a glimpse of a cell phone against Ezra's ear.

Nikki's cell pings. Even over all this noise I recognize her annoying ring tone. I turn and see her holding her cell but she doesn't answer it. Good girl.

Close but using dancers as cover, I see one of Ezra's watchers holds a palmtop, and has some gadget attached to his ear. The other guy seems to be scanning the room, perhaps looking for me.

I come up from behind – he quickly turns to face me. I look into his eyes and see digital orbs like mine. He's Government Issue just like me. Which means he can take pain just as well as I can.

I'm faster – I hit him with a vicious uppercut that spills him into his partner. Bodies and electronics crash to the floor. I grab people and toss their bodies at Ezra's watchers. Nikki moves through the panicked crowd like a kite on a blustery day. She reaches Ezra a heartbeat before I do.

"Ezra! It's me, Nikki. Let's go!" she shouts, tugging on his arm. His eyes light up after he studies her face for a moment.

"I thought I'd never see you again," he stammers, about to cry.

"No time for love. Let's jet!" I shout as I lead Nikki and Ezra toward the cellar exit. I shove them at the door – and feel a hand on my shoulder. It's not friendly. I spin away and avoid the punch. His recovery is great so no advantage on the miss. I jab, he blocks and counter punches. I quickly slide my right foot between his slightly parted feet as I grab his left shoulder. Our hips kiss and roll and I toss him across the room. He's lighter than I expected. He's a newer model with better composites. He also could be designed for a different application, say civilian control. Those units aren't built like me. I walk over to him. He stands and readies for my attack. I feign a kick and rocket my fist into his chest. He flails back into the wall and looks at me wide-eyed, he's having trouble breathing. Yeah, he's not built for hard combat. I step toward him, he prepares for the attack. I grab his right wrist and pull him to me – I greet his face with the crown of my skull. I hit him twice in the gut and he drops at my feet. He still has something in him, for he tries to rise. I pick him up and toss him across the full length of the room. He lands hard, rolls into a slide and finally slumps into a lifeless heap in front of the band.

His tekkie buddy slams into my back. We both hit the floor and roll. I sweep my legs out and upend the new guy before he gains his footing. I kick him in the face, in the back of the head, and again in the back of the head, and again.

Knee bent, I freeze because I note he's not moving. Looks

like the head kicks did it. I realize I may have used a bit more energy than necessary. I'm having a hard time today following that first rule. Sneak attacks just piss me off.

I rush down the stairs, into the basement. I glance at liquor boxes and cartons of snack foods. I note a couple having sex, her back slapping against the brick wall, as he holds onto a thin overhead pipe for support.

I find Nikki and Ezra standing at the bottom of the service ramp.

"Another minute and I would have joined the couple over there," Nikki says.

"I was surprised when I saw it wasn't you," I fire back.

Smiling, she nods up the ramp. "Locked on the street level."

I nod, then race up the ramp and explode through the metal doors. The doors had been bolted shut, little resistance to someone that can push over large military vehicles. I stand on the sidewalk, reaching back to pull up Nikki and Ezra.

I look around and note that no pedestrians were injured as a result of my exit. Yet, I only see one door.... Oh, there's the other one. Embedded in a silver mot. The vehicle is empty. No harm, no foul. The world got lucky today.

Nikki takes Ezra by the arm and they rush toward my mot.

As I step away, the blind fortune reader points at me and cries out, "Sun-god, heat all around you, but you control the flame. You heeded a fool's wisdom and secured deception. Deceit is a romance...close to heart." The blind fortune-teller is now quiet. Her blank, frosty green eyes drill into me.

"Thank you." I say. Not having a clue what she's just said. I give her a twenty and beat it down the sidewalk.

Nikki and Ezra stand by my mot.

I start the engine and open the doors on the run. Nikki and Ezra are in the mot a moment before I am.

I pull into traffic with a rush but without making too much of a fuss.

Nikki turns to Ezra in the backseat. The old man is taking deep breaths.

I scan the street for unfriendly types. And there they are, in my rear view monitor. I see three men studying the service entrance and the mot with the metal door sticking out of it and asking questions of the sidewalk vendors. I can already hear the conversation with the blind tarot reader.

"We're clear," I say to Nikki.

She exhales, and turns back to Ezra. "You okay, old man?"

"Yes, but running damn near killed me. Yet I am grateful for the shock to the system." He takes another deep breath.

I study his face. He appears to enjoy his new freedom.

"And who is your impressive boyfriend, my angel?"

"Ezra, this is Apollo. Apollo, Ezra."

"Hello, sir. Good to see you."

"A pleasure to be seen," replies Ezra as he studies me. It's almost like he recognizes me. It's an unsettling familiarity.

"Thank you very much for rescuing me," he says to me. He turns to Nikki.

"Nikki, they made me call you. They said that they would kill your sister if I didn't cooperate. I didn't know you had a sister. So I resisted. Then they showed me pictures of you at your sister's birthday party and other family gatherings. I didn't know what else to do. So I called you. I was hoping for a miracle – and you brought the miracle with you."

"Yeah, he is something special." Nikki pulls a pack of cigarettes from her purse. She tugs a smoke free from the pack and lights it.

I study the monitors, looking for a tail.

I feel a sharp prick at the nape of my neck and an icy vice seizes my throat.

I turn to see Ezra ease back into his seat. Needle? He's holding a needle?

I look to Nikki. Is she smiling or grimacing as smoke escapes from her lips?

My body sings pain. I can feel everything and my world is black.

There are known knowns. These are things we know that
we know. There are known unknowns. That is to say,
there are things that we know we don't know. But there
are also unknown unknowns. There are things we don't
know we don't know.

–Donald Rumsfeld. 02.12.02

18

The back of my throat is slick and salty. The wind is blowing and I smell the sea.

I open my eyes. The world is hot and white. Everything is super burning bright.

I close my eyes. I couldn't keep them open if I wanted to. Calm. Focus.

I feel the heat pressing my flesh. The heat is stifling and roasts my lungs with every breath I take.

Calm. Focus. I am alive, of that I am sure. Now manage the pain. Calm. Focus.

Moments to minutes to hours and the sun never change positions or intensity.

Calm. Focus. I open my eyes. The sunlight is so bright that it cancels out shapes and colors and depth. And yet I see that I sit on a chair that rests upon still waters. I sit upright and tight and lift my bare feet from the wet, solid sea.

In time, I relax and set my feet upon the calm waters. Yet I cannot contain my fear that my chair will drop into the sleepy water at any moment.

The brilliant light diminishes a few grades.

Then I …

I see a shadow.

Moments of indecision, then in a fit of exhaustion, the shadow wanes and reveals a thin man sitting across from me. He sits in the same type of chair as I do and his bared feet rest comfortably on the blue waters. I see that the man wears a yellow robe and a soothing aura rests about his stout frame. He speaks and it shocks me because it's not a pleasant voice; it sounds like a pickaxe biting into concrete.

"What would you do if you found a gold watch protruding from a giraffe's rectum?" queries the interrogator with the discordant voice.

I visualize the question. A very tall brown and white animal has a gold watch sticking out of its ass.

"I'd leave it there," I say. Quite sure that is the correct answer.

"The watch is real gold." The interrogator replies, adding an intoxicating hitch.

I'm confused as to the seductiveness of a real gold watch protruding from an asshole. "I'd leave it there." I state plain and resolute.

"Interesting. No regard for the giraffe's well being?"

"I'd call a vet."

"Then the vet would get the gold watch."

"Anyone willing to put their hand up a giraffe's ass deserves a gold watch."

I guess I gave the wrong answer for the calm sea begins to swirl and ripple. I feel dizzy, going under...

The blue ocean becomes a strange sky of scattered bright white clouds against a solid dull white ceiling.

I'm on my back looking up. Not wet but dry upon a soft white bed.

I see fuzzy people standing about me. Then one face becomes clear and vivid. The face is wide and plastic-clean. The man says, "You know, the initials P.I., really stand for Public Idiot." His voice, that familiar timbre of a pickaxe biting into concrete makes me realize I'm not dead. Just back in hell.

"Screw you, Griffin." I say. My throat hurts and feels packed with chunky salt. I want a drink of water. I smell high organic cleaning solutions. I feel clean and sterile. Downright divine.

"Well, well, well, it's alive." Griffin says with a rich laugh in his voice. Like the cat that gets the rat. Like the little boy who gets the most wanted toy. Like a man who has me by the short hairs. Griffin is my keeper. I'm supposed to report daily to him. I'm supposed to follow his orders without question. I'm supposed to consider him my friend and confidant.

I shun him like the plague.

This is the first time I've seen him in over three years. He is a man of medium height with a perfect pear-shaped body that suspiciously steadies on spindly legs. He is bald with thick blonde eyebrows and shallow green eyes. His skin is a taut sun-tanned buffalo hide. I hate this man. He is Satan in brown Forzieritti wingtips.

"Just shoot me, Griffin," I say.

"No way, baby. This is what I live for. Hell, you and Lynch going sour at the same time has us considering canceling the retirement program for you early model super studs."

Play stupid, a.k.a., act natural. "Lynch? What'd he do?"

"Your blood brother screwed a rich little blond girl to death then shoved her body under a hotel bed. Being a valuable piece of government hardware, like you, we just rescinded his retirement and sent his ass to space. He'll be space bound in a few hours, never to set foot on this planet again. And the same fate awaits you ... unless you can produce a miracle."

"Who do you want me to kill?"

"Kill whoever you need to in the course of recovering the Project Blue Book appendix sixty-three-A file. The same file you damaged eight agents for earlier today. The same file that we were attempting to recover at that bar about six hours ago. Get that file back – now! Then we'll talk about whether or not you get to remain on terra firma. But understand, fail and you will spend the rest of your half-ass unnatural days space walking."

I nod and bite the bitter bullet. Nikki used me then tried to kill me. She blinded me with a cool and fabulous ass. Nice set of tits too. Maybe I'll fuck her before I kill her.

"So, you ready to get to work, or would you like me to give you a sponge bath first?" he says as he lights a cigarette.

We stare at each other for a slow moment. I smile.

"Get the hell up!" Griffin shouts.

"Hey, don't offer if you ain't gonna deliver."

I see my clothes hanging in the closet. I sit up. Stand up and sigh. I walk over to the closet. Griffin and two uniformed and well-armed soldiers remain in the room. I'm obviously not going to get any privacy.

I undo the hospital gown and let it fall to the sparkling floor. I look up to find no underwear.

"What happened to my underwear?"

"We burned it," Griffin says with a laugh.

"And you didn't give me a replacement pair?"

"No. Shut the hell up and put your clothes on."

I sigh again and swallow the fire that wants to leap from

my throat.

Fine. I grab my pants and find to my dismay that they're dirty and torn at the knees and right hip. This is messed up. And so I put my pants on.

"Give me a snap detail of the events that led up to your ass being dumped on the curb," requests Griffin.

"I was hired to help find something. Once that something was found, I was hired as protection. At the bar, we met up with another contact that then tried to kill me. You already know what I was hired to find and who hired me to find it."

Socks are in my shoes. Well, that's something. I slip on the socks. I see the shoes are dull and shabby. I hate it when my shoes are beat. I gotta stop by home for a new pair. Hell, a new suit.

Griffin nods. "Yeah … What I don't understand is once you realized it was an official government document you had secured in that warehouse, why you failed to contact me? Apollo, where is your sense of national security? Where is your loyalty to the President and the party? You should've secured the file and immediately brought it to me. But that didn't happen, and now I'm the only thing standing between you and a count of treason."

I button up my shirt. No blood on it or stink to it. That's nice.

I say, "I had no way to be sure it was a true government file. It could have been a forgery."

"That's not your decision! You should have called me right away. You don't think. I do your thinking for you. That's rule number one."

My life is full of rule number ones. I slip my shoes on.

"What was I injected with?" I ask Griffin. I put on my shoulder holster and check my gun. Weapon is loaded and secure. I put it in the holster.

"Don't know. The lab is still analyzing your data. It almost did the job, whatever it was. I know that Davis and Sinclair are surprised you're alive. Serves you right for hanging out with vermin."

I put on my jacket and grab my overcoat – which is dirty as sin. Where'd Nikki dump me? I check the inside pockets and find my phone but not my wallet or the Bolt or the flash drive.

Well, I imagine Nikki has them.

Yet ... I'll know in a moment if Griffin has the Bolt. He'll tell me how illegal it is to own and how it's one more notch on my stick of doom.

Griffin walks over to the door of my room. One of the armed soldiers holds the door open for him. I follow. The soldiers follow us.

We stroll through the hospital corridors without speaking. I don't hear any other sounds. It's tomb-quiet in this facility. That's when I realize it's not a regular hospital but a company lab. Of course, why would they bring me to a regular hospital?

Griffin shatters the quiet. "Do you have Malcolm Space's flash drive?"

"What?"

"Your phone was ringing every ten minutes so I took the liberty of listening to your phone messages."

"You have something he wants bad. So what is it? What's on the drive?"

"Don't know. Haven't had the chance to view it. How did you figure out my password to access my phone messages?"

With a mean laugh in his voice, "Please ... We started with the obvious and it was a hit. Mr. Clean."

Nikki had called me prissy. And this nasty little asshole just tagged me pretty much the same way, or how else could he had so easily hit my password? I don't know why I'm pissed about this but I'm feeling tense. And this suit is dirty as all hell and I'm running without underwear.

Shoes are beat.

I'm not happy right now.

Griffin, agitated and tight, spits his question at the floor, "How long have you been working for Space? I thought Lynch was the only flunky on his payroll."

"I'm not working for Space. I secured the flash drive in question as a favor to Lynch. He gave me the word to pass it to Space. I was on my way to deal with Space when I got jacked."

Griffin gives me a disproving huff. He tries his best to walk tall. He sets his back upright and stiff and rolls his shoulders, too hard and square.

"He takes a backseat to me. You understand? Space is not important. I don't give a damn about his money. Your priority is the Project Blue Book file. Understand?"

"Understood."

We exit through a red door and emerge onto a parking lot.

My senses tell me it's night yet I must look up for confirmation and I find the ultra bright city lights make the night sky un-black and the stars invisible.

"Did you read the file?" Griffin asks me.

"No. Nikki found it and she was happy with what she found. All I had to do was get her out of the house and my job was done."

"Great job. If you like danger so damn much, why the hell don't you go into stunt work like Michaels and Becuá? Become a celebrity, get the women, get that money and be happy?"

"I don't like movies."

"You'd rather be a private investigator. You wanna help people. Michaels and Becuá are also volunteer firemen. That's helping people."

"To hell with the dynamic duo. I've done some good work."

"You found a missing child two years ago. Since then, nothing worth a damn."

On this count, Griffin is right. Most of my work is feudal justice.

"Catch." Griffin says.

I snatch the remote from the air.

"Black mot." He nods toward the low profile cruiser. It's flat deep black in color. The vehicle has no edges or angles. It's a smooth instrument that will slice through the sky.

"Damn. This is sharp, Grif. A Shorter Black Bullet. When did the agency start spending money on good mots?"

"We've always had good vehicles – we just never gave them to lowlifes like you. Now go get the file."

"Aye-aye." You little fat bitch.

"And you can't pull the seed out this time. It will explode if you mess with it. I want to know where your ass is at all times! If you go off radar I will stop the world to track you down. And when I find you, I won't waste taxpayer money on a spacewalker – I'll shoot your ass into the heart of the sun! Hell, that may be the only way left to kill you. And I'm sure the sun will kill your ass. Are we on the same page?" he asks with crystal cold anger. I believe he would scorch the earth to find me.

"Yeah. Doggie stay on his leash."

"Damn straight. Now get out of my sight."

"My pleasure."

I get in the mot and rip out of the agency's service lot.

Griffin hadn't mentioned the Bolt. And he would have given me much grief over the possession of an illegal weapon. So looks like Nikki has the weapon. Got to watch the way I approach her. Can't give her time to put the gloves on.

I punch up the office on the mot's phone. It rings once.

"Hello, Apollo Agency." The words flash from Liz's mouth. She looks good.

"Hi Sweetheart – man, it is good to see your face. What's the news?" I say.

"I want my flash drive, Apollo." Not Liz's voice and no longer her face.

This was the faceless voice of Malcolm Space.

"Hello Mr. Space." I hesitate. Here it comes. He wants to know where his drive is. Can't tell this man I don't have it. Take a deep breath. Decompress.

"I will trade you a live and healthy, and very beautiful business associate for my flash drive, Apollo. It's that simple. Liz's life for my flash drive."

"Understood." I say.

"Excellent. I await your arrival at my Madison office. Anytime is good for me."

"Be with you soon, Liz," I say.

I watch Space's finger grow fat then the monitor goes black.

Okay, one more reason to screw Nikki to death. But first I have to find her.

19

At sixteen hundred meters, the glow of the city is muted so I can see the true black of space. I can see space stations and orbit traffic and stars, planets.

Descending.

I come to a rest and hover above a rooftop in a residential neighborhood.

I hide behind a row of six huge wooden water reservoirs.

These high-rise condos are set in groups of four interlocking buildings. They have open-air food markets, schools, parks, pools and full athletic facilities. Nice place to raise a family and the rent won't kill you.

I open the Shorter's computer and call up my homepage. Let's see if Nikki is still using my old mot. I activate Port-trak. My old mot is exiting St. Louis City limits, continuing west at three hundred and sixty clicks.

I assume Nikki believes I'm dead.

Griffin said the techs that worked on me are surprised I'm alive. In fact, I remember hearing, *"I can't believe this thing is still working."*

I set the Shorter's trek log to match my old mot's course. The map states we're nine hundred and eighty-eight kilometers apart. Once I clear city limits, I'll be on Nikki's ass in about twelve minutes.

The Port-trak displays a hard rain in and around the St. Louis area.

I hate rain.

I lean back hard into the seat and close my eyes.

I can't believe I'm still working either.

This experience was not like a normal shut down. I feel unclean. What did Ezra use on me?

Deep breath. Relax. Reason.

Ding.

I open my eyes.

What the hell?

I guess I … napped?

That doesn't make sense. I don't nap. I enter rest cycles but I don't just nod off.

Snap to, kid.

Get organized.

I see the rain blanketing the sleeping farmland.

The Port-trak states I'm thirty seconds away from my old mot. I drop speed and cruise down onto the city grid.

I got suckered by a beautiful woman. Spiked by an old man. So much for detailed military training, general paranoia and common sense.

I dreamt of a gold watch up a giraffe's ass.

And napping?

I've never had a day like this.

I don't like it.

I don't get it. Nothing about this is right. It's not like me. I'm better than this.

I can see my old mot ahead through the fat splats that thud upon the windshield. It appears that traffic ahead is rolling over … my old mot has stopped.

I hover alongside the stalled vehicle and see it's empty. I ask the computer to advise occupancy within my old mot. The computer reads zero. Nothing. Nobody is in the damn mot. It's a decoy. Stupid.

Note to self: practice thinking.

I stop ahead of my old mot.

I pull away the top cushion of the rear passenger seat and expose the foxhole – a holdover benefit from the bad days of cars, credit cards and free television: long before I was around. And, as standard for government vehicles, I find one large white cloth towel, food rations for three days; three, two-liters of bottled water, two blankets, a first aid kit and a crank phone. Tucked in the upper right corner of the foxhole is what I need, a plastic poncho with hood. I remove the poncho from the package. I struggle to don the snug weather outfit, as regulation gear is always made for regular-sized people and I'm far from regular. I touch the door latch with a sigh. I'm about the get wet for no good reason but I have to check out my old vehicle. The door opens and I get out of the mot. The rain is dense, rough and warm. I'm sloppy wet after three steps.

Rapid moving expressway traffic flows overhead or arches away from the pair of parked mots. The large static advert on my right displays James Dean driving his iconic silver gray 1955 Porsche Spyder along a smooth black cliff side road, the calm Mediterranean Sea on his right, he wears Dikinikki's sport goggles and Dikinikki's exquisite Italian Umi-leather driving gloves. *Dikinikki – modo eterno.* This is the first time I've seen an expressway ad like this; then again, I've never had a reason to stand still on the expressway. While traveling, if an ad catches my eye, I watch it on NetEW. Company names scroll across the main monitor as the mot passes an advert. Just touch the advertiser's name to view the ad.

Of course I could always do what the neon orange mot before me is doing now, which is to travel very slowly to view the adverts as they are meant to be seen. It's an American thing. Groups of people in mots easing down the expressway and watching adverts. It's a party.

The orange mot has stopped before me. The passenger window is sliding down. A light rush of cigarette smoke escapes from the mot's cabin.

"Umm … why are you standing on the expressway in the rain at night?" asks the young and pretty blonde with shocking green eyes, holding a near empty wine glass and an unlit cigarette.

"Just waiting for you to ask me that question. Now all is right in the world."

The blonde turns to the other five people in her party. The glowing tips of cigarettes, fun whispers –"James Dean is so cute" – ride above innocuous pop music. Now giggles erupt from their mot.

"Shut the window the rain is coming in," someone says with a smile in her voice.

"Okay," says the blonde. Then she looks at me. "You're cute." The passenger window rises with a charge of high laughter. Their mot crawls forward and I become the; *'remember that guy standing in the rain on the expressway'* story.

I open my old mot door and confirm the vehicle is empty. The cabin reeks of cigarettes, piss and blood. I see the blood on the carpet and splattered along the backseat, and left door panel. I check the dash and see the battery is depleted. The autopilot is engaged and the disabled vehicle signal has been dispatched. A tow vehicle will be here to collect this mot soon. And of course, I'll get the bill for towing as well as a ton of other charges. I sit behind the wheel of my old mot and look about the cabin for clues. I pull up the trek log for the last twelve hours and send the data to the Shorter. I give my old mot another pat down and still find nothing.

At least now I'm sure that Nikki has the Bolt and my wallet.

I get out and walk back to the Shorter.

Across the expressway from the James Dean ad I watch a family of five enjoy a festive meal featuring Porterhouse cut steak at Coate's fine family dining, exit 38 on Ryeson Blvd. The bold lettered tagline reads: True Stock – FirstGen Meat only. No clone meat! Fresh live seafood!

I get into the Shorter and reset the autopilot for return to NYC. In a heartbeat the mot is airborne and zips off down the expressway.

Wet as hell, I take off the poncho. I open the foxhole and remove the large cloth towel. I toss the dripping poncho into the foxhole. I dry my face and hair.

I pull up the trek log from my old mot and advance the schedule to the bar. I send the time stamp, names and physical quadrants to MATRIX, NORA and PAUL; government databases for social affiliations, purchasing nuances, employment, all means of traffic, and the mass aliases of the world's citizenry.

The Shorter's phone pings. It's Griffin. I answer. "Yeah."

"So you followed your old mot to Missouri. What did you find?"

"Nothing. It was a decoy. I'm going to scan the trek log."

"Right."

"Anything else?" I ask.

"No. I just wanted to make you aware that I'm aware of your every move and I'm happy about that. And you want to keep me happy."

"Sure. Nothing's closer to my heart."

"Good." Griffin hangs up.

Asshole. I turn off the unit.

The Eye uploads my visual request and begins playing. The replay is like watching a shifting shattered mirror composed with a Time/Story program. The images courtesy of city and traffic cameras

I watch myself tumble from my old mot with the aid of a boot – Nikki's boot – square on my ass and shoving me out of the driver's side door. My old mot pulls away and I lie on the street like so much curbside waste. My old vehicle continues along Second Avenue. Then the mot heads uptown. At 52nd Street, Nikki and Ezra get out of the mot and run into the Fuji Hotel. The mot drives away.

PAUL's data log pings. PAUL informs me that Nikki is also known as Karen Davenport, Sabina Aveo, Emily Simpson, and Vanessa DiRay – this alias has licenses for prostitution, a personal protection device and traditional firearms. Yet, PAUL can't confirm her real identity. Birth records have not been found that agree with any of her known aliases. She is quite the chameleon. Each alias has a distinctly different face and demeanor. She can be a vixen super-goddess, or a reserved and shy woman. She has a great talent with makeup. She is an expert with firearms and explosives. She is known and watched by seven security agencies.

I see that NORA is loaded so I do a quick scan on the life and times of the person also known as Nikki Porter. She shops at trendy boutiques for her jewelry. She buys clothes and shoes from whoever is selling clothes and shoes. No brand or shop loyalty. Frequent visitor to the Underground. Narcotics, drugs, alcohol most purchased are hash, experimental, and all manner of liquor with whiskey at the top of the charts.

Her other alias, Vanessa DiRay, owns a Bettie .38. That's an expensive and painful weapon. The device has caused permanent disfigurement to the targets. Last I heard it was up for recall, but there's no flag on Vanessa's record so I guess the recall didn't happen. The traditional firearms are an Anton 9mm and a Smith & Wesson. 38, which is the gun she used when we raided Bobby's apartment.

I take a moment to add my two cents to the global law enforcement community regarding the person a.k.a. Nikki Porter. I open a new memo and write: See London Deep files – Pam Brown. Confirm Nikki Porter is Pam Brown.

I think about writing more. But I don't. All I do is sit and think.

The Nikki Porter I first met over twenty years ago was a waitress at a diner on 48th avenue. Like many young and pretty teens, she had also worked the streets for a fast buck and wound up on the bad side of a cat named Special K. Another little pimp who would be king. Nikki was running solo on his turf. Nikki came to my office one rainy night with too much color in her face. Special K had informed Nikki that she now worked for him. Nikki didn't know where to turn so she came to me. Well, I paid a visit to the little king. I broke his face, and both his legs at the knees. I took the money out of his pockets and left him mumbling in agony and coughing blood in the street as I drove away in his ugly green but nicely tricked-out mot. Nikki paid me with great sex and a wonderful breakfast.

That was in the last days of the pimps and gang run operations. Before the Underground and the Grid. The streets of Manhattan were toxic from commuters, constant construction, all manner of curbside vendors, homelessness – just too many people, plain and simple. The city streets were at constant gridlock, all day and all night. It got so bad that gangs were robbing people as they sat in their cars, stuck in traffic, the victims gave their money willingly rather than being shot through the glass and having their corpse violated. I did a lot of bodyguard work back in those days. People hired protection for their trips to and from work, as well as escort for their children attending school. That had been very lucrative work and I was allowed to exercise a lot of aggression. Those were good times. Then the city hauled in the private security firms for traffic enforcement and general civilian security.

The bodyguard worked took a real dive when The Commons instituted the Model Citizen/Recovery Agent program. It was the task of the MC/RA to secure enemies of the state. These guys took anyone of danger off the streets. They did it with overt force and blatant organized terror. I remember the insanity of muscle and violence that shook the city. Now those months of chaos and blood are called, *The Days of Hard Progress*. The result, for better or worse, the public has been tamed. I could have joined a private security firm or fallen into a contract program but I'm not a team player. So I continued to work private jobs for questionable clientele.

And it seemed like life accelerated after control and order was thrust upon the people. Aerospace technology led the pack in the applied sciences. A few years later, the global transport grid was started, eliminating traffic woes. The subway system became obsolete. What do to with all that underground real estate? The Commons decided to turn Manhattan's subway network into the world's first adult playground. *The Underground*. Seemingly overnight, laws were established for the people's health and prostitution legalized. The WHO introduced the international health initiative. This act provided sound and affordable healthcare to every human on the planet. Only those with a clean bill of health were allowed to work and play in the *Underground*. This had the effect of encouraging the populace to visit a physician, dentist and mental health professional at least once a year.

The global finance ministers redefined wealth as immediate and constant access to life-sustaining funds. Prostitution was now considered a legal occupation based on this dictum. Licensing fees, union dues, cabaret levies and a host of other subscriptions proved the sex trade more lucrative than first estimated. Laws were adopted to capture the narcotics industry as well. There is always talk about opening another

Underground yet it remains just talk. The *Underground* is exclusive to Manhattan.

A wavering ding pulls me back to the now. I see that PAUL has sent me a message. I open it.

This individual must remain active and unimpeded. By law – do not capture, restrain, and of course, do not kill.

The message twinkles away. Are you fucking kidding me! I can't believe what I just read. Nikki has me spitting blood right about now. That message told me that by law, I can't hurt her. This is amazing. Who does this woman know? Who does she work for?

Sure, I can muscle Space's flash drive from her, leave a bruise or two, but if I get strong, someone won't be happy about it and next thing I know I'm in space. And I don't like deep space. I've been there. Way, way out there in the ultra black. Running laps on padded steel floors and breathing the same air over and over. Listening to the same music over and over. Uploading this book and that book. Watching vid after vid. Enjoying the never changing view.

Look, Apollo, pretty stars.

Like the ad says: space, it's not just for heroes anymore.

Space is a great romantic weekend date. Space is for convicts. Space is time. Space is money. You get paid to go there and you gotta pay to go there. Space means pre-cooked food, no sunshine, no open windows but plenty of filtered recycled air. Space means living in a bubble. Sure, you can take a walk outside the bubble but you sure as hell won't get any fresh air. And yes, space is cool if you're orbiting the planet on a day trip. Mesmerizing phantasmagoric experiences and images of Earth and the black sky. But deep space is where I'll wind up and it sucks. It's black. Very black. I will do all I can to keep my ass here on Earth.

I can't touch her. Nikki. I know she wasn't holding the needle but she kicked my ass out of the mot and that is a clear statement that our years of friendship amounts to her foot up my ass and me bouncing off the curb.

I close the files on Nikki and spend quality time with Ezra Biconeer's profile.

Ezra is just as Nikki had described, a retired archival bookkeeper with a class six clearance. He is listed as deceased with today as his date of death.

He appears to be nobody special. He had a perfect employee attendance record for a straight twenty-two years. Collecting information was probably the easiest thing for Ezra to do, but it took some talent to remove the data from a secured area of a federal building. In particular *that* file. The only reason such a file is still around would be to frame someone. How did Ezra know about the file?

The satellite feed for the Fuji Hotel has loaded up. I hit fast-forward. Three hours running time becomes thirty seconds real time. I pause at three-point-six on the clock. Run view at normal speed. I watch Nikki exit the hotel and enter a cab alone.

I call up the cab's license plate and request a track log.

I engage fast-forward and continue to watch the feed on the Fuji Hotel.

Ezra doesn't leave the building and Nikki never returns. Then an ambulance zips into the roundabout for the Fuji Hotel. About a minute later, the police arrive. I know where this is going so I enter Ezra's name into the city morgue registry. His weathered face pops up on my monitor. His was the fifth body logged in today.

21

"Entering Manhattan." The computer informs me while the mot complies with the city's speed restrictions.

The cab's trek log pops up on the monitor. Nikki's cab ride terminates at 301 Park Avenue. The Waldorf-Astoria. I run a credit check on all of Nikki's aliases. Karen Davenport appears as a registered guest of the hotel. Room 404. Good ol' Dance Whore Karen. She plans to stay for a week.

I'll be at the Waldorf in two minutes.

#

I pull into the turnaround of the hotel.

I exit the mot and a valet approaches. "Official business," I say. "Leave the mot."

The young man with wispy blonde hair comes to an abrupt halt. He nods as I stroll pass him. I can feel his eyes upon my back.

"Nice ride," he says.

"Yes it is." I enter the lobby and walk over to the elevators. I can see that someone at the front desk is interested in me, but they don't leave their post.

I step into the open lift and push four. A moment later the door opens at my floor and I step off. Her room is just a few steps away from the elevator.

I stand before door 404. Like the old times I tap into the Allround. I think 'Command'.

"Griffin here." I feel the fat little bitch inside my head. It sucks.

"I need security to open door four-o-four at the…"

"Waldorf. Yeah, okay. I see that."

"My primary target is protected."

"Oh yeah, who told you that?"

"PAUL."

"Who's your target?"

"Karen Davenport, a.k.a., Nikki Porter."

"Hold." Command is quiet. I study the smooth texture of the peach-colored wall before me. I look at my shoes and sigh because these kicks need a real cleaning. The tension in my mind loosens. Command is about to speak.

Griffin says, "Then don't kill her."

"Right, I got that part. I may need to flex muscle to get info. How about torture?"

"Green light, just don't get stupid."

"Understood."

"See how this works, communication. All you have to do is talk to me."

"Yeah, the exchange warmed my heart."

I hear an expulsion of hot air from Griffin. If I could smell it, I'm sure it would reek like sulfur. "Get the files." He said.

"I'm on it."

Command is silent. I go offline.

Door 404 slides like a whisper into the wall. I walk into the quiet room. The door whispers to a close behind me. No one is in the living room. I walk down the short hall toward the bedroom. There she is, asleep on the bed. Face down, tight ass smiling at me. Her breathing is neat and even. She's dead weight. Nikki had been running hard for hours; this crash was inevitable.

I scan the room, never taking my eyes off her body. The ashtray on the nightstand next to the bed has a few butts and a half-smoked joint. The wine bottle is near-drained, no drinking glass in the room, so she was sipping straight from the bottle.

I see her laptop atop a small oval desk in the far corner. Her canvas bag is on the chair next to the desk. I walk over to it. A quick glance into the bag confirms that files and disc are intact. I slip her computer into the bag. Now where would she keep my wallet?

Yes. It's behind the wine bottle. Things are going my way. I walk over to the nightstand. Pick up my wallet and open it. Bingo. Space's flash drive and all my cash and cards. Nice.

I stare down at Nikki. You had the time of your life, girl. I'd love to give you a tattoo that would commemorate the event, but there isn't that much black ink in the world.

I just … ah man, I just wanna …

I walk over to the door, pause, stare at Nikki's sleeping body. So many vile thoughts run through my mind. And I can't act on any of them. She escapes my vengeance. She is untouchable.

I see myself in the mirrors set into the tall closet doors. Jacket, suit coat, pants and shirt are wrinkled. My shoes are beat. I got rude stubble over my cheeks and chin and even my eyebrows look left-of-center. And I'm running this game without underwear. I'm a mess.

I'm disgusted with myself and the situation and every fucking thing associated with it.

I leave the bedroom.

What am I forgetting?

I exit room 404.

Yeah, I'm missing something.

In the elevator. Going down. Something is not right. Just can't put my finger on it.

PING in my mind. Command is live.

I open up. "Yeah, Griffin."

"So what's the deal?"

I think about lying because something isn't right.

"Another dead end. I got a few more places to check."

"Quit cocking around and get the file! Space, it's such a lonely place."

At least it's far from you. I think. My silence is heavy.

"Get the file. Get it now," barks Griffin.

Command is silent. I go offline.

The elevator opens and I step out.

It dawns on me. He can't see. Griffin can't see what I'm doing. Otherwise he wouldn't have asked if I had anything. Griffin should be able to see and hear what I do in real time. I'm a mobile camera to command. Why isn't he calling me in for repair since I'm not functioning properly?

I look down at the polished black and white marbled floor of the lobby. The floor is a clean work of art. And so am I. I'm the same as this marble floor. The hand of man made me. Griffin and the technicians would not have released me without a clean bill of health. I'm sure they ran all sorts of tests on me. He can track me. I'm in the Allround. And yet

Griffin is blind and he's not calling me in for review.

Now I feel it's not in my best interest to turn this file and disc over to Griffin. I'm sure he assumes I've read it and that makes me a security threat. The moment I hand over the file I'm dead. He said as much earlier with the comment that the sun was the only way to kill my ass.

My cell pings again. The number is unfamiliar and there's no icon. Then I realize who it is.

"Yeah."

"Do you have my flash drive?" Space asks.

"Yes Mr. Space. I'm on my way to you now. May I speak with Liz?"

My cell now displays a silent moving view of a wood ceiling with exposed wood beams.

Then Liz's pretty face pops into view. "Hi Boss," she says with a strained smile.

"Hey you. How you holdin' up?" I study her face. No tears, her eyes are steady.

"I'm good. He's a gentleman."

"Alright. I'll be there in a moment."

"See you soon."

The line is dead.

Liz looked and sounded fine.

Cool.

I'm about five minutes from Space's office. I leave the hotel lobby – and stop in my tracks as I watch two guys wearing dark suits enter the hotel.

I turn toward the pair to catch a better look. They are familiar to me. I just cannot place their faces; so, I tap into the Allround. I run a visual comparison on the profiles I just captured against profiles from the pool. A heartbeat later I have a hit. This pair match the men that ran past me outside the bar. Space's men?

Going inside the Waldorf.

These guys are going to rough up Nikki looking for this disc. She deserves it. Yet, Griffin has me on record for requesting her door opened only minutes ago. So I'll catch the blame for her black and blue body. And if they kill her I'm in a world of hurt.

Screw me. Now I have to protect her deceiving ass.

I turn around and re-enter the hotel lobby. I grab my cell and call Space.

"Hello, Apollo."

He won't show me his face. I hate this guy. "Yo, call off your dogs. I'm bringing the flash drive to you."

"I don't understand. I have no agents looking for my property, other than yourself."

"You didn't send anyone to the Waldorf?"

"No I did not. Should I?"

"No. It's under control. I'm on my way to you." I hang up.

Okay, who are these clowns? I'm not hard to miss so it seems they're not looking for me.

And I still have to keep them from hurting Nikki. If that's why they're here.

I follow them to the elevators.

I get in the same car. The tall one pushes button four. I push six.

They step off at Nikki's floor. The elevator doors closes and I hit button five.

The elevator stops at the next floor and I jump out and sprint for the stairs.

In the stairwell, I leap over stairs. I'm on the fourth floor landing in seconds. I open the door, look both ways and find the hallway clear.

I rush down the hall toward Nikki's room.

Door 404. There is a deep black burn mark on the locking sensor. The door is ajar. I shove it wide open.

"What the hell!" I hear Nikki scream. Then her cry is cut short. I'm guessing a hand over her mouth.

I place her bag behind the couch in the living room.

I hear a slap.

"You bastard," hisses Nikki.

I pounce down the hall.

Right outside her door I hear the scuffle within intensify. I enter the bedroom hard and large. One guy has his back to me. I raise my right hand and bring my fist down solid upon the crown of his head. He drops fast and heavy to the floor … recovers, shooting an elbow at my knee. I jump back, avoiding his attack and snap-kick him in the face.

His neck flexes with the kick. He looks at me. We realize

we're cut from the same cloth. This is going to be fun.

Out of the corner of my eye, I note that the other guy is stunned by the way I dropped his partner. His moment lost in confusion allows Nikki – never a quitter – to worm a hand free and poke the guy in the eyes. She then lashes out with a wicked kick and plants her heel into the guy's knee. He buckles with a falsetto howl that rivals the best heavy metal singer. She bolts toward the bed as the guy falls to the floor screaming like all hell.

I block a punch from my sparing partner. He blocks my left hook. I kick, he blocks. He punches, I block. Punch. Block. Kick. Block. Thrust. Feign. Block. Miss. Block. Block. Block. I grab his wrist and try to turn him…. He shoves his palm under my chin and pushes hard, propelling me back, forcing me into the wall.

"Kiss my ass," Nikki hisses.

I see the energy blast slam my sparing partner in the neck. He falls to the floor with manic passion.

Nikki has my Bolt.

That's what I had forgotten earlier. I was so caught up with the files.

She points the weapon at me. My old sparing partner is still and quiet. The other agent is on the floor sobbing and cussing.

I say, "No thank you or, hey, what are you doing alive?"

"I wasn't really sure you were dead. Ezra shoved the needle into your neck. You went down. Then he came after me. But I remember something you taught me years ago – I poked him in the eyes then punched him in the throat. After that I kicked his ass."

"So you killed Ezra…"

"I didn't kill Ezra! Assholes like these killed him earlier. I've been running like crazy…" Her hands and arms are all over the place.

"Put the Bolt away and give me a pillow," I say.

The agent on the floor is squirming, whimpering and slobbering snot.

Nikki tosses a pillow at me and keeps the Bolt pointed at me.

I shove the guy's face into the pillow, not enough to kill

him but enough to settle him down.

The guy goes still. I remove the pillow. I let the guy's head rap the floor with a dull thud. He jerks and gasps. He's going to live. Good. I need info. But I want to hear from Nikki first.

"I assume you kept Ezra alive to interrogate him. And I know you asked this question, why did Ezra want to kill me?"

"You're a military tool. You can't be trusted. Something about your eyes tipped him off. He said your kind is connected to a large mind pool that is constantly monitored. You're a *creep*."

Creep, that lovely colloquialism denoting a human or non-human service drone. She's right. I'm a *Creep*.

The bolt is still in my face.

I think I can beat her. I think I'm faster than her reflex to press the trigger.

"That's what I told you earlier. The hook up to the Library of Congress. The mind pool is called the Allround, but I'm offline now."

Her pupils dilate – I wrap the Bolt within the pillow and drag the weapon and Nikki to the floor as the muzzled flash drills through the pillow and into floor. With sure and measured thought, I backhand Nikki across the face and that pitches her back on her ass. She sits for a moment then I watch her eyes roll white as she crumples to the floor.

I ease over and repossess the weapon. The Bolt detaches from the glove once the mental connection is severed. This is pretty much how I acquired the weapon in the first place.

Friends don't let friends kill them.

The difference is the first friend was an assassin. I had pissed some people off and he needed the money. Well, he doesn't need money anymore.

I peel the gloves off Nikki's hands. I shove the gloves and Bolt into the side pocket of my coat.

Okay, I can't carry her out of here. A big black guy with an unconscious woman draped over his shoulder may draw some attention.

Ah, I do have a government vehicle.

I pull the remote from my pocket. There it is, the good ol' blue button. I put the remote back in my pocket.

Now I need to talk to the agent.

I grab the guy by the hair. "Alright cupcake, time for you to play through the pain. Who do you work for?"

"Federal agent. Under arrest," he says in a weak and pained voice.

I check the guy's pockets. Find his wallet in the inside pocket of his suit jacket. I open it. Michael Robertfire. Special Investigator. AMBRE.

"What is Ambre?"

"You under arrest," he repeats.

Then it hits me. I turn him over. His other hand is on his belt buckle. He has signaled for help.

Time to go.

I pull out the remote. I tap the blue button. The number sixteen flashes in the tiny monitor. Then the countdown begins, fifteen, fourteen…

I pause to look at Nikki before I pick her up.

Blood trickles from her bottom lip, which is swollen. She also sports a welt beneath her right eye.

She's gonna love me when she wakes up.

I scoop her up and exit the bedroom, quickly set her on the couch, then grab her canvas bag.

The Shorter is hovering outside the window.

I walk over and open the window. Reaching out, I open the door of the mot and toss the canvas bag inside, before returning to collect Nikki. I carry her to the window, lean out, and pitch her into the Shorter. I ease onto the window ledge then leap into the mot.

I close the door and punch the green button. The mot floats down and enters traffic going north. Nikki rests on the rear seat with the canvas bag next to her.

Going with the flow. I like to cruise the city grid on auto drive. The mot travels with the sense of traffic, if the majority of vehicles turn left at a given intersection, then my mot will follow. It is almost feral, like running with the pack.

I note that Griffin hasn't checked in and that's strange. Why is he not questioning the fact that I'm just cruising around Manhattan? And Space hasn't called and I'm fifteen minutes past the time I said I'd be there.

The *personal* at my right invites me to a sneak preview of

the new Melissa Turaxo movie, *Deposit. (My Baby's Stolen)*.

I look away as the *personal* displays a clip of the movie.

"You know, it's always a party with you around," says Nikki slow and lazy.

"Welcome back. And they were after your ass – not mine."

"What, you came to save me?"

"Yes. I had the laptop and files…"

"What." Panic wrecks her face as she checks for her bag. Immediately found, she performs a slow inspection of its contents. She finds her computer and all the files intact.

She exhales. She pulls out her cigarettes. Lights one up. She pulls out a compact mirror. She winces as she studies her swollen face.

"Thanks for the new look", she snaps. "If you had everything, why did you come back to help me?"

"Because… It's complicated."

"Complicated? What the hell, are you in love with me?"

"No." I say with ease, but I speak the truth to myself and the truth is *yes. I do look forward to seeing you. Yes, I do enjoy being with you. Yes, I do judge other women against you and they all come up lacking. Yes, I do care how you feel and what you think. Yes, with you, sex is always a joy. You're smart and funny and very cool.* My brainstorm continues and I do my best to ignore it.

I say, "Somebody very important wants your skinny ass alive. Since I was there only moments before, I didn't want to get blamed for any undue harm that would have befallen you."

"Who wants me alive and why?"

"I don't know. It's in your profile."

"What profile? Where did you get a profile on me?" She moves to the front seat. Now facing me, I see that the right side of her face is swelled and highlighted with wicked red blush. Her lips are large and mean.

"Are you working for the government?"

"No," I say and I don't feel I'm lying to her. "I still work for you."

She is angry, confused and in a lot of pain. She lets out a heavy sigh. Smokes her cigarette.

I pull away the top cushion of the rear passenger seat; open the foxhole. I find the med kit. I pull out the instant ice. I twist the pouch and give the chilling bag to Nikki. She offers a low smile of thanks and places the cold compress against her face.

"Fine," she states at last.

My mind pings. It's Satan. I answer the call.

"Yeah."

"Why did you go back to the room?"

"Something didn't jive right and it took me a moment to figure it out."

"So what was it?"

"Intra-agency politics."

"What the hell are you talking about? All I'm interested in is a file that reads, Project Blue Book appendage sixty-three A. Can you do that for me? Just concentrate on that and only that."

"Ambre wants the same file." I say, joyfully ignoring him.

"Who is Ambre?"

"I don't know. But they got guys looking for the same file."

"They?" Command is silent. So I access PAUL via the Allround. It only takes a moment. AMBRE is the Alien Management Bureau Recovery/Evidence. Doesn't take a genius to figure out that mission statement.

I feel Command is back. "Okay, talk to me slowly," Griffin, says.

"I encountered a couple of Ambre guys in room 404."

The mot's trip meter pings; indicating trip time to Space's office is three minutes. The vehicle hovers like a turtle as it makes a left turn, then, flows into the rapidly moving westbound stream.

"Hey – I'm talking to you?" Griffin's whiny voice sounds in my head.

"What? Sorry, I was distracted."

"Distracted? I'm your master! Pay attention to me and me only. Tell me what you said to the Ambre agents."

"Nothing."

"Nothing," he repeats.

Hot silence.

"Just get me that file."

Command is silent. I go offline.

Nikki turns in her seat to face me. "I need the Project Blue Book file," she says.

I ask, "Why?"

"It's complicated."

I smile and shake my head.

"We'll be at Space's office soon. I'm going to give him his flash drive. He's going to give me Liz. We can talk about *The File* after that."

"Space is holding your secretary hostage?"

"Yeah."

"So you really came after me to get Space's drive to save her. The Project Blue Book file means nothing to you."

"What is it about you and this file? I get that it's incriminating to the President, but damn, I feel I'm missing a bigger issue."

"You are."

"Then educate me."

"Can't trust you. You're wired."

I remain silent.

"How long before your handlers catch up to us and take me in?"

That's a good question. Griffin knows where I am. I'm a blip on a map. Yet, it appears that he can't monitor my actions or else he could see that I have the file. That means I'm not leaving a wake in the mind pool. When I removed my first tracer, I also had Geek teach me how to detach from the Allround. I'm able to retrieve data without leaving any behind. It's been years and I've taken it for granted. Yet, is it something Griffin would be aware of? And I know that being denied access to my mind-stream would be a problem that he would rectify.

"Are you mind communicating with them now?"

"No. I'm thinking. Facts, you so rightly stated, are not quite right."

"What?"

"I'm being used. Again."

"If you share a common mind field, then your handlers are aware of your actions. They would know if you had or hadn't hurt me. So why did you come back and help me when your innocence can be proven?"

"All information can be manipulated. Just because they have the truth doesn't mean they will use it truthfully. You know the old saying, the better armed with the truth, the better lie can be told. It's in my best interest to keep you alive and healthy."

We drive in silence. She watches me, thinking…. "You are screwed up," Nikki states.

I nod.

A moment later we enter the turnaround for Space's complex. I disengage the autopilot, but I don't stop where the valet recommends. Instead I continue through the curved driveway and return to the avenue.

Now streaming in traffic heading downtown.

"What's going on?" Nikki asks.

"I gotta go to the Geek. He'll set me free."

22

I call Geek.

"Hola mi amigo."

"En route to Brooklyn. I'm not alone. I have an organic female aboard. Put me down."

The line is silent.

I leave my line up.

"What's going on?" Nikki asks with a worried pitch.

"Nothing pleasant." I reply. I keep my eyes on the road and the monitors.

"Wonderful." Nikki shakes her head in disgust. She wants to speak but she's too frustrated to form a sentence.

"You got any cigarettes?" she asks.

"No."

"What the…"

23

I wake up with mild discomfort in my chest.

I open my eyes to soft light. I hear the music of Recoil.

I say, "Subhuman. Nice."

"Welcome back. Yeah, thought you'd appreciate that. Also proves your drive and recall is in working order." The voice is even and pleasant. It's the voice of a man that has no worries.

"Thanks, Geek," I say. I look around the room. Same as it ever was. Geek is dressed in a red leather jumpsuit. His hair black, a short and neat Afro. Same as it ever was. He wears dark glasses, which he now removes, revealing quiet, light brown eyes.

Nikki is sitting in a metal chair, handcuffed to a metal ring protruding from a smooth steel wall.

"Howdy. Please tell Geek to let me go."

"No. You're right where I want you. Geek, meet Nikki."

"Both of you – assholes," she hisses.

"You keep such pleasant company, Apollo."

I smile. "She grows on you. Talk to me, Geek."

"The tracer was attached to your heart. I had to kill you to remove it. I used an EMP to stop your heart; then removed the tracer and deactivated it. I sewed you up a few minutes ago."

I look down at my chest. I see six inches of little black stitches.

"Can you help me get out of the Allround?"

"Yeah, funny thing about you and the Allround. You're live and swimming freely in the mind pool but you're leaving false memories. It doesn't make any sense. Unless you're becoming real, man."

"What the hell are you talking about and what the hell are false memories?" I try to sit up but I feel tight and weak. I decide to remain prone on the table.

"The real man thing is a bad joke. As for the false

memories, well, see for yourself. I'm in the Allround now and here are your entries. Since I restarted your heart you've left these memories in the mind pool. You've been to the beach. You've flown over the Grand Canyon. And right now, you're sailing along a coast."

"What the hell is that about?"

"Visual aphasia is a good way to look at your condition."

"I feel fine."

"You seem fine to me." The Geek lights a cigarette.

"Hey, can I have one of those, please?" Nikki pleads.

The Geek gives her a smoke. He sparks the flame. Nikki inhales deeply. She exhales slowly, as though kissing the smoke. The ceremony brings a smile to her face. I find the moment very erotic.

"Geek." I nod at the cigarettes. The Geek obliges. He even sparks the flame for me. Good guy, the Geek. I take a deep hit off the smoke, let it roll through me, then, exhale long and slow.

Yeah, that's a good drug.

"So Geek, what did you use to knock us out?" I ask.

"I put you down with a localized Sonny. I left her awake." He shrugs his shoulders, and his face crinkles around his nose and mouth. I get the feeling he's suggesting an organic female poses no threat, so there was no reason to put her down.

"She didn't give you any trouble?" I ask.

"Not much. I think she was in shock. I just cuffed her and brought her aboard."

"Yeah, shock, that's it." She sighs and shakes her head. Hits her cigarette. She looks around the warehouse-like cabin. She sees the dense rows of bookracks against the walls and massive block servers and a workstation adorned with dozens of tools, gadgets and doohickeys.

"You created him." She stares at Geek but points to me. "You did all this by yourself?"

"By myself, hell no. It's my design and overall concept but there were thousands of medical doctors, psychologists, physicists and technicians of every trade involved with his creation."

"Well, I dig your work. But I gotta say, he's a bit glitchy at times." Nikki looks at me with a certain curious inspection. "So he's a natural construct. Where'd you get the source material?"

"Donated egg and sperm. Nothing nefarious," Geek replies with a smile. "He's one hundred percent organic human, save a few dozen microscopic computer implants. Science just played with the natural design. Just imagine every cell, every drop of blood, every oxygen molecule, has a superman complex. To the world at large, he is invincible. Yet certain elements can immobilize him, allowing people like me to kill him. It's not an easy process. You need the right tools and have to know his design." Geek hits his smoke as he points to my chest. The stitches are gone. The scar is not prominent either. He's so proud of himself. And me, I guess.

"What did Ezra use on me?" I look at Nikki

"I don't know – and it took me by surprise too! I mean how did he know you were coming and why did he have a needle? I don't know why. I get that I was used. That part I get."

"What happened?" Geek asks.

"A friend of hers shoved a needle into my Mjac and injected me with something that nearly killed me. Griffin said the boys at the lab are surprised I survived the attack. He never told me what was used on me."

"I can tap into the lab database and pull it up." Geek stands up and comes to me. I feel his fingers do a spider dance over the nape of my neck as he examines my Mjac.

"I didn't notice anything wrong when I hooked you up earlier. Pretty smart attack. The Mjac is an Achilles' heel. Someone knows more about you than they should. When did it happen?"

"Less than twelve hours ago," I say.

"Really?" Geek replies as a sick smile sneaks over his lips.

"Yeah, why does that make you happy?"

"I just marvel at your recovery time. Your Mjac looks fine. Also the chest scar is gone. Healing time after major surgery, seven minutes. You're getting better with age. Exceeding all expectations for your model. Amazing."

"How many are there like Apollo?" Nikki asks.

"There are many," Geek states.

"There were fifty in my platoon. One was killed by remote

control just to show the rest of us it could be done," I say, with a memory of that long ago moment as clear as the last second.

"Yeah, but I didn't put a bomb inside of you. You're my first, my baby boy; no way I'm treating you like that. That's why I'm no longer part of the program. Persona non grata to party and state."

"And that's why I come back to you." I take a short hit off my cigarette. "So what's up with my mind? Is it possible for me to nap? I think that's what happened to me after they released me from the shop. It was very weird."

"I – what do you mean, nap? You mean you just nodded off?"

"Yep."

"That is weird," replies Geek. He moves to his main computer console and presses one button on the keyboard. An image of a kite dancing in the wind appears above his workstation.

Geek says, "See, you're still leaving false memories. Right now you're flying a kite. Let me scan for any, *downtime*."

Nikki asks. "Can you see into the memories of all the freaks like Apollo?"

Geek nods.

"How about a peek at Lynch Alstor?" I say.

"I heard they just sent him into space." Geek says. He hits a few buttons on the keypad.

"Do you know why they turned him starman?" I ask. I reach up and feel the remote plug protrude from my Mjac. For some reason, I just can't get used to the insert. I want to pull the plug out but that would screw me up. Damn irritating.

Geek shakes his head. "I haven't heard anything."

"They think he murdered Fury Randall," I say.

"What?" Geek replies as he continues to work the keypad.

Blackness fills the monitor yet distant sparkling illuminations puncture the inky pitch. Geek manipulates the controls with an artist's touch.

Lynch looks into the mirror. The image reflected back at him is a different Lynch.

"What is that blur? Is that Lynch?" Nikki asks.

I realize that she can't see him the way I do. And Geek is so used to the sight that he thinks nothing of it. I say, "This is what I was talking about at Lynch's place. It's the blonits in our blood and skin. The units interfere with electronic transmissions so we can't be properly photographed or recorded and, the blonits mask our body heat, so we run cold as far as heat sensors are concerned."

"But within that *blur* is a code that tells Command who the soldier is," states Geek. He manipulates the controls and, a moment later, a fourteen digit alphanumeric code appears within the static smoke that is Lynch.

Lynch looks down and slaps Bobby's rigid member as he screws his pretty boyfriend. Bobby's beautiful pixie face is fixed in ugly ecstasy: eyes scrunched, front teeth bared like a rabid beaver.

"Well, I didn't see that coming." Geek says with a laugh.

Nikki and I laugh.

"Does this come with sound?" Nikki asks.

"Not in search mode." Geek replies.

A succession of remembered images flash across the monitor ...

Blood saturates the monitor. Rings pulled from the pasty fingers of a dismembered hand.

Slapping ... rough sex with blonde Bobby.

More blood and body parts.

I run with the rest of the unit into a building. I look over my shoulder and use my fingers to tell Lynch: two at eleven.

Oral sex: looking up at redheaded Bobby.

Nikki smoking a cigarette across the room.

Looking down at a pained Fury Randall. Lynch holds both of her wrists with his left hand and clamps her mouth with his right. Geek captures this memory.

The image remains still on the monitor while the memory pool continues live around the frozen image. Geek continues to tweak the memory pool.

The monitor is black behind the frozen hardcore scene. Then the black dissolves into a hotel room and the full moment comes to view. Malcolm Space rapes Fury Randall as Lynch holds her down.

Geek stops the pool. Now, he runs the memory feed at real

time.

"That's my bitch. Yeah… That's my bitch!" Space pounds his sex into Fury's thin body. Each violent thrust into the skinny blonde's body is like a boxer's punch. Fury snorts, her face is wet, her eyes are swampy and red.

Space slaps Fury's face. He continues to ravish his lean victim. Fury's body resigns to the abuse.

Geek jumps out of the moment. Moves forward. Fury is prostrate on the disheveled bed.

Geek slows back into the memory.

Lynch watches Space smoke a cigarette. Space seems, well, confused, and he smokes his cigarette like a man avoiding work.

"I'm gonna finish this." Space tells Lynch as he snubs out his cigarette in the ashtray.

Space returns to the bed and eases over to Fury. He studies her for a moment. And then it just happens. Space grabs Fury by her hair and pushes her face into the mattress. I don't count but I figure the assault lasts better than a minute, most of that time, Fury doesn't protest. Space crawls off the quiet bed. He walks stiffly to the bathroom.

Lynch approaches the bed. He doesn't really look at Fury's body. He checks under the bed. He picks up Fury's limp body and stuffs the dead girl beneath the bed. No ceremony. No remorse. No concern.

Lynch walks toward the mini-bar and pauses to study the mirrored closet door. The coded mist that is Lynch pulls out a cigarette. He lights up and smokes, as he stares at his reflection in the mirrored door.

I wonder if he's looking at himself or sensing something – someone – on the other side of the glass.

I see Geek flick off the contact. The monitor returns to swirling black water.

We remain silent as we smoke and consider Lynch's memory.

I see my shirt hanging on the wall.

I walk over and put it on. I reach into my inside coat pocket and pull out my wallet. I remove Space's flash drive.

"See if you can read this." I hand the drive to Geek.

He studies it. "Odd," he says as he continues to inspect the drive. "Where did you get this?"

"It's a Space creation. It's the recording medium for a special camera. Special probably means one-of-a-kind."

Geek nods and says, "I'm sure it does." He looks around his lab; in time he finds the proper hardware. He places the drive into a reader.

"So Space killed Fury," Nikki states. "And you say they exiled Lynch into space for the crime? Why didn't they look at the memory pool like we just did? That's a sure defense. It's obvious he didn't do the deed."

"I know but Space has friends in high places. So Lynch would need other evidence to save his ass and I believe that's what that drive is all about." I reply, pointing to Geek's reader.

"Bobby filmed the rape and murder. That's why he had the drive. Remember the way Lynch had stared at the mirrored closet? He must have sensed that Bobby was hiding in there and he just let it be."

"Can I get released here?" Nikki asks as she rattles her handcuffs.

I glance at Geek, nod my okay. Geek reaches into his pocket and pulls out a remote. He pushes a button with his thumb.

The cuff about Nikki's wrist pops free. "Thank you," she says as she massages her wrist.

"Why would one of the richest men on the planet kill a socialite?" she asks.

"Men have been killing women for asinine reasons for centuries," I reply. I turn to Geek. "You got anything for her face?"

Geek looks at Nikki. "Yeah." He stands and walks over his mini-bar. He reaches under the counter and pulls out a medkit and a bottle of rye. He fills three shots of rye. He opens the medkit and produces a popshot.

Nikki and I walk over to the bar. Nikki takes the shot glass offered. Geek and I pick up our glasses from the countertop. A round of cheers is said and we empty our glasses.

Geek takes the cover off the popshot, exposing the needle. He hands it to Nikki. "Just tap it into the side of your neck," he instructs her.

Nikki studies the needle, and asks, "Anywhere?"

"On either side. Not the throat," Geek advises.

Nikki injects herself with care. She hands the spent needle back to Geek. He places the cover over the needle and drops the popshot into a metal container.

We hear a ping. We follow Geek back to his workstation. A note is posted on the main monitor that reads, *Unable to read.*

Geek says. "I'm going to have to make a call for help." Then, with creased brow and thoughtful gaze, he says, "You know, years ago, Elizabeth Hudson-York and Malcolm Space were the king and queen of New York; a beautiful power couple. The story is that Elizabeth rejected Space's proposal for marriage and left Malcolm for Denson Weller Randell the very next day. Later, Elizabeth, pregnant with Fury, became instrumental in Randell's successful presidential campaign."

"You think Space killed Fury because her mother rejected him, what twenty odd years ago?" Nikki asks.

Geek shrugs and slips on his headset and gives his attention to his main monitor.

Soon he is talking in tech-speak to the friend he has asked for help. His fingers are a silent blur as they strike the flat keypad.

Geek meets opposition with each technical maneuver. The drive remains inaccessible.

The technical speak between Geek and his friend becomes compact hard code and line data. Geek's fingers hover then sporadically tap dance upon the keyboard as he talks with his friend.

I ease Nikki aside. The redness and swelling of her cheek and lips is receding. Her face will be healed in moments.

Nikki says, "So Bobby was going to blackmail Space over Fury's murder. That's the lifetime insurance he told Piss-Tommy about. Now it seems Lynch has been setup for Fury's murder. Yet, I'm sure Space still considers Bobby a liability; he is a live witness to a crime. And without the flash drive Bobby has no protection from Space."

I state the obvious, "He's probably already marked for a hit."

"Right," Nikki says with a nod. Then her brow crinkles, her

eyes pinch at the corners and her head sweeps the air with a soft stir. "I still don't get why one of the richest men on the planet would kill Fury Randell – of all people. It makes no sense. It's insane."

I look over at Geek as he places the flash drive into a different reader.

"Okay, enough about Space's problems. Educate me on the Jump One file. Why is it important to you?"

She looks me in the eyes. She's ready to tell me. Being here, in Geek's mobile home, she probably feels like she can trust me. She looks at my chest. She gently runs her fingers over my smooth, scar-less skin. "You're an absolute freak. I watched him crack your chest open just a few minutes ago."

She sighs, shakes her head in resignation and says, "My real name is Alima Āl-i Buyeh. My father was Burhan al-Jamil."

"The pilot accused of firing the nuke from Jump One at the base in Puget Sound." I say as it starts to come together. Burhan al-Jamil is also known as Lieutenant Colonel Adam Rose. His backstory regarding the Event is that had changed his name so he could join NASA.

Nikki says, "Look, my father was a level-headed, boring man. He was a damn good pilot, that's why he was selected for the Jump program. I've been on this path for years but I've never learned why he was accused of this insane crime. Now at least I can prove my father is not a terrorist. The flight log and the video prove he was following orders from US ground control."

I look at her, as if looking at her for the first time. I smile. She smiles back.

I ask, "Does your dad have a dirty past? Why was he made the bad guy?"

"I don't have a clue. He had an amazing record as a pilot. Before NASA, he was with the Royal Air Force and was the Queen's pilot of choice."

"We're in," Geek says with a hint of amazement.

Nikki and I look at the monitor above Geek and see Space chasing Fury onto the bed. The point-of-view is from the closet.

"Is that where the drive begins?" I ask Geek.

"Yeah. This is the start," he replies.

"So Bobby *was* in the closet. Good call, bodyguard," says Nikki. Her eyes never leave the monitor.

"*You* think you can cheat on *me!*" Space screams into Fury's face as he wrestles with her on the bed.

"You think I don't know you're screwing that pretty boy model! You think I don't know? Dumb bitch! I know everything!"

He turns to Lynch, who is just entering the bedroom, and screams, "Hold this whore!" Space's face is bent with pain, his small black eyes pop and burn and spittle flies from his razor thin lips as he yells at Lynch.

Lynch rushes over to the bed and grabs Fury's frantic arms. Lynch holds both of Fury's wrists with his left hand and clamps her mouth with his right.

"Good man!" cheers Space.

"Jealousy," says Nikki.

"Geek, you got a secure phone?" I ask. I don't want to use my phone. I don't trust it.

Geek nods. He stops the program and the monitor above his head goes black. No need to watch that again.

Geek tosses me a small black unit. It's heavy and looks like one of those archaic cell-phones from the turn of the century.

I hold Geek's phone and consider the options before I place the call. Of course, Liz is priority one. After that, the world is my oyster, via Space's money.

"What did you mean when you said I have a profile?" Nikki asks me.

It comes out of left field and it takes me a moment to recover, after all, according to the monitor displaying my streaming live input into the memory pool, I'm currently nude sun bathing on a white sands beach. And who can say I'm not. The Bible states there are more things in heaven and Earth than man has dreamt. And if I channel the Aristotelian binary school of thought, then I can realize the dualistic relationship between the sublunary and superlunary realms. Placing me here and now as well as anywhere at anytime.

Sitting on a sandy beach, it's nice to know there's a side of me that just wants to chill. I haven't had a vacation in … forever. I always work. I'm on call, in motion, in action all the time. Sleep mode is my holiday. Life is all about the next time I can go to sleep. But that involuntary thing that happened earlier, *the nap*, that is scary. That's like blanking out; like being offline. Not a good thing.

I break from my sad existential wonderings to answer Nikki.

"PAUL told me. It's one of the global citizenry databases used by law enforcement. I have access to those resources because my primary protocol entails domestic peacekeeping situations. Anyway, there's a big Do Not Disturb sign on your file. That's why I didn't kill you when I grabbed the file and your laptop."

"Wonderful," she says low and hot. Then, not looking at me. "Who wants me protected?"

"I don't know, but your ass is secure by law."

She huffs and storms away from me.

I look back to the phone in my hand. "Geek, get ready to send a sample of that file to an email address I'm about to receive."

"No problem," Geek says. "Nikki, I can hack PAUL. Give me a moment. For the record, I never believed that whole terrorist scenario."

"Thank you Geek," she says. She eases over to him.

I call Space.

"Yes, who is this?"

"It's Apollo."

"Where's my drive?"

"What's your email address?"

"What?"

"I want your secured email address. I want to send you something."

Silence.

"And does this something regard my drive?"

"Yes."

Heavy sigh. "Very well. Malcolmonlyatnightdotein."

"Malcolmonlyatnightdotein." I repeat to Geek. He nods.

A moment later. "File sent," Geek says.

"Check your email." I tell Space.

"I am."

Silence.

Then I hear Space swear; a vile, curt clip.

"You still with me?" I ask Space.

"Yes."

"Good. Now, you're going to let Liz go home. After that, you and I will make arrangements. Put Liz on the phone so I can tell her the good news."

Silence.

"Apollo?"

"You're going home." I say. "Just give the phone back to Space and walk out. I'll call you again soon."

"Okay. Thanks boss."

"Sorry for putting you in the middle of this mess. We're going out to dinner as soon as I lock down this affair. Now get going."

"I'm out."

Silence.

"How many people have seen this drive?" Space asks.

"Three to my knowledge," I reply. "Took some time and experience to hack it. They tell me it was like pulling teeth from a rabid bear.

"Speaking of which, you looked very rabid as you killed Fury. One of my colleagues is very disappointed that jealousy is the motive. Thought you'd be bigger than that."

"To hell with you and your colleague. What concerns you is money. How much do you want?"

"This can't be quantified with a lump sum. We're dealing in terms of years. Many, many, many, many years. Consider me an invisible life mate. So another thing I want you to do for me is to not kill Bobby. I'm sure he'll try to squeeze you for money. Just remind him that the people that made Tommy piss have the flash drive. He'll understand and that will keep him quiet. I'll call you again when I need to." I hang up.

24

Geek has hacked PAUL.

I look over and see the face of Nikki's alias, Karen, on the big monitor.

Nikki looks over at me. "Liz okay?"

I nod.

"Good," Nikki and Geek say in unison.

I set Geek's phone on the clear countertop.

"Keep it." Geek says. "It can't be traced, and you'll never pay for a call."

"Nice. I love free stuff. Thanks Geek." I put the phone in my pocket.

"And I thought I was being clever with the aliases. They completely know who I am. Every little thing I do." Nikki lights a cigarette and takes a quick hit; she blows smoke at the large display of her life, as PAUL knows it.

I'm not saying a damn thing. I'm not apologizing or anything. But that's only because I don't have to. My comments are not dated or signed, just part of a larger pool. I wrote what I wrote and that's it.

"It's all about national security. All of your activity is fed into one registry, then, summarized into this profile. The right panel of the page is personal entries from undercover contacts you've met over the years. Damn, you have been a bad girl." Geek says to Nikki with a smile.

"You try to get the truth out of the government and let's see how angelic your ass remains." She walks in a tight circle with slow and measured breaths. She wants to explode but she's keeping it together.

"Who put the don't touch tag on me?" she asks Geek.

Geek taps a few keys on the keyboard. Pages in tech-script flow over the large display.

"Looks like an executive order," Geek states.

"The President?" I say, and I'm surprised by the shock in my voice.

"Doesn't get more executive than that." Geek replies. He opens page after page of tech-script.

The perk in Geek's voice betrays his surprise "You know what? Glidden placed the do not disturb sign on you Nikki. And look, former President Cresthaven created a secret division called Ambre. It appears that Ambre's top mission is to secure the file titled *Project Blue Book appendix sixty-three A*."

"Ambre? Oy, again with Ambre." I say.

"Is this going to be a bad story?" Geek asks me, with a cocked eyebrow.

"Yes," Nikki answers. "We met two Ambre agents and really messed them up."

Geek nods and continues to finger-tap the flat keypad. Then he pauses to light a cigarette.

"Nikki's disappearance is listed priority one with WEB as of today at seventeen forty-eight hours. You're hot priority all over the world." Geek says as he smiles at Nikki.

"What's WEB?" Nikki asks.

"World Enforcement Bureau," I reply. "The last people you want to dance with."

"Great." Nikki shakes her head in amazement. "So the President wants me alive – or just wants the Jump One file?"

"I gotta say he wants the file in his hands and you dead. Now that WEB is involved this whole affair has escalated from cool quiet to blood riot. They're about a dozen of my pod brothers looking for you. And probably me as well."

"So the WEB is made up of individuals like you?"

"Yep." Geek and I answer in unison.

"WEB captured Lynch." Geek states as Nikki and I read along.

"He offered no resistance," Nikki says with a touch of disbelief.

"What was the point? All that would have happened is a lot of things would've been destroyed and in the end he would've been secured," I say.

"Secured?" Nikki asks.

"Rendered either temporarily or permanently immobile. Incapacitated." Geek informs Nikki.

She nods. "But not dead?" she asks.

"No." Geek replies.

"Lynch, Apollo, these WEB things can't be killed?"

Geek replies, "They can be killed, you watched me do it. But what's the point? Just put 'em to sleep. They can lay in stasis until duty calls. None the worse for wear. These guys are expensive. Killing them is just pissing away good money."

Nikki nods her approval.

I feel good about Geek's response. Too bad Griffin doesn't share Geek's point of view.

Nikki looks straight at me, yet her gaze is somewhat vacant. Her eyes are steady yet she's not there. I've seen that gaze before but always in more unkind situations. It's the look someone has as they sum up their life. A shit or get off the pot moment.

Nikki walks over and retrieves her laptop.

"How long are we safe here, Geek?" she asks after a long exhale.

"Indefinitely. I'm mobile and off the grid." Geek replies.

"Good, but I'm still going to create a new look." Nikki states as she opens her laptop. She ejects a thin silver wand from a hidden panel on its side. She finger taps the side of the wand and tiny tines jut out. She runs the wand/comb through her thick, curly black hair and her hair immediately turns early autumn red.

Geek and I look at one another with amusement.

"That's a neat toy." Geek says. "Where'd you get it?"

"From Japan. It's called Body Flourish. I'm a show model. It goes on sale next spring. The thing is, in order to effect pigmentation, you have to get tiny implants under your scalp, and eyes, lips, nails and skin."

She spins the lower end of the cylinder. She removes her shirt. She then makes a broad swipe with the wand over her face, neck, arms, the front and whatever should could reach on the back of her torso. This takes the August California tan out of her flesh, becoming a winter New England pale.

She puts on her shirt.

She pulls out a compact mirror and studies her face. She's very pleased to see no swelling or bruising. She pulls tweezers from her bag. She plucks her eyebrows with mirror in one hand and the small silver tool in the other.

Satisfied with her brows, she drops the tweezers and picks up the wand. She studies the tool, makes and adjustment. She holds the wand up, arms length before her face and stares at its tip. She taps the wand with her forefinger. Her brown eyes turn Nordic blue.

She makes another adjustment on the wand. Now she swipes the wand over her lips, reducing the volume out of her pout.

She inserts the wand back into her laptop. She opens the color pallet and selects a soft pink. She ejects the wand and swipes the tool over her lips, painting them soft pink.

In far less time than it takes me to heal from open-heart surgery, Nikki becomes a different woman.

She smokes her cigarette, yet, she does it differently, demure and elegant. She looks at me with a smile.

Amazing. She is not the same woman.

I think I'm in love – again. And like an idiot I ask, "Is there a new name for the new woman?"

She shakes her head, no, and says, "Nikki's fine." She takes a short hit from her smoke. "Okay, now what do we do?"

"Well, your plan is to expose the President and to clear your father's name. To that end, let's get the dogs called off. Give Geek the disc."

I turn from Nikki and face Geek.

"Can you get the President's personal phone number? I want to play the same deal with him as I did on Space. Just send him a snippet of the evidence."

Geek nods as he receives the clear disc from Nikki.

"Damn, I haven't seen a clear disc in decades. What's on it?" he asks.

"It's not as graphic as Space's but you'll find it interesting," Nikki says. "Do you believe in UFOs?"

Geek smiles. He looks about his workstation for the proper reader for the disc.

The room is quiet. Each of us locked into his or her mind. I feel a noise and pressure in my brain. I guess the Mjac plug is bothering me more than usual.

The new Nikki sits cross-legged atop Geek's workstation,

smoking, and watching Geek work his magic.

I pace the room, trying to quiet the white noise that is my thoughts. My mind being so unfocused is not normal. Even stoned I don't suffer this … deranged static. It's like someone is trying to contact me but the signal is being blocked. It's annoying as all hell. Must roll with it.

Nikki wants to punish the President. That's a losing battle. They will claim the disc and file are forgeries. Nikki's past will be exposed and she will be presented as the maniacal daughter of a villainous air force pilot.

Geek is enjoying the situation. His defiance is legendary. So he's in this little escapade for the long haul regardless of the no-win outcome.

And Griffin will cancel Geek's breathing privileges, unless Geek decides to come back to work for The Administration. Geek's brain is more renowned than his insubordination.

As for my fate, I'm looking at termination. Griffin will put an end to my lifetime contract unless I disappear completely. And with my newly acquired wealth, and Geek's aid, I may be able to do that.

25

"What's our status?"

"Well, Mr. President, I'd like to begin by stating that protocol for this type of event was followed to the letter."

I turn to see the Security Council conference in progress on the far monitor above Geek's workstation.

I hear a ping. One of my phones needs attention. I pull them both out. A green button on the new phone blinks. I check the phone. It's a message from Geek. It's the President's personal phone number.

"Thanks Geek," I say.

He acknowledges me with a nod but his attention is dedicated to the Security Council conference.

I call the President.

"Yeah." It's a statement, not an inquiry. Gliddin answers the phone like I do. I suppress the urge to laugh.

"I got something you want, and you got something I need," I say.

"Who is this?" Gliddin asks in a none-too-happy tone.

"Not important. What's your private email so I can send you details?"

"Who is this?"

"Damn – I didn't realize you're such a bitch. What's your email address?"

"You're talking to the President of the United States. How'd you get this number?"

"I asked someone for it."

Silence.

"What's this about?" Gliddin says at length, calm, as if he is lovingly placing bullets into the chamber of a gun before an execution.

"I have Nikki and the Jump One files. Gimme your email address and I'll prove it."

Silence. I can't even hear him breathe.

"Is this Apollo?"

Well, at least he's well-informed. "Yep."

"Okay …" The line goes blank. Dead silence: like a stone tomb on Pluto. I look at my cell phone.

"What's wrong?" Geek asks.

I put the phone back to my ear. "Not sure."

"Apollo. Send it to *zelayamd@pre.org*."

"Spell that." I request and he obliges. Then I hang up.

Geek sends the file.

I decide to wait a few minutes before I call Gliddin.

"Earlier, the line went dead for a moment there," I say to Geek.

"He probably tried to trace it," Geek replies with absolute ennui.

Yet, there's something about Geek's demeanor that betrays his confidence regarding the *invisibility* of his cell phone. And so I play on it.

"Let's say he can track this cell phone. How long before we can expect company, Geek?"

He doesn't stutter or flinch when he answers. "It's not that simple. I'm mobile, and projecting global shadows so they can't get a true setting. If they are able to track the signal, their best hit would place me in the country but they can't ID the state, county or city."

"You think they were able to trace it?" I ask.

Nikki takes a short pull from her cigarette as she studies Geek.

Geek rubs his eyes and sighs. "No. Relax and have faith, I've been living like this for decades. You can use the phone. It's cool."

I nod. That's good enough for me.

"Show me the snip you sent to the President." I ask Geek as I call Gliddin.

"I sent a stream, so he's watching what we're watching," Geek says.

I watch the monitor as I listen to the phone ring.

"Well no kidding. I'm not telling the world we fired on a UFO with nuclear missiles. The truth is not an option," the President states.

Third ring – he's not answering the phone.

I hang up on the fifth ring.

"He's not answering his phone. That can't be a good sign," I say.

On another monitor, Geek studies the local transport grid, no doubt looking for incoming trouble.

Nikki paces the room as if she's trying to stay warm in a meat locker.

I set my mind for fighting. I will destroy a lot of crap before I'm secured.

"Why wouldn't he answer the phone?" Nikki asks no one in particular. She spins around, approaches to Geek's workstation and asks, "Did he receive the file you sent?"

"Yeah. I can see that he did," Geek replies with a curt clip. Never one to lose his cool, this is a bad sign for the home team.

And Gliddin knows who I am …

My mind is unquiet. Static, or is this white noise? Damn Mjac plug… Can't think.

"Geek – are you sure I'm bug free?" I study his eyes. No, he's not sure.

Geek reaches into a drawer beneath his workstation and pulls out something that looks like an antique Colt .45.

He looks at me.

Then a shadow crosses his face and I know Geek and I have reached the same conclusion. I'm being used.

Geek aims the .45 at my face.

I see a bright blue flash.

I don't feel a thing.

Dead again. I love being right.

26

Slow and lazy guitar fades in and out as Jimi Hendrix invites me to Electric Ladyland.

I open my eyes and see Geek and Nikki.

Alive again. Naturally.

But no dreams this time.

"Griffin really had you tagged. I pulled seven very well designed tracking units from your monkey ass. I inadvertently disabled one unit when I shot you in the right eye. My scans didn't pick up any signals until you called the president, then all the bells and whistles went off. Good thing I have a deep security blanket over my traveling home. That's the only reason we're not in custody or dead, right now."

Geek hands me a lit cigarette.

I take a deep hit.

My mind is quiet. No static or white noise. I reach back and feel the Mjac plug is still in place. It doesn't bother me now.

Nikki smiles down at me.

"You're not human. You know that, right?" she asks with a smile.

"Yeah, I know that." But I feel so real. Aww, Geppetto, why did you make me? And what is this performance we're engaged in? I know you're directing this madness. Who am I playing in your production, the fool, the tool? This puppet must learn to cut his strings.

Yet I don't speak my mind.

So I say, "I didn't think I could be put down with just a plain gun."

"It's not a plain gun, I just fashioned the device to look like an antique. Your right eye is a reset button. It's the fastest way to secure you. And I got a million eyes for you." Geek replies as he eases back to his workstation.

Geek pulls a bottle of scotch, from the same drawer that had contained the weapon, and pours shots.

Nikki steps up to Geek's workstation as if she's a regular at the neighborhood bar. We pick up the shot glasses and drink.

I take a moment and drink in Nikki. The new look is stunning. Yet, it's somehow easy to believe that she's always looked this way. She's just beautiful and it doesn't matter what she wears.

"So where do we stand now?" I ask, loving the fire that courses through my gut and lungs.

"We're in Nevada, just south of Reno. We're in the clear." Nikki replies with a cool air. "We're heading back to Manhattan soon."

Sensing her pleasant, almost jovial demeanor, I ask, "So, did you and Geek bond while I was shut down?"

"You could say that," Nikki replies with a neat smile. "We watched the Security Council meeting."

Silence. We drink without looking at one another. Then she says, "So thanks to me, Gliddin is now certain the disc and transcript exist and he will stop at nothing to get it," Nikki states.

"Yep," I reply.

Then something hits me. "I need to call Liz."

Nikki reaches for the phone that Geek had given me earlier from the desktop. She holds it out to me.

"Is it good to use?" I ask Geek.

"Yeah," he says with confidence.

I take the phone from Nikki.

I call Liz.

"Hello." Liz replies.

Good, she sounds safe. "Are you okay?" I ask.

"Yeah, why shouldn't I be?"

"I think you may get a visit from some assholes that will use you to get to me."

"What – again! Are you kidding me?"

"No. This time it's the government so stay very low."

"Damn! Damn it Apollo! What the hell is going on?"

"I'll give you details later. Right now, just make yourself invisible."

"Fine." She hangs up.

"She's not pleased, is she?" Nikki says with an impish grin.

"No, she's not pleased." I reply. I pour another shot.

"You see, as much as they need to destroy the evidence,

they can still deny it if it's released to the general public," I say.

"The American media will ignore it. It will get play internationally but that's not enough to sweat this Administration. They'll just keep stating that the disc is doctored, all the while continuing to hunt us down in hopes of killing us and destroying the disc."

"So my glorious plan to make the government pay isn't going to happen." Nikki says.

"No. You're not going to get an apology or collect any money." I'm more delicate with my next words.

"And you'll only win a slight victory for your father. Yes, he was under orders to fire on the UFO, but he could have denied the order. He launched a nuclear weapon and he had to realize that if he missed the target, the nuke would strike American soil. Trust me, he will remain a villain in the eyes of many."

"I agree," Geek says.

"What about the fact that he thought he was shooting at a UFO? He thought he was protecting America," she says.

Nikki finishes her drink. She takes a cigarette from the pack, lights it.

"So I'm on the run forever," she states.

"I can help, with Space's money. I have to vanish too."

"I'll help in any way I can," Geek says.

Nikki begins to get angry. "I can use Space's money to fund a political campaign against Gliddin. Force the truth to see the light of day." She takes a short hit from her cigarette and stares at Geek and me. Then her eyes brighten and the mystery fades from her brow. Looks like someone has had an epiphany.

"Is anyone from that Security Council meeting, other than Gliddin, still alive?" Nikki asks. "And Thorosen – what can you find out about that guy?"

"I can answer," Geek says. His fingers dance over the keypad. Web pages pop up on the large monitor above his head, each page dedicated to a Security Council member. A quick glance at their birth/death stats shows that Gliddin is the sole survivor from that clandestine conference.

"I don't see Thorosen's name on that list, " Nikki states.

"Searching," replies Geek. "Oh, we're back in Manhattan."

"That was quick." Nikki says. "Won't that kind of speed register with ATC?"

Geek replies with bored confidence. "Yes, but shields deflect true position. We arrived in the city before Command captured the real signal."

I call Liz. She picks up on the first ring. "Tell me good news, Apollo."

"Coming to your home."

"Don't. I'm on the move and I'm being tailed."

"Has anyone made direct contact with you?"

"No."

"Good."

"I hate that statue." Liz says.

And now I know exactly where she is.

"Tell you what, I think you need a drink."

"Right."

We hang up.

"Liz says she's being followed. She's at Fifty-third and Eighth. There's a statue of Thom Rudi in the Hoover courtyard. Liz says that with his arms outstretched, reaching and gangly, he looks like Frankenstein stepping off the pedestal. It freaks her out. So I sent her to the M1R."

Geek nods and dials in the course.

"It's an Underground club. We'll be there in three minutes," he states.

"Nikki, you'll go into the club and pick up Liz and bring her back. You cool with that?"

"Yeah," she replies with a nod.

I grab the cell phone Geek gave me and stare at it. I can't remember Carol's number.

"Geek, are you sure I'm getting better with age? I can't recall a phone number."

"Oh yeah …" He pulls up the mind pool, according to which, I'm ice-skating at large indoor facility.

"What's wrong with you?" Geek asks, not looking at me, the physical me standing right next to him. We all look at me, as I appear on seven floating screens. "Well … All systems are green. You're running well. No abnormalities, nothing glitchy. You can't recall a phone number? That shouldn't be possible."

Nikki has a sweet laugh to herself.

"What?" I ask.

"I dunno. You have a sharp dress code and you're always neat, even your nails are fine. Let's face it; you can be a little prissy and fussy. You're a flirt, which makes you cute as hell. The mind pool indicates you're leaving false memories, which is deceit. Now you're exhibiting signs of forgetfulness. You have a lot of human traits for a construct."

"Good to see you're enjoying yourself."

"You're very good in bed." She winks.

Geek laughs, then says, "Interesting catch Nikki. I've tracked all forty-nine of the originals since day one. Each has acquired distinct personality quirks that programming should have prevented. The newer models don't exhibit any of the characteristics that plague the originals. Also, the newer models don't visit the Underground unless ordered and seem to abstain from drugs, alcohol and sex. A few of the originals were like that for many years but the clean living lifestyle didn't take. With the exceptions of Michaels and Becuá. Those are the only two original units that remain clean."

"Oh please, don't you start praising those assholes," I say, shaking my head in disbelief.

"What? I'm only saying that out of the original models, only two have continued to live a clean lifestyle. Let's see if these new models stay on that straight line over time."

"Was Apollo a bad boy from day one?"

"Yes, yes and yes. He gets the blame for bringing down the top ten. He was first out of the gate and everything he did was shared over the mind pool. And since he was having so much fun, others followed his lead."

"A bad seed with high self esteem," Nikki laughs.

Geek agrees with Nikki by nodding and smiling.

"Okay… back to Carol," I say.

"Just look at your phone for the number," Nikki says.

I stare at her. Exhale. Pull out my phone. Get the number. I punch the number into the phone that Geek gave me.

Nikki applauds.

Carol picks up on the first ring. "Hello?"

"Hi Carol, Superbad here."

"Well hello, stranger. Good to hear from you. You comin' in?"

"No. Got a situation and I need your help. Liz is coming to you. I need you to give her a make-over so she can shake her tail."

"Not a problem." Carol's reply was confident. And that's what I wanted to hear.

"Thanks. I'm sending a friend down to pick up Liz and bring her back to me. Her name is Nikki. She's beautiful. You'll know her when you see her."

"Very good."

"I owe you, lady. Just call."

"I know. I'll talk to you soon."

Carol hangs up.

I turn to Nikki. "Look, when you get inside the club, ask for Carol."

"First, thanks for the compliment. Second, and more important – Superbad?" Nikki howls.

"You telling me I'm not?"

Nikki smiles big. Then says, "So give Liz a new look and bring her back here."

I nod.

"And your friend will have a wig, make up, and clothes handy?" Nikki asks.

"It's a strip club," I state.

"Of course it is." Nikki chuckles. "What's Liz look like?"

"Damn, all these years and you've never met Liz?"

"No."

"Neither have I," says Geek.

I think about it. He's right.

I look back to Nikki. "Well, you saw her earlier, on the car phone."

"That wasn't an avatar?"

"No, that was true Liz. She's a lean and hard Spanish beauty with long, curly red hair. She's about as tall as you. She's has kissable thick lips."

"Easy, Skippy, I got it."

"Okay. We're parked." Geek states. "The Underground entrance is right outside the door."

Geek escorts Nikki out of the cabin.

27

I stand alone in the lab, waiting, listening to the cold hum of electronics.

Scanning twenty-seven monitors that display the earth. I count ten monitors that deal with this vehicle. I'm still on display on seven screens.

Geek returns to the cabin. He sits at his workstation. His fingers play over the keypad. A moment later, a new picture appears over Geek's workstation. It's a three hundred and sixty degree, live image of Nikki walking down the sidewalk. Up, down, north, south, east, west and all points in-between is presented in one flat, storyboard view, sans panels or overlapping windows or upside down shots. I watch Nikki's shiny hair bounce with every step she takes, the people approaching her, the people behind her, the constant traffic and cumulus clouds above and the sparkling sidewalk below as one continual view. The tall guy approaching Nikki is just as clear and in perspective as the nattily dressed teenaged boys behind her. I watch the tall guy pass Nikki on her left and he is now behind her nearing the boys, he turns his head to get a look at her ass. The boy closest to the tall guy notices the tall guy's glance. The young boy gives the tall guy the thumbs up.

Nikki descends the clean stairs into the Underground. Her eyes are scanned as she waves her Lifecard at the sensor. Green light – the clear force field shivers — and Nikki zips through the barrier. Nice to see she's disease free. If her health-line had been negative, she wouldn't have been allowed to continue. The cops would have held her and arranged immediate transport to a medical facility for a mandatory checkup.

"This isn't the city's feed." I state.

"That's correct. It's a camera I created. It's fixed to orbit Nikki."

"Cool and it doesn't seem to annoy her."

"It shouldn't. It has the same visual warping program as you."

"It's invisible."

"In a fashion." He shrugs. "The camera floats on the grid. There are some maneuverability issues to iron out but I expect to have units available to uplink within the year. It's going to change the way we view sports because as you see, the camera can sit right on a player's shoulder so the viewer is truly in the moment of any athletic event. Dozens of cameras can be placed on the field so a viewer can choose their favorite player and the angles they want to watch. The viewer can sit on the quarterback's shoulder, watching and listening as an angry defensive end delivers a punishing blindside tackle as the unaware QB is checking off his eligible receivers. Hell, a viewer can even *be* the ball in play. Yet, that's the tracking issue I'm still working on. It's easy to hitch a ride on a football tucked under a running back's arm. My goal is to smoothly track a fastball hurled from a pitcher's hand then being launched from a solid wood bat."

"Damn man, this is great. So how big is this camera?"

"Twenty-nine millimeters in diameter and weighs seven point six seven grams, about the dimensions of the human eye. And no, I didn't tell Nikki there would be a camera following her."

"You know every government on the planet will want this toy."

"Of course. That's why I control all use. You have to buy the service and cameras from me. Period."

"All for the money." I say without disapproval. No condemnation from me. I like money.

"Yes. Even you."

Even me. Geek created me because they paid him. Selfish behavior and economic incentives rule every aspect of life.

We watch Nikki pass Mr. Tony's casino on her way to M1R.

Mr. Tony's is a high-end establishment. The spot is solid with players. The bouncers turn people away.

The camera's point-of-view is over Nikki's shoulder, at the ultra-thin cashier for M1R, as Nikki pays the five-dollar cover charge. The cashier is a skinny black queen wearing an intricately looped sterling silver choker.

Nikki steps into the M1R then pauses to take in the busy scene.

Perfect breasts bounce to thumping afro-cuban drum and bass. Warm flesh offered for inspection. People of all types toss back shots of cheap alcohol and smell of scented and unscented crotch. Happy sweaty faces absorbing nasty memories as evidenced by the miles of thick wet smiles.

Nikki walks up to the bar. "Martini," she says to the willowy albino bartender.

"Sound quality is amazing." I say.

"I can filter out everything and focus just on her voice." Geek replies as he tweaks the controls.

The bartender gives her the drink.

"Is Carol in?" Nikki asks. Then she sips her drink.

The bartender studies Nikki. Then, after the tall waif pours a beer for another customer, she nods toward the right.

I study the monitor. I spot Carol against the wall wearing a long silver dress. She's cut her jet-black hair real short since last I saw her. Yet, her eyes and mouth remain unchanged; they droop softly at the corners, giving her a perpetually cheerless countenance, an expression she wears with erotic wit.

Nikki leaves a tip on the bar and having recognized Carol, walks across the crowded room toward her.

"Hey, hey ... hey – when you dancin'?" A semi-upright Neanderthal slurs at Nikki.

"I'm on at eight, love. I hope you stay and wait for me." She rakes her fingernails across his moist cheek as she walks away.

"Hell yeah I'll wait!" The drunk shouts at her back. "Show me your tits!"

Nikki spins and lifts her shirt for a flash. She turns away from the applause and continues toward Carol.

"Damn," Geek says.

I nod with a smile.

Nikki approaches Carol.

"Carol, I'm Nikki. Superbad sent me."

Carol studies her. In time she gives Nikki a cool smile.

"How is Superbad these days?" Carol asks.

"Sometimes he's alive, sometimes he's dead. It's weird," Nikki replies.

Carol looks at her with a cocked eyebrow and something akin to a question forms on her lips but dies.

The house music gets madder so the dancing girls become more frenetic. Of course dance whore Nikki has the beat.

Carol looks at Nikki. Something in Carol's gaze changes, perhaps brightens, then, is muted. I have the feeling that Carol *knows* Nikki.

Carol says, "I like the way you handled that customer a moment ago. You remind me of someone from that London Deep scene a few years back. You ever dance DUK?"

"I've danced all over the world." Nikki says, then, sips her drink. "Yeah, I've twirled around a London pole or two for fun and profit. I may have done a gig at Dark."

Carol nods to no one.

Quick as fire, a young girl appears at Carol's side. The happy waif holds open a slender silver case. Carol removes a thin filtered cigar from the case. She offers one to Nikki. Nikki accepts. The pretty cigar girl holds the lighter at the ready. The women light their smokes from the single flame of a penis head lighter. The young girl goes away.

Nikki exhales a fine stream of smoke. "I didn't think anyone remembered the DUK," she says to Carol. "That was so long ago. Parliament has moved onto much larger sex scandals."

"Yes they have," Carol replies with tight lips. She takes a hard and clipped hit from her cigar and exhales a soft puff of smoke.

Carol snatches a fresh drink off a waitress' serving tray. She knocks back the shot. "You're a strange little bitch," she tells Nikki.

"Yeah, I hear that a lot." Nikki replies. She sips her martini.

The ladies smoke in silent cool as they scan the doorways for Liz, as does Geek's camera.

Carol snatches another drink from a passing serving tray. "Why did Superbad send you? What did he tell you about me?"

"Well, he told me nothing about you. And he sent me

because, hell, I don't know why I got elected for this."

"Well, I remember you from the Dark. You're volatile. Downright hostile as I recall."

Nikki nods. "Yeah." She smokes and drinks and bounces to the beat.

Carol looks away. She smokes and drinks and studies the floor.

I say, "I forgot ..."

"What did you forget?" Geek asks.

"I forgot Nikki's time in London. You know Nikki as Pam Brown."

"What? Oh man – wow!" Geek says. He calls up PAUL's profile on Nikki and reads.

I say, "Carol owned a few shops in LD. Nikki used two of Carol's shops to stage her play. Nikki doesn't know Carol from the Virgin Mary, she just used Carol's shops because that's where her targets went."

"Damn. Nikki is a sick little girl." Geek lights a cigarette. "I will be very careful with her."

"You're golden now. Just don't cross her."

"Or try to make an example of her." Geek says.

I nod. That was the crux of the London Deep. Pam Brown had been set up as the corrupt whore selling corporate and government secrets. Truth was; Pam acquired her knowledge as payment for very deviant sexual favors. And she got caught when she tried to exercise an inside stock tip. She tried to barter her freedom with information but the more she revealed, the more this official or that authority found new ammunition and so bottled Nikki up even further, offering multitudes of clauses before they'd even consider a reduced jail sentence. Eventually she tired of it all and decided to burn the whole thing down. She set up an orgy with twenty high profile members of Parliament and law enforcement, as well as corporate leaders attending what had been a tame bachelor party. The whole affair was recorded and released online. Thousands of copies of the six-hour sex party were received in mailboxes around the world. Scores of lives were ruined by the scandal. Six of the men in the recording committed suicide. And it was the suicides that had been the most shocking thing about the scandal. Suicide was an abnormality. It just didn't happen anymore. And here were six within three months. Pam Brown became the most hated woman on the planet. So Nikki made her disappear.

I see Liz walk into the main room of M1R. She walks over by the bar and takes in the scene. She's probably looking for me.

Nikki and Carol look at one another, having spotted Liz.

Then Liz sees Carol. She walks toward her.

A few moments later the three women are up close and personal. We look down on the trio as Geek's camera is above the women.

"Good to see you, Carol," says Liz.

"And you, Liz. You look well."

"Thanks," Liz replies with a nod. She looks at Nikki.

"You're Apollo's infamous traveling partner." Liz says to Nikki. Perhaps a little frosty, but I could be imagining things.

The greeting doesn't faze Nikki. "Nice to meet you too, Liz. Do you know what your tail looks like?"

"Which one? I swear I got six guys on my ass."

"Doors. I want visuals on all the men that followed this woman inside and are showing interest in her," a discreet Carol says into the wire of her headset.

I note nine men take positions around the club interior. A few of the bouncers nod or motion to certain seated or standing men, five by my count.

Carol leads Nikki and Liz from the main room and into heaven on earth. The dancer's dressing room. Dozens of women in various states of dress and undress perfumed and coifed to cock-hardening perfection. The whole room, even the ceiling, is mirrored. You get a fabulous view no matter where you look.

"I gotta share this," Geek says with a thin grin. His fingers glide over the keypad. "This is going live over the net. I'm clouding out Carol, Liz and Nikki. And no sound."

"Man, you're Santa Claus today. This is gonna cause a masturbation wildfire." I sure as hell want to pet my puppy.

"I'm notifying TV producers to this link. The same guys I pitched the camera to last week. This should drive up the bidding war."

New screens appear above Geek's workstation. The live

images on the left screen are a silent feed of the dancers. The live scene on the right screen is dedicated to Liz, Carol and Nikki and has sound.

"The images on the left are the live feed to the net," Geek says, confirming what I'd thought.

Carol introduces Liz to the endless wardrobe. "It's all yours. Knock yourself out."

"Thank you." Liz says as she studies the selection.

Geek's camera continues to scan the dressing room. As soon as I spot a perfect set of tits, the best ass on the planet strolls by and once I lock onto that, the sweetest little girl pout stops the world. Then the camera angles shifts to close-ups and askew vistas of faces and bodies are captured in the many-mirrored panes. I'm in love with the elegant geisha sitting on the divan, and now the extremely tall Brazilian beauty gives me a warm fuzzy feeling, and definitely the profile of a thin Nordic ice-doll smoking a cigarette is exciting, and my-o-my, the smoky amber eyes of that petite Black girl are luscious.

In my mind I'm screwing them all right now and forever.

"Looks like our girls are ready to go," says Geek.

And like that I'm crashing back to reality. I see Liz has a blonde wig. She wears red bikini bottoms and a black leather vest. She works her feet into tall stiletto heels. Then she dons a blue fisherman's cap.

Nikki puts on a short plaid skirt and a tight and plain white shirt. She set her hair in unbraided-pigtails. Now she pulls out her wand/comb, makes an adjustment on the instrument. One pass along her hair and presto her hair becomes the color of stardust.

"What the hell? How'd you do that?" Carol asks Nikki.

"It's called Body Flourish. Very teeny-tiny implants under my scalp, eyes, nails and skin." She begins the demonstration with her eyes: she aims the tip of the wand at her eye and taps the wand with her forefinger. She then applies eyeliner and eye shadow. Now Nikki changes the color of her fingernails. The whole change of appearance takes about fifteen seconds.

"That's great!" says a tiny dancer. "How much for the whole job?"

"The deal goes on sale next season, but you can get hooked up now if you place your order with me – right now. I'm a basic model number nine B. Fifty gees and you're set like me but there is so much more that you can do. It's a Japanese outfit so you know the science is good. There are two offices here in the city." Nikki pulls out her phone.

"This unit can talk to anything on the market so just hook up with me and I'll give you all the details. And when you place your order, you'll get an appointment right away. It's a two-hour procedure with very little inconvenience."

The other girls scoot away to get their phones. They quickly return and patiently line up to hook up with Nikki.

"She's got more horses running than an afternoon at Belmont." Geek says with delight.

"Yeah, she's special alright." I reply.

And Nikki's so smug when she tells me I'm not human. She's got a ton of implants too so what's the difference? Even Geek has had modifications made to the original unit. In most cases, the only truly organic humans are babies.

Something occurs to me. "Does this invisibility include electronic detection? This camera must show up as an anomaly on the security units, especially the barrier entrance."

"You're right. I'm sure there are security technicians scrambling like mad to pinpoint this camera. It emits shadows, like my transport, so it will take them sometime to place the camera in the strip club."

"Unless someone at work is watching the feed," I say.

"And that's not happening," Geek replies with certainty.

"But web traffic…"

"It comes up as a porn link."

"Right, no one pays attention to that," I state with a knowing nod. Porn sites come and go like the breeze.

"Ladies …" Carol gets everyone's attention. "Nikki and her friend need to make a hasty exit, so I want everyone to go out and blitz the floor. Give it the midnight polish. Leave no dick unturned." She snaps her fingers and more than forty beautiful women leave the dressing room.

Geek kills the stripper-cam.

"I'm going out this door. You two exit anyway you can.

My doormen and the other girls will run interference. Sissy will show you the dancers' exit. You both look good so go ahead and make some money before you ease your butts out the door. And tell Superbad to drop in and say hello."

"Thanks for your help." Nikki says.

Carol nods then exits via a mirrored door.

"Here, put these in." Nikki hands Liz a pair of contact lenses. "Geek said they'd beat all security scans."

Liz dons the clear lenses. "Thanks. You've met Geek? I've never met Geek."

"He's cool. You'll like him."

Liz and Nikki follow a short redhead from the dressing room. Geek's camera is one and half meters above and in front of the women.

Our girls meet the bristling crowd with smiles. Sissy nods toward the left, at the end of the runway that disappears behind the curtain. Sissy then dances her way toward a lap begging for attention.

Nikki and Liz hit the floor like regular working girls. And Nikki, or rather, Vanessa DiRay does have a license to thrill. Nikki slides her ass over the lap of a skinny guy. He slips a five-dollar bill in her bra then squeezes her breasts.

Right behind Nikki, Liz smacks her tits against the face of dapper man waving paper money.

I knew Liz would be up for this kind of fun but Nikki's subtle expression says she is surprised by Liz's play.

"Nikki and Liz are coming back here, right?" Geek asks.

"Oh yeah. And I'm brewing up unspeakable sex acts involving me and the ladies."

"I got some unsavory thoughts of my own."

Nikki massages the crotch of her play as she peels single greenbacks from the guy's free hand. His other hand is engaged.

Meantime Liz is nursing her play. Liz has the perfect tits for this job. Her girls cut a slender upward swoop, offering fat brown areolas and thick nipples. I feast on that lovely set as much as possible. The guy supports her breast with a palm flush with dollar bills, a cushy green nest.

Geek and I watch Liz and Nikki ease away from their marks like a succubus, leaving behind mean smiles and warm, wet crotches.

At the end of the catwalk, behind the curtains, Carol approaches Nikki and Liz. She hands the girls small tote bags.

"Don't forget your clothes," Carol says.

"Thanks," Nikki and Liz replay in unison. The girls rush toward the exit.

Muffler waves wash over the exit gate; the music switches from M1R house pop to Balkan lounge dub without bleed.

The girls run down the bustling tube, stuffing cash into whatever pockets they can find, constantly checking their backs, racing past long metal bars that jut from the walls of both sides of the tunnel, offering liquor, narcotics and drugs from around the world. Some people consume their purchases at the bars while others have packages to go.

Liz takes advantage of the moment. She runs her card over a small black patch on the bar's metal surface. A menu appears in the black area. Liz makes her selection. The fat bartender hands Liz a cube of hash. And just like that the girls are back on the move.

"I didn't figure you for a party girl," Nikki says to Liz.

"I work for Apollo."

"True enough." Then, "You two sweet on each other?"

"We party. It's good," Liz replies with ease.

"I like you," Nikki says. "Give me your tote."

Liz hands it over. Nikki dumps both bags into a nearby trash receptacle.

"What the hell?" Liz says.

"I've had a hell of a day due to tracking devices. You can't trust anything that someone gives you."

Liz nods as she stares at the trashcan. "Right. Good call."

The ladies jog up the steps as soft red beams sweep over them.

Green light – the clear force field shivers – the girls glide through the security barrier.

Nikki and Liz sashay pass a group of cops. The cops nod at the girls. Nikki and Liz smile in return. They trot up the stairs toward the Underground exit.

The girls approach, then walk through the red, white and blue Sing-Cola logo.

Nikki and Liz wade through the crowd that is heading into the Underground.

They stand curbside on the busy avenue. Mots, *personals* and people pass by them. They receive hard and leering looks from the guys because they are still in their stripper outfits.

"This is where they dropped me off," Nikki says. "I assume this is where they plan to pick us up."

On cue, a big ugly yellow transport appears before them. I look at Geek and ask, "We haven't moved, right?"

"Technically. We hovered at about twenty meters above the underground port. We descended and I dropped the cloak."

A panel slides away on the side of Geek's vehicle. Nikki and Liz rush into the transport. Geek kills the Nikki-cam.

Nikki and Liz enter the main cabin.

"Welcome back," I say to Liz with a smile.

"Screw you," is the sweet reply I receive, accompanied with a hug and tender kiss.

"Hi, I'm Geek." Geek spreads his arms and waits for the love.

"Hi, I'm Liz. About time!"

They hug.

I feel good. It feels like a family reunion. Liz, Nikki, and Geek are my family. Albeit incestuous because I've had sex with both Liz and Nikki, and plan to continue having sex with both of them well into the future.

"So what do we do now?" asks Geek.

"How about giving me the highlights on why I was held hostage and then chased down?" Liz replies.

"We have dirt on President Gliddin and dirt on billionaire Space." I state. "Gliddin wants Nikki and me dead but if Space pays me for my silence we may be able to cheat the hangman."

Liz looks at me. Then she glances over to Geek and Nikki. They nod.

"The President wants you dead. What the hell do you have on him?"

"The truth about the Glass Shore. It wasn't terrorists. The Glass Shore is a result of an aerial nuclear blast. The target was a UFO."

Liz just stares blankly at me. Her lips are parted and I can see her processing the information. "When you say, UFO, you mean, something not from Earth?"

I nod. "Technically that's right."

Liz exhales deeply. I can see she's not comfortable with the idea. "Aliens – like in the movies?"

"No, not like that. I imagine the spacecraft was a drone. I'll give you my theory later. Right now, we got other stuff to deal with."

Liz nods. "Of course." She looks at Geek, Nikki and me. "And what about Space?"

"He killed Fury Randall."

"Damn! Are you serious?" Liz sits down on a steel chair next to Geek's operating table. Watching her sitting there sends a shiver up my spine. I can't count the times I've been resurrected on that table.

Liz snaps a stern scowl at me.

She says, "You have to turn Space in. You can't take hush money for murder."

I look over at the Geek and Nikki. Geek tosses his hands up and Nikki nods in agreement.

"Alright … sure. I can turn him in and collect on the reward for information leading to arrest and conviction."

"The big problem is that there are two very rich and important people that want you and me dead," Nikki says.

"And both of your adversaries can afford to keep bounties active." Geek states.

Liz says, "Get as much from Space as you can before you turn him in."

Geek pulls a cigarette from his pack. He sets the pack down on the counter. Nikki and Liz each take a smoke. I pass.

The trio sparks up from a single flame.

Silence.

"Geek, set up a few ghost offshore accounts. I'll get money from Space to feed those accounts."

"That's a plan I can get behind." Geek replies. He locates his keyboard. A moment later a web page appears above him. "How much money are we talking about?"

"Millions," I reply.

"Good boy. Okay. I have established businesses that sprouted from a few of my patents. We can easily hide big money in those ventures. Give me a few minutes."

I nod. I set my mind to work on the Gliddin and Glass Shore issue.

"So what are we going to do about the President?" Nikki asks.

"Yeah, I'm pondering that myself," I reply.

"Well ponder aloud dammit. I hate hearing my voice in my head asking the same damn thing over and over." Nikki says. She takes a long draw on her cigarette.

"Like I said earlier, you're not going to get an apology or compensation from the government."

"So my only recourse is a private campaign to spread the truth about the Glass Shore." Nikki says.

"Only conspiracy nuts will believe you. There will be no public outcry to re-open the case," I say.

"Well I gotta do something. I'm not gonna let this die."

She smokes her cigarette.

Nikki says, "We concentrate on the other plan. We have to prove the UFO was created. We have to prove Mkeyinc created the UFO. Like you said, dollars and cents – let's mess with Space's business."

"So what is the great Malcolm Space like?" Nikki asks Liz.

"Want to get to know your target?" Liz replies.

"Oh yeah." Nikki sits next to Liz, like an old friend.

"I was a captive, not a lover. I don't know anything about him." Liz looks at me, then back to Nikki.

"He's cute. Sharp dresser. Very, I don't know, refined I guess you'd call it. I found him cold, yet, I didn't think he was a killer."

Nikki asks. "What did you talk about?"

Liz sighs, smokes, "He asked me about Apollo. I told him you'd bring him the disc. Or you'd kill him."

"What did he say to that?" I asked. Thinking about it, if Space had hurt Liz, I would have killed him.

"He said he knew that by the fact that you didn't say it. He said most people, when threatened, will issue some sort of bloody revenge. You didn't. And he seemed aware of your reputation, so that obviously didn't sit well with him." She laughs a little. "He was very pissed that you cracked the security on his flash drive. He was raging over that. And now I got some questions. How did Space kill fury and why do you think he created a UFO? What exactly does that mean?"

"Accounts are live," says Geek. "Nikki, Thorosen doesn't exist in any database I'm aware of. And yes, please explain why you think Space created a UFO."

The moment brings a smile to my face. "Nikki, bring Liz and Geek up to speed. I'm gonna call my best buddy. Time to get paid."

I grab the phone. Dial up Space.

"Yes," Space answers with a cold note.

"I need one hundred million. Just got a hot lead on a sweet investment."

"One hundred million?!"

"Your net worth is estimated at twenty-seven billion. And let's just say that your mining firm did find gold on One

Ceres – which we both know is highly improbable – well, that would be a mighty find worth billions. Yet the reality is that in a few days, the news will say that a dozen very smart geologists misinterpreted a data stream and long story short, no gold on the asteroid. No matter to you because over the last month your stock has soared up, up and away due to the rumor. Don't play with me, just pay."

"Is this going to be a regular thing?"

"Now you know why they say *silence is golden*."

And so I receive a golden moment. I can't even hear him breathing but I know he's still there. I give it another heartbeat and right on cue.

"Fine. What's the account?"

I look over to Geek's monitor and then read the digits to Space.

"Give me time," he says.

"Make it work." I hang up.

I address my family. "Once we get the money, we'll make our moves."

"And what moves would I be making?" Liz asks.

"I was just getting to that." I reply with a smile.

I look at Nikki. "You got two commissions waiting for you, Liz and Geek. Set up appointments for them to get the deluxe Body Flourish deal. And you might was well get an upgrade too."

"Good thinking, and I've got the perfect doctor. She's uptown on Riverside Drive. And what about you, Apollo?" Nikki asks. Then she winces, "Sorry. Body Flourish can only be performed on organic humans."

"No matter. I reason Geek will pick their brains, allowing him to rig something up for me."

"I believe I can turn you into a chameleon now. I think I have the right hardware for the job. But you're right; I should get the science on this deal. Then I'll be able to adapt a clean program for you."

"Nice," Nikki says with a nod.

"Okay let's go back a step or two," Liz says, wide-eyed, her mouth a soft oval of confusion. "Apollo, you're not an organic human?"

Nikki says. "I've watched Geek *kill* Apollo and then

resurrect him twice today."

Liz and I stare at one another. "Wow. I never imagined. You're so life-like." Liz chuckles. "I'm sorry, I know how that sounds, but the Housemaid ALUs are so weird. Kinda creepy."

Everyone nods.

"Apollo debuted a decade before Dejann created the Housemaids series." Geek says with solid pride. "Of course, he cost a helluva lot more money than what it cost to build the average animated life unit."

"You created Apollo?" Liz asks.

Geek nods with a smile.

"Cool. I like your work," Liz replies. Then, "This is one insane day. My boss is a *creep*. I was held hostage by the richest man on the planet, speaking of which, you're saying that Space created a UFO to be shot down by American air defense, to secure roughly four states for his corporation. Is that what you're saying?"

"In a nutshell, yes. I doubt he imagined such extensive damage. But it was nothing more than a power play," I say.

"It's an interesting theory but Space didn't create the UFO. I saw some of the physical debris from the Glass Shore event. It was amazing stuff – it was thin metal and it floated. It was not of this world." Geek states.

"Space created the grid. That comes after the Glass Shore. He affected selected debris with then unknown technology. You just confirmed it. Metal that floats. At that time, he had two orbiting space stations and mining operations on Mars and some asteroids. Of course the source material was off-world," I say.

Geek considers this. His face sours. "What the hell." He taps on the keypad; moments later, web pages dedicated to Malcolm Space appear above Geek's workstation.

I study the small picture of a self-satisfied Space. Malcolm has a small, oval-shaped face, gently pinched at the ears and chin. His hair is sunlight blonde, wavy, and cropped close. A blade thin nose splits his tiny black eyes that are seemingly devoid of eyelids and eyebrows. His lips are sharper than his nose. He looks like a genius.

I point to the Wiki-page. "See, Global Magnetic Transport

Grid established in Phoenix, Arizona in twenty sixty-nine. I point to the page at the upper left. "Glass Shore happened in twenty sixty-two."

Silence. Geek, Liz and Nikki read.

"I had always thought that Space's success was a combo of good education and hard money. And, of course, I believed he had access to the same debris from the Glass Shore as I did," Geek mused, "but he knew what to do with it. Hence the grid. But, looking at the timeline of his patents with a conspiratorial eye, I can see that your theory has merit. It's very unnerving."

Nikki points to a page. "What stands out to me is the patent for True Balanced Metal, granted in twenty fifty-nine."

"Yeah, that's big. There is also the Harmonic Actuator, granted the same year as the Event. The Harmonic Actuator is the operating platform that allows for undisturbed motion throughout the grid."

I say. "Both of those elements would also make a convincing UFO."

"Yeah they sure would," Geek says as he expels a shot of hot air. He continues, "This article is over twenty years old. I never knew this. Little Malcolm changed his last name from Wauglauneetz to Space because, and I quote, 'I don't want to be forgotten. When this generation and generations going forward look to the stars, they will speak my name and see my face'."

"Arrogant little shit," Nikki says. "Is it possible to have something greater than a god complex?"

"Well, unfortunately he's right," I say scanning the web pages before us. "He is the space industry. He has more operating space stations and mining companies than any other corporation. He owns the only off-world prison. He owns Celestial Fields, the only off-world graveyard. He owns the most transport ships and he may as well own the military, no one else gets the contracts like he does. His fortune is as vast as space and billions of people follow his lead. He lives up to his name. Everything he is; is off-world."

"Except for being a rapist and murderer. Can't get more terrestrial than that," Nikki says with that special venom that could burn through concrete.

And kills the conversation.
Nikki walks away and consults with her phone.

191

30

A bouzouki plays softly in a distant section of Geek's cavernous transport.

"Why are you listening to Greek music?" I ask.

"Running a language program." Geek replies as he continues to read about Malcolm Space.

I wait … and now I hear vocals but I still don't get it. "What kind of language program?"

"I'm exposing new *germs* to archaic and dead languages. You're not listening to modern Greek."

I absently nod with slight understanding. I'm made of *germs* – organic microprocessors. Live, learning organisms. I think I get it. "Dozens of translation programs already exist. How is this different?"

Geek shakes his head. "This is primarily about language preservation. There was a big push in the last century to save dying languages. English has wiped out thousands of the world's minority languages. From North America, to Hong Kong, Eurasia, to the Pacific Islands, indigenous speech was captured on audio and video, but no one has done anything with the recordings. I'm going to offer the treated germs to linguistic scholars and tribal ancestors. Keep the voices of the past alive."

"What are *germs*?" Liz asks.

Before Geek can respond, we hear a ping and a red dot appears in the middle of the air above his workstation. Geek taps the space bar and the disembodied red dot explodes into a web page. It's a bank statement.

"Damn – the money is in!" Geek slaps his palm on the desktop and lets out an evil whoop.

The four of us gawk at the page. One hundred million dollars. Solid. Real.

"That was fast," says Nikki.

"Well, now we know how much Space wants to keep the murder a secret," Liz says.

"Too bad that's not going to happen." I reply.

We absorb the moment in silence.

Money. Changes everything.

"I made our appointments for Body Flourish," Nikki says as she checks her phone.

"I'm sure he expects to re-claim this money," I say.

"So let's turn him in now. Give the evidence to the cops and the media. Let him concentrate on staying out of jail." Liz says.

"Yeah, good idea. Let him dance with that whirlwind. That will give us some breathing room, for a day or so." I say.

"I'll send a copy to NYPD and the FBI now," Geek says.

I nod my approval as his fingers tap dance over the keypad.

Man, this is going to get real ugly, real quick.

"Did I mention that our Body Flourish appointments are in fifteen minutes?" Nikki says.

"Send the address to my travel log," Geek says.

Nikki nods. She touches the keypad on her phone.

Ping. 00:15:00 minutes appears on a screen on the lower left. The countdown display fades to a ghost image.

"What are you going to do, Apollo, while we're getting upgrades?" Liz asks.

"Monitor the situation. Try to figure out how Space manufactured and launched a UFO."

"I'm gonna spruce up for the appointment thing," states Geek. He leaves his workstation and disappears down a corridor.

"Where's the potty?" Nikki asks. And Liz looks at me with interest.

I point in the direction that Geek went. "At the end of that hallway."

"This mot is massive." Liz says. She follows Nikki down the hall.

"I like your stripper outfits," I say.

"You'll see 'em again," Nikki replies over her shoulder.

"Maybe at the same time," Liz states with a grin in her voice.

I like being alive.

I turn and study the tabletop of Geek's workstation. It consists of fourteen touch-pads. Letters from four different alphabets, along with numbers, symbols, and the odd writing in Geek's shorthand; are written above the various keypads or etched into the tabletop of the workstation.

Now let's see if I can remember how to decipher this multi-language tech-junk graffiti.

I think what I'm looking for is the series of red keys. So I gravitate toward the keypad at the far left. Sixteen red keys are etched with Geek's shorthand.

I press the first one. A new screen appears above the workstation. It's black with a window. Within the window a cursor blinks. Next to the blinking cursor: *Enter address.*

Space had told me to delivery the flash drive to four-forty Madison.

Okay, which keys do I use to type in the address?

DISPLAYS is written above a keypad at the lower left. I look up and scan the screens. I see page numbers at the upper right of each screen. The traffic camera trained on Space's building is page twenty-three. I press 23 on the DISPLAYS keypad. The cursor within the black window stops blinking. I type in the address.

The black window immediately displays a street view. I watch traffic roar down the avenue. Nothing out of the ordinary.

Geek enters the main room. He looks dapper in his simple black suit. Nice black leather shoes.

"Where's that?" he asks.

"Space's place. At least that's where he had wanted the flash drive delivered. I'm waiting for the cops to show up."

Geek nods. He taps a few keys at my right as he says, "NYPD dispatch. Let's see what we hear."

The first conversation we hear is peppered with laughter.

"Woo.... Damn. What type of incident would you say this is?"

"It's a . . . it's a . . . battery. He got beat up."

"(jaunty pause)... By assailants unknown?"

"Ah, well, in there lies the rub."

Geek slides his finger over a blue bar, changing the frequency. The next conversation is more sedate.

"... Your ETA?"

"In three."

"You two go easy. Be respectful."

"We hear you. Treat him like the Pope."

"No you don't hear me. Treat him better than the Pope."

"Treat who better than the Pope? What is this?" Nikki asks. She and Liz are back in their normal clothes. No less sexy. No less beautiful.

"You clean up nice." Liz says to Geek.

"Merci," he replies.

I say, "We're listening to NYPD traffic for any news on Space's arrest. The street scene is Space's place."

Liz snaps back. "Sure is. I just left the place. It's beautiful inside. Few furnishings but a lot of art. A lot of space."

We all laugh.

Liz continues. "You know what I mean. The short tour his hired goons took me on was through rooms that had no furniture so it's just open, like a gallery. High ceilings too."

"Unit four-twenty stand down. Repeat. Do not engage suspect."

"Unit four-twenty, we copy. Will await further orders."

"See chief on site for further orders. His ETA is seven."

"Understood. Four-twenty out."

I can see on the monitor that there is no traffic on Madison Avenue. At least nothing is moving before Space's building.

"We're late for our appointment." Nikki states.

"I guess we're going to have to catch the highlights. I can see they've stopped traffic." Geek says.

We nod as a group and continue to watch the traffic window.

"Let's go ladies," Geeks says. He leads the way out of the main cabin.

"See you soon." I say.

"Peace," says Nikki.

Liz gives me a kiss on the forehead.

And now I'm alone.

31

"Base, what's the chief's ETA?"

I ran my finger over the bar and shut down the cop talk.

I pull up the Wiki homepage and enter *Glass Shore terrorists*. The page pops up, prominently displaying the images of the four alleged architects of the tragedy now called *The Event*.

I'm pretty sure these guys were framed.

Adam Rose – Deceased. (*In commission of The Event*)
West Syde – Safe House A – New Mexico and Arizona border. *Alleged.*
Harvey Houseman – Safe House B – Baja, California. *Confirmed. Deceased.*
Kamru Q'lam – Safe House C – Maine. *Alleged. Escape unconfirmed.*

Secured in separate federal safe houses. Authorities have admitted that eight assaults have been attempted on those dwellings, resulting in the deaths of two federal agents and twenty-six assailants. The incarceration of these subjects is an expensive order due to unique electronic surveillance applications and ever present L10 human security. The possibility that Kamru Q'lam has escaped is low.

I didn't realize that they, well, two of them, are still alive. And who helped Kamru escape – if indeed he has?

I scroll down to trial entries and click the link. A picture of the courthouse of Runyon County appears at the left of the web page. It's an impressive structure, fortified by high concrete walls and gates of black metal. I select a random date. I have the option of transcript or audio file. Why no video? Probably because cameras were barred from the trial. I click audio file 1A. The speaker's voice – district attorney Donald Pathney – is well trained, smooth and engaging, and carries an air of clean certainty.

"Well, we have given you gentle people a mountain of factual data. Truth. Indisputable evidence. For the last five weeks, you have had speed courses in nuclear science, digital linguistics, the stock market and the Ziptrading scam, military psychology, radio technology, satellite technology, NATO Comlink, and extraordinary security procedures.

"We've discussed the personal motives for each defendant. Each reason, in and of itself, nothing more than revenge for an imagined injustice. Kamru Q'lam blames his father's death on our government. The truth is Safir Q'lam had been a double agent, working for the United States as well as Egypt. His body has never been found. He is declared dead. So, with a deep-seated resentment toward America, Kamru manipulated his way into a government contract that concerned the security of America's military defenses. It was during this time that Kamru inserted a command code so well hidden, that it remained undetected for years. The code disabled our satellites and early warning systems. Short wave, microwave, all radio waves were down and out. But it only affected our systems. And, by the grace of God, the Italian satellite was in position and was able to record the missile launch.

"West Syde was accidentally injured by Senator Woolcyk during a hunting trip. He was crippled from the waist down. Sentenced to a lifetime in a wheelchair in the prime of his youth. Does he have a right to be angry? Sure. But understand, Mr. Syde has received the best of care, and all his medical bills are covered. Yet, this didn't sate his want for just punishment concerning the Senator. We have read a few of the letters he sent to the senator; you know the depth of Mr. Syde's anger. And still the fine senator reached out to Mr. Syde. He introduced him to Malcolm Space. Mr. Space hired Mr. Syde and placed him on a then secret project that was to become the Apricot Wind.

"During an awards ceremony at an amateur aviation convention, Mr. Q'lam and Mr. Syde discovered they had a lot more in common than model planes. That being an absolute disgust for American government. But the two men were missing one essential element: leadership. They found that quality at the very same convention, in the person of Harvey Houseman.

"Colonel Houseman gave these revenge-driven men a way to strike back at our government. But what was Houseman's reason for hating his country? This Rhodes scholar, this highly decorated war hero, Harvey Houseman, continued to fly in the dangerous missions. He never ordered another man into battle if he wasn't standing the line himself. Harvey Houseman truly earned the rank of an American champion. Now he suffered from the horrible Suf-cancer, like so many NATO warriors. What would make this true American bomb his homeland?

"Guilt. Houseman remained regretful for the nuclear strike during the Reconstruction. He found contentment with his jail sentence; he openly expressed that his sentence of life imprisonment was just. Yet, while in jail, he secretly reached out to Syde, Q'lam and a new man – a man unknown to Syde and Q'lam.

"Houseman used a series of confederates with whom to communicate and set his plan in motion. As fate would have it, Syde was already in place at the Apricot Wind project site. Mr. Syde used his connections to secure a job for Kamru Q'lam. It was during a three-year period – the length of their contracts – that West Syde and Kamru Q'lam sabotaged the spacecraft known as the Apricot Wind. These men believed they were the plan. They thought that the plan was to take command of the Apricot Wind – via remote control and crash it into the Puget Sound installation. And as the evidence proves, Mr. Q'lam's dirty work did disable the command center computers, and Mr. Syde crashed the spacecraft into the military installation.

"Yet for Houseman the Apricot Wind was just part of a bigger plan. His true instrument of destruction was to come from the best that the military had to offer.

"So Houseman and an unknown man made a pact. The unknown man changed his name. And using old and true friends of Houseman, the unknown man successfully infiltrated our space program. Yet he didn't attain his position because he was a friend of a friend. No, this man was a superior pilot and a model citizen. So it was logical for this man to be chosen for the Shield program.

"I speak of course of, Burhan al-Jamil. Also known as Lieutenant Colonel Adam Rose. The pilot of Jump One. The man who fired the missile on Houseman's command. It was a suicide mission, but this was in accordance with Colonel Rose's agenda. An agenda that we're still trying to understand.

"So I close with something we do understand from Houseman's own journals. These laborious tomes betray the torment of his soul during his seven years in solitary. He wrote these prophetic words while incarcerated: 'If I set a hundred bombs in your front yard and, with willing naïveté and faith in God, you believe that you and your family are safe, then you're stupid and deserve all the hell that will most certainly blow up in your face'.

"We have established history, motive and method. We have displayed solid evidence regarding execution of the plot. The photographs from the Italian satellite clearly show the missile was launched from Jump One.

"There is nothing more I can say or do. Harvey Houseman, West Syde, Kamru Q'lam and Adam Rose are solely responsible for the missile bombing of Puget Sound, Washington. Thank you for listening."

Silence save for soft whispers and the sound of typing.

"You're up, Mr. Tyler."

"Thank you, your honor.

"Ladies and gentlemen of the jury, I'll begin where my esteemed colleague stopped. Let us examine Harvey Houseman's statement. 'If I set a hundred bombs in your front yard', is the first line. This is a true statement. Military bases, missile silos and mercenary arms dealers are literally in your front yard – right now.

"Second line: 'And, with willing naïveté and faith in God, you believe that you and your family are safe'. Well, is that not how we all feel now? We trust that those who protect us are competent, vigilant, and safety-minded. It is the last line that sets it truly in perspective. 'Then you're stupid and truly deserve all the hell that will most certainly blow up in your face.' That, my friends, is exactly what happened.

"We are complacent. The bombs have been in our yards for

decades. They are so commonplace that we have forgotten how to fear them.

"We are so wrong.

"The former naval base at Puget Sound had been the most advanced military installation on the planet. The government will never expose all the projects in which the facility was engaged. They're protecting national security, of course.

"Pardon me, ladies and gentlemen, but we *are* stupid. We give our hard-earned money to a government that builds bombs and God knows what else. Then, when a horrendous accident occurs, this very same government expects us to believe in Donald's wonderful tale of terrorism. Four men, who exhibit enormous capacities for originality and decisive thought, are chosen to take the fall. Given, these men aren't saints, but think about their lives, imagine how much time they must spend on their individual endeavors. When would they have time to make all this happen?

"I don't care how precise, smart and determined these men are, the prosecution is giving them too much credit. That is one hell of a project for four men to design and execute. Never mind how they enlisted others in their scheme AND how they maintained silence and security during the entire operation. Not one article or communiqué from one man to the next has been presented. No letters, emails, or phone conversations. Due to their dubious past experiences both Houseman and Syde were under constant surveillance from authorities. Since they were so closely monitored, why don't the authorities have a communication trail? I guess we're to believe that telepathy was their means of interaction.

"Why didn't they immediately trace the transmission spikes to West Syde's residence after NADD command received a cryptic message the day before the Event? Of course, now they want us to believe that had been a test message from Mr. Syde and they can confirm the link.

"This is all too easy and simple. It's great fiction but it can't fly in real life. Think hard, ladies and gentlemen, your government is solely responsible for the tragedy in Washington State. Make them accountable. Make them prove to you that this won't happen again.

"Remember, the bombs are still in the yard."

Silence. The audio file is over. That's odd. I check the feed. Yeah, that's it. Well, for what it's worth, I thought the defense was more eloquent. Better expressed than the sterile authority of the DA.

I scroll around until I spot the evidence files and I am about to click on but a blinking link catches my eye.

Conspiracy Theory Alert! *Diary excerpts from General Pug Bradshaw. Discovered after his death on 12/25/2075.*

I click the blinking link.
The General's diary opens.

The world was commiserating the fifth anniversary of The Event. Gene and I tired of the spectacle that is the tribute ceremony. So we decided to visit the Colonel. Just hang out for a few days and escape the bullshit.

The first time I saw the Colonel, I remember thinking he was just an old fisherman standing on the breakwater with his fishing rod planted deep in the moist sand.

The sun was setting as Gene and I approached the old fisherman. I remember a warm wind at our backs.

I remember Gene and I saluted the old fisherman that was Colonel Harvey Houseman. The Colonel turned to look at us, Lord... I... The look in his eyes was ice hard loathing. He had nothing but disgust for Gene and I.

I'll never forget the look of those eyes.

It felt like a blessing when his attention returned to the sea. And so Gene and I took that moment to ease away from the Colonel. It was hard for Gene and I, we men of power, to remain cool under Houseman's silent dismissal. And there is no doubt that we deserve the Colonel's venom. His aim is true. We lied. Our testimonies damned him. Read their testimonies before the Senate.

Nonetheless, we came to Baja to relax.

A silver Airstream trailer was Houseman's permanent residence. It was parked a few hundred meters from the breakwater. A wooden picnic table was planted before the trailer. Gene set up the folded chairs while I continued to the trailer. We had arrived empty-handed, reasoning that the Colonel could not have consumed the cases of various liquors that we'd sent to him over the years.

There had been a few pairs of shoes on the concrete stoop outside the trailer door. So I took off my shoes before I entered the trailer.

Inside the trailer, to my surprise, I found dozens of liquor cartons stacked neat against the far wall, unopened.

The Colonel wanted nothing from us. Not even a free drink.

Well, I came down for a drink so I opened the case of whiskey.

I remembered Gene had sent a set of shot glasses. I found the package, also unopened.

Harvey's jail cell was clean. I don't recall a TV, but he did have a small radio.

There was only one picture on the walls. I remember it because it was almost – no it was – a shrine. It was a black and white photo of a beautiful young woman grooming a black horse. The picture was set in a plain gold frame. It was a picture of Sara, the Colonel's dead wife. She was killed during his arrest.

I left the Colonel's hell and found Gene sitting at the picnic table. We started drinking whiskey.

It was night when Gene said, "Our lies made it a better world, Pug."

"Yes." I agreed then and I remain convinced it is true to this day.

The Event changed everything. Of course, Pii helped. The Positive Image Inducement was a program developed to avoid major mental breakdowns amongst the people after the tragedy. (Click here: Doctor Ayni Rouessua discusses the Pii theory.) The government bombarded all media sources with subliminal messages. These blips were loaded with coping with loss, and recovery tenets. They were also primers, stimulating one to help others in need and to find solutions to the environmental concerns for the devastated region. The program was then installed into all reflective surfaces like household and industrial glass and mirrors. So that when people see themselves, they receive a flash, or twinkle, of good will. Platitudes like: You're a good person. Help as you can, when you can, all you can. You are not alone. Reach out, someone is there for you. Believe in yourself and others. We will not let you down. You are an asset. You are loved. These sayings are constantly washing over people. And in short time, the hidden messages paid off. Healthy, pretty people everywhere you look. The government finally saw the big picture and dealt with the fact that sick people cost money. Unhappy people aren't productive. Keep the people in the best of health and fix all of nature's imperfections. This produces a happy productive worker. And a person who's very easy to control.

Healthy, happy, sexy people building the future and no one notices the change in attitude. Hunger will be eliminated within the decade. People have homes or at least a roof over their heads. Sex is fabulous. And it seems like every woman on the planet is pregnant or damn well wants to be.

And so everyone has a purpose. City streets are clean, no litter, graffiti or bums. Stories of bad people and bad things are few and far away. The tribes, gangs and cults are all but done. All vice is restricted to the Underground; where you can easily acquire any illicit service your heart desires. It's a wonderful world.

I tipped my glass to Colonel Houseman. Thanks for taking one for the home team.

The action on the other screen pulls me away from the General's diary. A well-dressed officer walks an angry Space toward the police cruiser. Space yells at the officer – then shoves the officer into the edge of an opened door of a police mot. The officer drops hard to the ground as Space races away.

I laugh out loud. This is so cool.

Two other cops tackle the fleeing Space, slamming the

Man-that-is-the-Future to the sidewalk.

"Treat him like the Pope!" I shout at the monitor. I laugh to tears as I watch the officers secure Space in a full-body restraint suit.

The rugged grips of the suit are located at the shoulders and hips. Four officers grab a handle of the leather suit and lift the jacketed Space off the ground. He pitches and yaws against the police, so his transport detail look like men trying to navigate the deck of a boat caught in a maelstrom. Blood smears Space's face and he appears to be cussing up a storm. I look at the page for the volume control and see none. I search the keypads and find nothing that indicates how to switch the sound on this screen. No big deal. Seeing it is good enough.

The officers deliver Space to the rear of an ambulance, and fasten him onto a waiting gurney. The gurney is slid into the vehicle and the doors shut. I wonder if they're going to transport him to the hospital or to jail?

I return to Bradshaw's diary. There is a disclaimer stating no verification of authenticity.

The clip of the Security Council would add weight to this excerpt, even though the webmaster will tag the clip with the same disclaimer. I have to show this site to Nikki. It will boost her spirits. It could be the place to launch her story.

I've heard the Pii rumor before. It makes sense in some ways but I don't see how it could be implemented. I get subliminal messages, that's easy but it often doesn't achieve the desired response. A program set in all reflective surfaces, glass, mirrors, metals and gemstones, how do you make that work? For Bradshaw to drop two major conspiracies in one diary entry is amazing. Almost unreal, yet, the nagging thing is that I can wave a flag of truth that Houseman, Syde and Q'lam were not the cause of the Event.

And I shouldn't disregard the possibilities of Pii. What if Pii is part of the overall plan? Bradshaw states the Pii program was put in place after The Event. What if the program was in play long before The Event? Preparing the public to calmly accept and reasonably respond to a major incident. The Event should have triggered a major economic breakdown, perhaps even global war. Neither of those things happened and that was due to the cool response of the people. President Cresthaven gave his speech, asking for help from private citizens, corporations and other governments. He apologized to the world for The Event. And so everyone related differently after The Event. The market did take a hit but all the new jobs, both government and private, reversed things seemingly overnight. People hunkered down and fixed the problems and generated a lot of fast and hard money. And once that design was in motion, it was easy to introduce new science and lifestyle programs alongside the tried and true living plan, and so fashion the future.

If Pii is real, Malcolm Space and Geek are affected by the program and look what they've created.

I wonder if the program affects me?

Sometimes I really don't like the way I think.

I need a drink or a hit. Or both. I get up and walk over to Geek's mini-bar. I pour a shot of whiskey. I slam back the warm liquid and set up another.

I don't know whether to read the Senate testimonies of Bradshaw and Orison, or dig deeper into Kamru's escape from his safe house and subsequent disappearance, or look into the Pii program. Somehow I have the feeling I'm going to dive into all of the above.

I slowly sip the second shot until the little glass is dry. Good tasting booze. I walk back to the workstation and take a seat.

I look back at the traffic monitor and traffic is back to normal flow on Madison. I close the page.

I check the desktop for broadcast controls. I know Geek has them.

I see TV etched above a keypad at mid-right. I press 1. NY1 appears above me. *LIVE from East 51st Street* is displayed on the lower left corner on the silent scene. I watch a sour and defiant Space walk tall, calm and hard into the police station. No attempt to conceal his identity. No shame. No concerns. He is escorted by two very large officers and with his hands secured to his waist and a wire attached to his ankles that allows only half-a-step of liberty. It's obvious that a medic has bandaged him up, yet, even with the gauze and tape plastered over his face, the disfigurement of his nose is like a blaring horn. It is clown-large and bright purple. The way those cops had slammed him to the concrete during the arrest, I'm surprised he's not missing teeth and suffering from a concussion.

Just as I find the control for sound, I hear a whoosh, followed quickly by the familiar voices of my family. I look at the clock. They've been away for better than two hours.

Time flies when you're having fun.

32

"This is Winston Belmont, live in Midtown, standing before the Seventeenth Precinct on east Fifty-first Street where, only moments ago, mega-billionaire industrialist, Malcolm Space, was brought to this police station in restraints, his face bruised from a fracas with authorities during his arrest earlier today at his office on Madison. At this time we have no word on the charges against Mr. Space."

Geek enters the cabin first. He carries six clothing bags. Of course they went shopping. A new look requires a new wardrobe. Geek sports a classic Latin flavor. Deep caramel skin with a head of healthy silver-hued hair set off by hard gray eyes.

"Damn, new and improved Geek." I say.

"I think so too," he replies. "So what the hell did we miss? Is he in jail?"

"Yeah, the arrest was hilarious. He knocked a cop down and then other officers just dumped on him."

"His face is all messed up," Liz says, looking at the monitor replaying Space's arrival at the police station. She is now a lovely Asian doll with a smooth, light yellow-brown complexion and wide, alluring sea green eyes.

"Beautiful," I say to her. She gives me a kiss. Her arms are also loaded down with bags. "We got stuff for you too."

"Thanks."

Then I see Nikki. The color of her skin is that of burnt sage. Her hair is now jet and cropped short and thin. Her eyes are white as ice. She is, as ever, drop-dead sexy.

"You look good," I tell her with a smile.

She runs her fingers along the nape of my neck and along my shoulders.

"So what the hell are you looking at?" she asks, dropping her bags by the servers.

I point to the pages floating before us. NY1 replays the scene of Space being escorted into the police station.

"Watching Space's arrest. Checking out the trial of the terrorists. I found something very interesting you should see."

"You got a lot going on here," Geek says. "Get up and fix me a drink." He mutes the volume of the NY1 page.

I get up and head for the bar. Geek sits down and resumes control of his desk. Nikki and Liz crowd around him.

I stop to look at the quiet trio. Seems they've bonded. It's soothing to see this. It's an odd feeling. I've never thought of anything as *soothing*. Even comforting. And that's where I'm at, right now.

Liz smiles as she looks at me.

I grab three shot glasses and walk back to my crew. I hand out the glasses. I pour and receive a round thank you for my generosity.

The trio reads and sips their whiskey shots. It's very quiet.

"I can tag the Security Council tape and the Jump One transcript onto this diary," Nikki says. "I've been chasing this rabbit for years. How did I miss this?"

I consider Nikki's question. We've uncovered a great deal of information since we've been with Geek. The next moment I find myself glancing at our host. Our Information Agent.

"You should see the disclaimer at the bottom of the page," I tell her.

She reads, nods. "Of course. I don't care. The data I have supports Bradshaw. The three items make a solid case for my father."

"Señor Geek, please send the Security Council clip and the Jump One transcript to that link," Nikki requests.

"Yeah, okay," replies Geek.

"You guys have had an insane busy day," Liz says. "You've squashed the richest man on the planet. The president wants you dead. And it's not over yet. I'm nervous you know. I mean so much money and all the conspiracies. This never ends well in the movies."

"This isn't a movie. We're in control. We just have to stay on top of it," Geek says. "Gliddin will use WEB and other official sources to get to Nikki and Apollo. That's easy to track. I also have a good idea of the pros Space will contract for your execution. We can monitor them. No surprises. No accidents."

So that's where I get it from. *Like father, like son.* Geek has all of his ducks in a row and has a contingency plan for each duck. No surprises. No accidents. I think the same way. Yet, I know it's my programming. Once again here I am pretending to be human. Trying to connect with dad.

Liz sighs. She pulls out her pipe and the hash she purchased in the Underground. She loads up. Sparks up. Deep coughing and a cloud of smoke later, she passes the pipe to Geek. He accepts and tokes up.

Geek passes the pipe to Nikki.

Nikki has a hit then passes the smoking pipe to me.

I hit it.

"So is the Pii thing real?" Nikki asks Geek.

"Yes." His reply is quick and sure.

I ask, "Bradshaw states it was initiated after The Event. Could it have been in play before The Event?"

Geek is silent. At length, he answers, "Yes. I've always thought so at any rate. Why do you ask?"

"Because it fits my theory."

Liz asks, "How do you know it's a real program?"

I pass the pipe to Liz.

"I first heard about the Pii theory about sixty years ago. Apollo was still under construction in my mind only. I had been good-friends with Ayni Rouessua and she frequently discussed, more like vigorously debated, how governments squandered the potentiality of people. She was sure she could harness more from people by making them feel better about their work, their bodies, their social and private affairs. People just need constant positive support. She just couldn't figure out an unobtrusive way to provide affirmative endorsement during the day and soothing encouragement while sleeping. She also said that people shouldn't be aware of the support.

"Years later, when I was working on Apollo, I considered bringing Rouessua aboard, but she had fallen off the face of the planet. And I was so busy and so deep into his construction that I didn't have time to follow up. So I let it go.

"I heard about the program for the second time, right after The Event. I've confirmed the use many times over the years. And like Bradshaw says, even knowing about it can't stop the program from being effective . On that count, Rouessua was wrong.

"Then as now, the Pii program is distributed through television, the net, radio, ring tones, any intonation or modulation that has a minimum duration of three nanoseconds carries a Pii code. People are bombarded with passionate props."

"Prove it," Nikki says.

Geek nods. Works his keypads.

"Does the program work on me?" I ask.

"I believe so. Your brain works like mine, albeit faster. I can't see how you'd be immune to the program.

"Here, watch." Geek points to the NY1 broadcast. It is a commercial, sponsored by the New York State tourism council. The on-screen guide is a beautiful blonde woman in a black body-suit with a flared collar. She runs across the green field and says, "Visit Lake George, the gateway to the Adirondacks. An immense blue and green space in which to relax, play and plot an adventure." The camera pulls out and away from the guide, offering a verdant pasture and rolling green hills in the distance.

Geek pauses the commercial, capturing a still of the beautiful valley. He then removes the color. Then peels away degrees of gray. We can now clearly see the words, *Love You*.

"You understand that is constantly displayed during this commercial. Now tell me, how do you feel about Lake George?"

"I'd like to go there. It looks nice," replies Liz. "There's nothing sinister about that."

Nikki says, "Right. Yeah, I could see myself up there. Sure, I'd like to go there. Yet, I like to travel. I like everywhere."

"You like Earth?" asks Geek.

None of us answer but my answer is yes. And that's why Nikki, Liz and I are silent. We get it. We like the planet because we've been told to. And we know the earth likes us. If fact it loves us. Says so, right there on the monitor.

Silence continues. We stare at the screen. Perhaps waiting for something alarming to happen in the calm valley.

Love You.

I say, "I can't hate the situation. I feel I should be mad right now but I can't find the anger."

"Why should you be mad?" asks Geek.

"Well, I'm being programmed."

"Programmed to love, yeah that sucks," Nikki says with a smile.

Geek is the only one laughing. "Apollo, son, you are one big program. I'm about to install an upgrade in you for appearance control. You're telling me that this," he points to the gray valley, "is unforgivable."

I know my mouth is open but whatever I was going to say is cut short by Nikki's laugh.

Liz is smiling too. She looks at Geek and says, "This is why that friend of yours said we shouldn't know about it. It's gonna bug me forever."

"You'll get over it. You'll even forget about it. I forget about it all the time. I've been affected by it much longer than you and...." Geek shrugs his shoulders.

"How does the program work with glass?" I ask.

"Glass, mirrors, reflective metals and jewels carry germs with the program. My favorite is wedding bands. Every time a husband and wife look at their wedding bands they receive the message that they are loved. You know that divorces are rare. You know as well as I do that people still have affairs and they get caught but obviously it doesn't matter. They follow the program. Love conquers all."

Geek cancels the still shot and just as the broadcast is about to jump live I see something that makes me shout out, "Stop!"

Geek does, but the valley is now in color.

"Go back to the gray scale," I say.

He does. I point at the picture and say, "See, just over the trees."

"Oh, wow," says Liz.

"Damn," Nikki states.

Geek just nods.

The faint words brush the treetops; *The Meek shall inherit the Earth.*

"So, why aren't we a non-violent society?" Nikki asks.

"Ego and passion. To become non-violent, we'd have to eliminate both qualities and that makes no sense. Let people love and lust, let them have secrets and desires; those passions fuel the machine. The goal is to generate money every way possible. People work to support their desires, which supports the machine and increases profits across the board. It's a win-win scenario.

"Hollywood still makes movies about them but when was the last time you heard about a real serial killer? Unfortunately lovers still kill lovers, and there always seems to be the street-fight that ends in a death. Terrorist attacks and suicides are almost non-existent.

"Abortions are a rarity. Women know they are loved and they know the child they bring into the world will be loved so it's all joy."

I nod. That case of the missing child I found a few years back; it had been the first Amber Alert in the Commons in many years. The abductor didn't harm the child. She had just wanted to hold the kid. The woman had been sterilized due to a rare infection and she just lost her mind over it. They were having a tea party when I found them.

"I thought mind control was all about making everyone the same," Liz says.

"Once again, ego and passion. You don't want to mess with that," is Geek's sure and fast response. "Some people receive the life-affirming messages in a much different way. And yes, we can detect and amend brain abnormalities very early in life but human robots would be unproductive.

"People need to be independent. Freedom to create, work and play in their unique way. Independent people are a sound economy. Each person will find his own way and not be reliant on family, friends or the government. The Pii program ensures that people maintain one perspective, duty now for the future. People engage their lives with pride, energy and confidence. People are aware of themselves and they like themselves so at work, or concerning creative and athletic pursuits, including sex, no one gives less than their all. People are satisfied. That's real mind control. That's power you can't laugh at."

Geek stands, then walks over to his wall of old-fashioned accessories and gadgets. He rummages through a small metal pail. I can see he's frustrated – he removes the pail from its holding spot and dumps its contents over his workstation. My sisters and I gather around dad and check out the swag. Slender vacuum tubes, film capacitors, unmarked transistors, tiny incandescent glass bulbs, chunky computer chips, silver discs – which I believe are batteries – flash cards, memory sticks, zip discs, square glass, bobbie pins, paper clips and dust bunnies.

Geek singles out two small squares of glass. He hands the glass chips to Nikki and Liz.

He scoops up the spilled contents and sets the stuff back to the metal pail. He returns it to its proper place.

Geek ask, "How do you girls feel?"

"Very good," states Liz. She takes a deep breath. I can tell she's happy. I'm sure everyone in the room can tell she's happy.

Nikki nods in agreement. "Feeling sexy," she says.

Liz nods, "Yes. Yes."

"Let me hold one of those," I say and find they both gave up the glass chips rather quick.

"Take it," Nikki says as she drops the chip in my palm.

"Yeah," Liz utters short and with fire as she thrust the chip into my palm.

So I look. *Twinkle.*

Sweet. Nice buzz. *Twinkle.*

Twinkle. I take a deep breath. Feeling good....

Twinkle.

Yeah, hell yeah. *Twinkle.* I'm warm and my dick is getting hard....

Twinkle. This is amazing.

I hand the chips, more like mirrors I guess, back to Geek. He drops the mirrors into the pail without glancing at them.

Geek says, "I believe those were first freely distributed during the global New Year's celebrations in twenty-forty. And every year since then, but of course, with time and technology, better versions."

"Twenty plus years before the Event," I say. "That works

with my theory. I believe the game plan was to mentally prepare the masses to deal with utter catastrophe and, to accept and learn all the new technology that was in the pipeline. You can't place idiots in space. And space is where the big money is."

Geek shakes his finger at me and says. "You really don't know how right you are, Apollo. There are programs detailing all levels of math problems and scientific applications. People see these images from birth. People have come to equate hard math and science with leisure activities and comfortable surroundings. The hard work is satisfied by subliminal phrases of praise, confidence and love."

"What about blind people?" Liz asks.

"Rouessua had thought that the blind and the mentally challenged would be easy to win over with pop music. Catchy little ditties that make people sing along. And if someone can remember the song, then they've accepted the program."

"So a sighted person looking into a mirror and singing their favorite song…" I start but Nikki finishes.

"Is getting slammed with equations, phrases of love, diagrams, and symbols setting them up for even more information to come later, at a different location."

Geek nods and says, "The learning set of the Pii program is structured on a mathematical analytic function; a bridge between simple and complex power series. Think fractal geometry, and you'll get the picture on how information is written."

"We receive small pieces of random data and our mind places that data in an order we can understand," Nikki says, her eyes focused on Geek as though her vision could cleave him in half.

"Yes. Each person will process the data differently, in their own time, eventually piecing together what they need from the information. Around kindergarten or so, we have a clear view of one's aptitude and so fashion Pii programs more suitable to the individual."

"Where'd you get those mirrors?" I ask.

"Off the beaten track," Geek says. He walks back to his seat. "Got any more hash Liz?"

"Sure." She sets out to prepare a bowl.

"You know, that song from ME? The Mirror is Lovely. Could that be about the program?" Liz asks.

"In the eye of the reflective surface, I am love. I am strong. I can do anything," I say flatly. Not attempting Marilyn Elvis' falsetto and timbre. "Sure as hell sounds like it. Then again it could just be a song about loving yourself too much."

"Don't know the song," replies Geek. He unfreezes the commercial, returning to the live broadcast from the street outside the Seventeenth Precinct police station.

"… Richard, we're working with the understanding that Malcolm Space is considered a prime suspect in Fury Randell's horrific murder. This is a most disturbing development. We have not received any official word, but trusted sources will not deny it."

The broadcast is now a split screen, with the on scene reporter at the right and the studio anchor on the left. The anchor asks, "Winston, have you been given a time, or any indication when the authorities will hold a press conference?"

"No Richard, nothing of that nature. The situation thus far has been hush-hush."

Geek laughs and mutes the broadcast. He stands up. "Nikki, Liz, let me show you how to work this panel."

They smoke hash as Geek runs a tutorial on his keypads. The ladies nod as Geek details the buttons and switches. The pair doesn't ask him to repeat the instructions. One is a hacker and the other is a published programmer. They get it.

Geek turns to me and says, "Come. Time for an upgrade."

We walk to the familiar workbench.

I lie down.

Geek checks the connection of my Mjac.

"See you in a moment," he says.

And right before I go silent, deep in the fleeting distance, I hear, giggles and laughter and, "Good night, sweet prince."

#

Standing on the beach looking at suddenly erected mirrored walls and ceiling – Twinkle – inflaming my desire for decadence. I give in to the Afro-Cuban rhythms that are the soundtrack for the now Purple Room. The room is heavy with the scents of jasmine and hash. Liz massages my dick with a warm clear cream. A moment later my mind is white fire and I shake. I stand, wobbly at first, but then I get my feet and face Liz. I dance ... we dance to the beat, dance back toward the wall mirror. Twinkle. I pin her against the cold glass. Twinkle. I grab her thighs and lift her off the floor. I stare into her brown eyes and find her pillow-soft lips. A hard kiss, a soft kiss. She bites my lower lip. I press into her flesh. Press, kiss and hold. Her thick red hair is all in my face and her breathing is shallow. I feel her nails in my flesh. I peel her off the mirror and toss her onto the bed. I rush her. Fall upon her like a predator. No grace, no style, no art. She smells of cinnamon. She pulls my hair. My flesh begins to itch and I'm nude beneath a hot sun. My skin reddens and blisters develop. Wisps of smoke trail from the ends of my hair. Shock as I smell my hair and flesh burning. I drop to my knees, suffocating as heat takes all of the air. I watch and feel my pinky nail violently curl and explode from the swollen digit. Like a popcorn kernel ejected from the popper. I want to yell but fused lips trap my screams. My body collapses. I lie quivering voiding my bowels. Unbearable pain.

"What can we do you for?" asks the thin man who reeks of garlic.

I pull my hand out of my pocket and display a large, solid gold coin. It's old and dull in color, inscribed in Latin and engraved with the face of a Roman emperor. I put it on the table. "Grothman sent me. He wants to talk to DeMillo about a deal."

"Right," replies Garlic. He picks up the coin and studies it. "This is beautiful." he says with awe. Even simpletons appreciate good work, I muse. "You wait right here." He stands quickly. Walks over to the near wooden door and raps on it with urgency.

"What!" a voice roars from behind the door.

"Serious business," states Garlic.

"Bring it on." the voice commands.

Garlic steps into the room. A moment later, he opens the door and waves me in. I walk in and see DeMillo sitting in a thick leather chair. He wears a simple black suit. A plain gold ring adorns his right ring finger. His nails are smartly manicured. Small, round glasses soften a wizened face. He smokes a thin cigar and holds the gold coin like he owns it.

"How many are there?" DeMillo asks as he looks into my eyes.

"Thirteen, including that one." I reply.

"What's the offer?" Those are DeMillo's last words. I'm not there to make a deal. I am there to settle a debt. I pull my guns out. I fire each gun once. Sinking bullets in DeMillo and Garlic's foreheads. I turn to the door and wait. The rest of the muscle surges into the room. I fire four times, shooting the last guy twice. Silence. No dying gestures or words. I walk over to DeMillo. The dead man has fallen sloppily into his comfortable chair, blood streams from the hole in his head. Blood. My blood. Not bad. I can deal with it. Just wish I could breathe better. I take a long slow pull, suck in all the air I can. A pair of trackers race past me. Single tracker is two meters on my left. It senses something amiss. Probably smells the blood. It's scanning for me. I'm well-concealed even for a tracker's heightened senses. Yet there are many trackers and they won't leave this sector soon for I'm not the only one they seek. I'm just the one with the answers. My arm is starting to annoy me. How much blood have I lost? Six girls and two boys. Eight volleyball players. Eight basketball players. One marathon man. One ballerina. One psychologist. One pediatrician. Two singers. One lawyer.

One more lap around the track as Dionne Warwick asks if I know the way to San José. "La-la-lala, la-la-la-la...."

33

Dream crash is a sudden snap from a languid, romantic discovery to a bright and brazen exposure. I scan the room. So is this real? Looks real. Three perfect nude bodies just out of arm's reach. And I can smell them, like the electric scent of near rain. I hear the Belgian duo called The Glimmers warp a disco throb, the bass kicks like a little frog in my chest.

This is real.

I watch Nikki slowly swallow Geek whole. The girl has no gag reflex. She twists her head from side to side, mocking a corkscrew turn. Geek tenses up and shudders. Nikki lazily pulls back, releasing the tension on his member.

"Damn girl," Geek hisses with a smile.

Liz takes her turn on Geek. She can throat dance too.

My dick is hard and I move in to taste the action – yet I'm stuck in place. I'm still in stasis!

This is real and I'm only a voyeur. Geek is just streaming the live sex show to me, no doubt courtesy of his tiny invisible floating camera.

What a greedy bastard. This . . . this is hell!

Nikki turns her attention to Liz. She flicks her tongue over Liz's nipple. Liz caresses Nikki's head, drawing her in and never letting Geek's cock feel lonely.

Nikki slides from erect nipple to harder flesh, sharing Geek with Liz.

I can't even masturbate right now. This is wrong. I thought these people were my friends.

I watch Geek enter Nikki as Liz pleasures herself.

I feel the heat, hear the passion and smell the slapping flesh. I feel the energy. I'm in sync with their beat. Geek is pumping a marathon atop Nikki.

Stunning heat in my groin as Geek uploads into Nikki – I shudder and jerk and ejaculate. Hands free. Never did that before.

Now it's black and silent.

In life, you have to do a lot of things you don't fuckin'
want to do. Many times, that's what the fuck life is: one
vile fucking task after another. But don't get aggravated.
Then the enemy has you by the short hair.

–Al Swearengen. *Deadwood*

34

I awake.

I sit up and locate Geek. He and Liz sit at the workstation, smoking cigarettes. Liz sits on a stool at his left, phone in her right hand, her thumb taps out a tattoo on the tiny keypad.

"The dreams are getting stranger," I say.

Geek pokes his head from around Liz's hip and asks, "How so?"

"Weird stuff like ghosts and being hunted," I reply, now realizing, "It's hard to recall the dreams."

Geek says, "Nothing strange about that. You are being hunted. And I've killed you twice in the last, what, six or seven hours; so you're a ghost. Just your subconscious mind doing its thing."

I want to talk about their sex play while I was locked down, but I keep my mouth shut. I'd just wind up sounding like a hurt child. And I imagine that Geek didn't tell the girls they were streaming live to my mind. Yet I doubt either lady would mind.

I rise and sit upright on the workbench. "Can I pull the plug?" I ask.

"Hold on." I see Geek's fingers dance over the keypads.

I look over to Nikki. She sits on a rattan chair by the servers. She works on her laptop, smokes a cigarette.

"Okay, you're clear," Geek says.

I remove the plug from my Mjac. I'm back in the world and all is well.

I stand and walk over to the mirror. I look the same. I turn to Geek and ask, "So, where's my wand? How do I make this work?"

"Think about it," is his reply.

I stare at Geek, dumb written all over my face. I exhale. Think about it. So I think blond hair. My hair fades to lighter shades until I settle for the color of summertime hay.

"This is cool." I turn toward Geek and find Liz and Nikki

225

watching me as well.

"You can do more than your hair," he says.

I think about my skin and my flesh lightens. Then darkens.

I change my eye color.

This is insane. I can see how this could get addictive.

"Thorosen doesn't exist," Nikki states.

I look over to her and say. "He was listed as the special consultant to President Cresthaven. What do you mean he doesn't exist?"

I remember my original form and so I become that once again. That leads me to reason. I think about Geek.

I now look like Geek.

"I wondered how long it would take you to get there," Geek says.

"That's not good," Nikki says. "Precise impersonations. You can already blend into the shadows and you're a blur to monitors."

As she talks, I become her, sans breasts and I still have my cock. Which is the most important thing. Don't want to go messing around with that.

"Now that's screwed up," Nikki says with a laugh.

Liz and Geek laugh too.

"More elasticity of the skin and hair management. All I had to do was install two chips," Geek says, as he looks me over. He's very happy with his work. As well he should be. I kick ass. I'm Superbad.

I become me again. I step away from the mirror and walk over to Nikki.

I stand behind her and read the monitor of her laptop. From the page's background, soft pink with a black imprint of the bust of Venus, I know she's at her website called Venus Imperfect, working her blog.

Text along the left column of her webpage reads: *There is nothing to fear except the persistent refusal to find out the truth, the persistent refusal to analyze the causes of happenings. – Dorothy Thompson.*

Text along the right column of her webpage reads: *The truth will set you free. But first, it will piss you off. – Gloria Steinem.*

"Idiots!" With a cigarette between her fingertips, Nikki

points to the webpage. She smokes her cigarette.

"So far, all the hits about the Jump One flight transcipt concern the UFO. Some people believe the UFO was a returning contingent of the alien race that spawned humans. Can you believe this?"

I say, "Did you expect a more intelligent level of conversation? C'mon, you're a big girl. You know better than that."

"Still sucks to see it in play," she replies.

"There are other voices, Nikki. Look here," Geek says and points to a page above his workstation.

"This discussion is about the pilot's actions. This guy sees Lieutenant Colonel Adam Rose as a man caught in a difficult situation. Rose had to follow the order to fire, plus no one knew if the alien spacecraft was friendly or hostile. Reasoning also that if Jump One had not engaged the alien spacecraft and allowed it to continue on its path, perhaps more devastation would have ensued, more lives lost, and everyone would have asked why the government didn't protect Americans from such an attack."

"True enough. I'm still mad at them for allowing terrorists to blow everything up," Liz says and holds up her hands. "I know the truth now but until today, I believed the terrorists story and I was – am – still bugged by it.

"The government is responsible. That's the only real truth."
Silent nods.

"What is the word on the Security Council clip?" I ask.

"Go to padotgov," Nikki says. "There is a live feed from the Senate floor. It's pretty boring. They all agree that the Jump One flight document is a forgery. The Security Council clip is doctored. And Bradshaw's journal entry is also crap."

"Well, that's what we expected," I state.

"Yeah…" Nikki nods with her reply.

Silence. We all read various web posts. Geek has one up from a guy who claims that the Pii program is modeled after the Kinjo Glimmer. The KG was tested and rejected back in twenty forty-seven. The only test subjects for KG were the submarine crew of the USS Marshall. The Marshall ran aground in a small atoll in Indonesia in twenty fifty-one. No one has seen the recovered logs but this writer states that

Senior Lieutenant Ellis Hauk went nuts due to the program and killed thirty-three men before running the boat ashore. The USS Marshall was a weapon. Pure muscle wrapped in sheer stealth. The best and last of her class. She was one hundred and seven meters long and ten point five meters in diameter, weighed 6,032 metric tons. She carried 24 Trident 2D5 missiles, along with an assortment of vicious conventional missiles and mines. She had a crew of 10 officers and 110 enlisted men.

The US recovered the Marshall but all her crew was lost. Two Tridents and a great deal of conventional weaponry had been removed. So began another war.

"That's it, I'm done. To hell with these people. You know what the new one is? People are posting that the UFO Jump One destroyed may have held their abducted loved ones. Yeah, I'm done." Nikki closes her laptop. She sits in her chair and smokes.

Geek bursts out laughing. He keeps laughing until the laugh turns into a hacking cough.

"Nice to know my distress brings you such comic relief," Nikki says as she smiles at Geek.

"Oh Jesus…." Geek says with a weak, scratchy voice. He rights himself in his chair and wipes the water from his eyes.

"So what are we eating?" I ask the group. It's been quite a while since I've had a meal.

"I know a good Thai place," states Geek.

"I second the vote for Thai," Nikki says.

"Thai is good with me," says Liz.

"Let's do it," I say.

Geek taps his keypad then says, "Back to Manhattan. We'll be there in fifteen minutes."

"Where are we now?" I ask.

"Lake George," Liz states.

I nod. "So show me the clothes," I say. "We have fifteen minutes to dress for dinner."

"Oh, cool," Liz says as she hops off the stool. She walks over the mound of bags against the wall. Nikki meets her there.

Geek and I ease over to the girls.

Liz spins to me, offering a yellow button down shirt. Long

sleeve. Light cotton blend. I take it from her.

I check the collar tag, Carl Close. "I like it."

"Cool," Liz says. She holds out the pants. Flat black, the fabric looks and feels like leather but it's not.

I nod approval and take the pants from her. "Did you get shoes?"

"You prissy little bitch," Nikki says.

"What, I don't deserve new shoes?"

"Relax, we got shoes," Liz states with fun in her voice.

I sense that she and Nikki had a good laugh expecting this very conversation and moment.

"Love you both," I say.

The girls laugh.

Nikki hands me the shoebox.

Liz sets a clear bag atop the shoebox. I see socks and underwear in the bag.

"Bless you child. May good fortune smile upon you for the whole of your life."

Liz chuckles "Go get dressed."

"Yes ma'am." With bounty in hand, I leave the main cabin. I take a right, and head for Geek's room.

#

I strip down, tossing my soiled clothes into the corner by the closet.

I turn out my pockets, dumping everything onto the dresser.

I dress slowly and with a sense of purpose. Clean underwear and socks make all the difference in the world. The pants are utilitarian, department store stock, but look sharp and fit very well with good flex. The shirt is spot-on. The shoes are low cut, black leather loafers from Mikal Pip, and are exceptionally comfortable. It is so sweet when your lovers buy you clothes. They know how to fit you and what suits you. They know what works.

I grab the Bolt and gloves and walk out of Geek's room feeling fresh. And I know I look good.

I'm the last one to return to the main cabin. I spin for my audience.

"Very nice," says Liz. Nikki nods approval.

"You girls look edible," I state the obvious.

Liz wears a plain white tee shirt, dark blue leather jacket and dark denim pants. Her stiletto heel cowboy boots are white. She's still rocking the Asian look.

Nikki has also kept her look, but of course sports new clothes. She wears a light gold shirt, a black mesh silver glitter skirt beneath a lean, black, body-hugging duster. She wears smooth black leather boots with a low heel.

Cuban Geek sports fat leather pants with a huge black belt, a simple black shirt beneath a black leather vest, and rigid mud-stomping boots.

"What's our ETA?" I ask.

"We're here," says Nikki.

"Then let's do this," I state.

"One moment, got a surprise for everyone," Geek says. He displays a rectangular case with a seashell finish. The case is about the size of his palm. He opens the case and we see two sets of contact lenses.

"Nikki, Liz, these contacts are for you and will register with your new identities. They won't interfere with you Body Flourish implants."

"Nice. Thanks," says Nikki.

"Yeah, thank you, Geek," says Liz.

The girls give him a kiss.

"You're welcome." He looks to me. "I installed your new eyes with the appearance upgrade."

I nod. Of course he did.

I watch the girls apply their new contacts. Then they pull out tiny mirrors to check themselves.

"All good?" I ask.

"Shut up and wait," Nikki replies.

We exit Geek's mobile home like the Kings and Queens of the World. The cobblestones beneath our feet are glossy black due to on and off showers. Geek presses a black button on his phone. The door of his mobile home closes. His mobile home then jumps into the flow of westbound traffic. A moment later the blue metallic covering of his mobile home shimmers, bends and flexes. Now Geek's mobile home is invisible.

I look up and see a slate gray sky crowded with air traffic and *personals*. I look southwest and find the bright, towering city.

"Is this the Bronx?" I ask Geek.

"Yep," he replies

The neighborhood is bustling with people. Small shops specializing in fine jewelry, clothing, day spas and other ways to spend time and money.

Accosted by *personals* for financial services, IPOs, personal management advisors, and health spas; Nikki, Liz and I follow Geek down the sidewalks. From time to time, the sexy and sinister rhythmic clicking of the women's heels striking smooth stone captures me. I just wanna get nasty when I hear that sound. I have a very low threshold for erotica. Cigarettes, heels, skirts, bras, red lipstick; all that makes me very happy, really fast.

We hear the roar and rush of music and cheering people yet noise is muted due to the sound-absorbing properties of the reconstructed white stone façade of an old fort. I look up. A few meters above us, in what had been the fort's main courtyard, now converted to a multifunction sports ground, a Dominican kid rules the handball court.

Back on ground level, people mill about, the crowd grows thick, and so we know we're about to dive into the heart and heat of the street. We turn a corner to find a huge gathering of people surrounding a lone musician. The music is hard and hits you like gravity but has a catchy guitar riff with a bouncy bass line and a solid, no-nonsense skip beat. Large cameras float overhead, dodging banners and balloons, a basketball sized orb that randomly fires confetti, and small hovering spheres that shine colored lights on the singer. All of this fanfare announces the musician's presence, Marilyn Elvis, live on the Hudson.

"In the eye of the reflective surface, I am love. I am strong. I can do anything," sings the tall, thin man.

Nikki, Liz, Geek and I look at each other. We wade through the bopping people.

I yell at Geek, "Did you know this was going on?"

He shakes his head. "Not at all. Is this a new song or an old song?"

"About four years old. It's his breakthrough hit. He's been around for better than ten years."

Geek nods.

I'm not bumping into people. How cool is this? We ease through the crowd and I'm not leading the way, the girls are. They are beautiful and people peel away from them as though afraid of their touch. I'm bringing up the rear, so I watch the men and women stare at Nikki and Liz with smiles and whispers and looks of awe. And the gawkers cast approving eyes upon Geek, and finally they see me, think about, and then nod as if it all makes sense. The girls take us front and center stage.

I look up and note the cameras trained on Nikki and Liz. Okay, how do I tell my little dance whore that we should not stay and enjoy the show?

Looks like I don't have to. Nikki is shaking her super bonbon but she's not hanging around. She and Liz shimmy with some of the boys in the crowd then move on.

As the four of us move by, I can see ME plays a clear multi-string device with a long neck and box body. His instrument is attached to a half dozen silver cubes by a hydra of colorful cords. Six black amps are suspended behind and above him, powering tsunami sound upon the masses. I have to say Marilyn is not the most beautiful boy to look at. His head is round and he's basically pie-faced; set down by a poor complexion with wisps of hair along the sides of his flat face and on his puff-knob of a chin. I chuckle because his thin body, round head and pie-face remind me of a sunflower. Marilyn's hair is long and unkempt and unwashed. He wears a hot white shirt highlighted with gold and silver threading about the neck, cuffs and hem. His trousers are tight and black. And true to his rebel agenda, he's barefoot. I understand the barefoot thing is related to his non-regen agenda. He wants to age naturally, like that Ezra asshole.

I realize his agenda is inline with the Pii program. It doesn't matter what you look like; do your best and never give up and you will be rewarded. And so Mister Ugly up here on the stage is kicking the Bronx in the ass and they love it.

We pass the musician, the small LCD display before his instrument case states, Give Your Money to ME. I see that the name inside his case, Marilyn Elvis in big gold letters. I'm feeling good and I like his music so I give him a few twenties. The money falls silently into the instrument case, mixing with other bills, credit flashes and panties with phone numbers or emails addresses scrawled upon them.

Geek walks with Liz, leading us away from the concert.

I keep step with Nikki.

We exit on the violin diminuendo for "Mirror is Lovely". I turn to see ME draw a bow across the strings of his instrument. Knowing the ending, I watch as he drops the bow, flips a switch and using only the fingers on his left hand, plays the last few *piano* notes as he sings, "Lay down your weapon and lay down with me."

Nice. The beat breaks into a rapid hi-hat riff and I turn away.

The music pauses for only a second then ME kicks back in with a song that brings a smile to my face. My pod used to play this tune whenever we hit hard resistance.

Rock Lobster. Good times.

I have to jog a bit to catch up to the trio.

We make an abrupt left and our trail ends at the start of a dirty side street. A small mountain of wet bagged trash is staged sloppily against the wall at our left. I look to my right and up and see a large square hand-painted sign in Thai above the shabby front of the restaurant. I imagine that the hand-painted sign translates to Banana Cup, as indicated by the yellow neon sign in the window to the left of the door.

The handwriting on the chalkboard to the right of the door is shaky and erratic as though it had been the first time the writer had used chalk. And English is not the writer's first language. I laugh as I read the chalkboard. *Flesh fishfood daly. No yesteday fish. No sosaa meat! No cat, dog, rat meat! Dont axx!*

"You want to eat here?" Liz challenges.

"Trust me. They're clean and the food is excellent." Geek says. He opens the door. Liz and Nikki enter, I follow.

Shredded dry banana leaves in shades of green, yellow, sunburst orange, sunset red and brown pad the weathered wooden floor. The interior is a honeycombed grotto with a high ceiling and has a feel as old as time. Faded and decaying posters and party banners (Happy New Year 2000) are fixed on the thick cherry wood beams overhead. The old hardwood walls are dust free, dark and hold the scents of thousands of meals. The restaurant is crowded and noisy. Solo, couples, parties of ten or more. Everyone is dressed in fine clothes. The place is hopping. The food must be good.

A skinny waiter with thin black hair that lies flat and lifeless on his head quickly approaches us. "Gee tee krap?" he says.

"Four," Geek states as he displays four fingers.

The waiter seats us at a table by a window with a view of the rear of an apartment complex. He deals out the menus and hurries away.

"You speak Thai, Geek?" I ask.

"Just enough to get fed and laid," he replies. Then with a polite raise of his finger to a passing waiter, he says, "Sung aa-haan krap."

The waiter nods with a smile. He eases over to a bank of waiters standing by the bar. He speaks to the very skinny guy on the far left.

The waiter appears at our table with his order pad at the ready.

"Four Singha. Large bowl of tom kha gai for table." Geek makes a circular motion with his hand about the table to accentuate *for table*. "Moo sateh, mieng-kum, fried quail eggs and tod mun," Geek says.

The waiter nods and exits, weaving his way toward the kitchen.

"What did you order?" Liz asks.

"Four Thai beers, soup and a bunch of appetizers," Geek replies.

"I heard fried quail eggs," Nikki says with a sour scowl.

"Yeah, top 'em off with soy sauce and black pepper. Brilliant." Geek says with a tasty grin.

Nikki, not convinced, shakes her head and says, "No thank you."

We sit in silence and take in the action of the Banana Cup. From what I see around me, the portions are huge, plates thick with veggies, nuts, fish and meat, accompanied by dozens of tiny ceramic bowls filled with a multitude of sauces.

Appearing like an apparition, a tall thin waitress serves our beers. She exits the scene in the same fashion.

"A toast to life," Geek says.

And so we do.

The waiter who took our order appears with friends. The servers place the food on our table with effortless expedience.

I study the utensils. Chop sticks. "The old scoop and shovel, hand to mouth, school of dining." I say.

Geek nods and fills a soup bowl. He hands the bowl to Liz. Geek says, "Sip slowly, it's hot."

He fills bowls for Nikki and I, then for himself. He takes a slow, dignified sip of the steaming brown liquid.

I point to the red, hollowed, oblong dish placed in the center of the table with a dozen dainty and attractive shells covered with chocolate-brown speckles and stuffed with their fried former contents neatly plated.

"Quail eggs?" I ask Geek.

He nods. He reaches out with his chopsticks and snares one. He sprinkles ground black pepper over it, then dips it in soy sauce and pops it into his mouth. Instantly his face is awash in ecstasy.

"Great," he offers as if some hard-won victory has been achieved.

I reach out with my chopsticks and follow Geek's plan. And damn, it does taste great. It's like being kissed by god. In my reverie, I notice the shell has a delicate shade of blue inside.

"That's a pretty shell," says Nikki.

I nod as I toss it aside and dive in for another. "You should have one before me and Geek knock 'em out."

Liz reaches out with her chopsticks and picks up a quail egg. She dips it in soy sauce then dusts it with black pepper. She pops it in her mouth. She smiles, her head tilts to the side. She seems very content.

It happens rather quickly, yet, I note the movement in slow motion.

I see the two WEB agents enter from the left quarter, as we had.

I see three more agents approach from the right. Now I can see four emerge from the kitchen. Geek and Nikki's eyes tell me agents are behind me, just a sheet of glass between us.

There is a family of seven at the table to my right. I can reach out the touch the child in the highchair. There is another large group of civilians at the table on my left, behind Liz. Geek and Nikki are hemmed in by a row of dining couples.

Looks like I have to sit on my hands for this round.

One of the agents places the barrel of a gun to Nikki's temple.

In sync, all around our table, barrels of slender, nasty black metal kiss flesh, except for me. The barrel of the weapon with my name on it points at my right eye.

The restaurant grows from quiet to absolute silence.

"Clear out the diners," orders the all-too-familiar voice of the man I call Satan.

Griffin eases into view. "Apollo. You had me thinking you were some kind of voodoo machine. Can't track you, not even with the dozens of bugs planted on your ass. Not in the Allround and what is with your mind – petting puppies and flying kites? The memories you're leaving in the Allround are jacking up the system."

He pauses, rubs his right temple with the whole of his palm. "Hell, I can't even blow you up just for shits and giggles. It's frustrating. Then it all came together when I learned you were with Geek. Geek and his special freak boy."

Griffin stands next to Geek. "My god man, I thought you had learned your lesson. What was her name – oh yes, Ofilia. She was a lovely woman. The House is very unhappy with you and we all wonder why you're involved with Apollo. I look forward to discussing that later."

Griffin turns to Nikki and with a cobra flip, backhands her across the face. She takes the slap like a kiss. She smiles and him and I know she's laughing inside.

"And you're the chameleon making life so miserable for the good guys. Where is the Jump One file?"

"On Geek's mot," Nikki shoots back.

"On Geek's mot," Griffin repeats. "Okay, Geek, where is your mot?"

"I need to reach into my jacket pocket for my remote," Geek replies.

"No. You stay still. Just tell us where you parked?"

"The mot travels. I call it when I need it."

Griffin nods, as if that's the answer he expects. "Sergeant, please reach into – what pocket?" Griffin asks.

"Right."

The sergeant locates Geek's remote.

"Show it to him." Griffin instructs the sergeant.

Geek studies the remote.

"It's about two clicks east of here."

"What button will call it back?" Griffin asks.

"Blue."

Griffin nods at the sergeant, the sergeant presses the blue button.

"How long will it take to get here?" Griffin asks.

"About two minutes."

"Fine."

"How did you find us pork-butt?" I look at Griffin. "Not only the restaurant but we got this whole new look happening and you easily pick us out of the crowd."

"With a little help from your friend." He walks over to Liz and extends his fat paw to her. "You're a good citizen. You can go."

The agent withdraws his gun from her head. Liz doesn't take Griffin's hand. She stands unaided and with stone dry eyes she stares him down.

"Tell them why I did it," she says.

Griffin smiles, it's not a pleasant type of smile. He looks at her, then, glances at Geek, Nikki and I.

"You did it because you are sensible," states Griffin.

"I did it because you promised to release my mother! So let her go!"

Griffin is shocked. I don't think I've ever seen that face. It's funny. Then he spits his reply.

"Don't get demanding with me, citizen! I will put your ass in the cell next to her. Loving conversations without physical contact for the rest of your fucking lives. How does that sound to you?

"Breakin' my balls – I haven't got time for this bullshit. Get her outta my sight," he says with an offhand dismissal.

The closest agent grabs Liz's bicep and rushes her from the restaurant. I get the feeling she's trying to resist but she can't match his muscle. She's truly doing a good job to keep up with him and not fall to the floor and then get dragged from the room.

Liz glances back at me before she flies around the corner…

I'm not a happy man right now.

"How long has she worked for you?" I ask.

"I secured her services before you came out of the coma. Then Space snatched her and I didn't know what the hell to do. Now, I understand what happened there. You rolled over on him after taking the man's money. Have you no honor? What was it, oh yeah, one hundred million. You know you can't keep that money."

"I knew about it." Geek says to me. "I knew Liz was working with Griffin."

I study Geek and try to figure out his play. "Yeah?"

"Oh yeah. I monitor all communication to and from my rig. Liz had sent fifteen text messages to Griffin. Her contact lenses are cameras. She's really scared…."

"She's a smart girl who'll listen to reason," Griffin interjects. "I'll lay it all out for her in a neat little package.

"Once I retrieve the disc and files, I'll personally hand them over to the President. Then it's a cushy cabinet post for me. Respect. Perks. No more handling riff-raff." He looks at each of us, just in case we don't realize we are the riff-raff.

The greedy bitch snatches a quail egg with his fingers. He even takes the time to dip it in soy sauce.

"Damn – this is good." He states with a flick of his wrist. Then he uses my napkin the clean his fingers.

I say to Geek, "We gotta help Liz."

Geek nods. "Shouldn't be much of a thing for you, me and princess."

"Sweet. I'm a princess now," says Nikki.

Griffin laughs. He says, "You better think about helping yourselves."

We are, asshole. I don't know the play but I have a feeling Geek's got the game in hand.

"Where's this mot of yours?" He snatches the remote from the sergeant's hand and studies it. "What's this? It's blinking."

"That means the ship is outside." Geek says.

"Who's outside?" Griffin asks the sergeant.

"Mercer," the sergeant replies.

"Don't tell me! Call him and confirm the vehicle."

The sergeant nods and does as he's told.

"Mercer. Do you see a …" the sergeant looks to Geek for assistance.

"It's big and silver with twin, fat, horizontal red and yellow stripes," Geek says.

"Big, silver vehicle with red and yellow stripes?"

"Negative."

"So, what's the deal?" Griffin asks.

"Have a quail egg." Geek says to Nikki.

"What? Hell no. I'll take a cigarette."

"As the fat man will testify, they're damn tasty. A little taste of heaven before Griffin sends us God knows where," Geek says. "Did you know quail eggs were successfully hatched in space on the Mir, back in nineteen ninety-two?"

"What is it with you and the damn quail eggs?" she snaps back.

"If you have it you can't share it and if you share it you can't have it." Geek says with a laugh.

"What?" Griffin asks.

"It's a secret." Nikki says with a laughing sigh. She reaches out and grabs a quail egg. Drenches it with soy sauce and pepper. She looks around the room, closes her eyes and pops it in her mouth. She chews, swallows … opens her eyes and says, "Wow." Then she goes quiet, entering the gates of bliss.

"See, settle down girl. I wouldn't steer you wrong," a smiling Geek says to Nikki.

Soft tones from the new Cambodian pop singer, Jeeya Sukapatana, ease through the anxious soldiers in the restaurant. I can feel all eyes on me. The man directly across the table seems to be monitoring my breathing and watching my eyes for any signs that I might just reach out and kill someone. I think about the music. Her notes float and swell, connecting like smoke rings then wrinkling and slowly dissipating from the air.

Jeeya's spellbindingly beautiful voice could captivate and soothe all but the coldest and hardest of hearts. Naturally, it has no effect on Griffin.

"Where's your goddam ship?" he snarls, shaking the remote at Geek.

"It's still in stealth mode. Hit the blue button again." Geek explains to Griffin with a good-natured smile.

"Of course, you've got an invisible ship." Griffin replies as he hits the blue button.

Hot blue flashes wash over the restaurant. Everyone that didn't have a quail egg falls to the floor like fat water balloons clumsily dropped by a gleeful toddler.

Griffin looks around, disoriented, then fast mad. He reaches into his coat.

I jump up, trample over our dining table – I see Geek and Nikki save the beers – I hit the fat man with a head and shoulder tackle. The crown of my head busts his nose and his blood flows down his face like the waters of a ruptured dam. Flat on his back on the banana leaf-padded floor, dazed and in pain with my right hand a vice grip around his meaty throat, tears well in Griffin's eyes as he coughs and spits and slaps at my arm using a breakaway technique that is taught in self-defense classes. I'm a breath away from punching his lights out but Nikki speaks up.

"Easy, Apollo. Don't hurt him yet. I want to talk to this asshole." She comes around, stands at my side and sneers down at the broken Griffin.

"Guess who's not going to hobnob with the President?" she mocks. She sips her beer. Hands one to me.

I look out behind me and see the agents outside are in the same condition as the agents inside. Geek and his science. I sip my beer.

I pat Griffin down, pull his weapon from the inside pocket of his jacket and put it into my pants pocket.

"He'll make a good hostage as we make our exit." I say as I yank Griffin to his feet.

"No need. Everyone within a three hundred meter

perimeter suffered the same fate as the agents around you if they didn't have a quail egg."

"Alright, this is driving me nuts – what's in quail eggs?" Nikki asks.

"A pesticide that was used in the last century has mutated the bonding enzymes in the eggs of water fowl, specifically marked in quail eggs. The thick white strands that anchor the yoke to the eggshell are rich with diflubenzuron, or *Debbie*. Debbie raises the colletenzinite levels in the frontal lobe. Blue light at the right frequency and strobe rate can induce a minor catatonic fugue, except if the brain is tainted with Debbie. That giddy feeling that you had after eating the egg is a by-product of Debbie. A sign that you won't be affected by the blue strobe."

"Science is pure evil," Nikki says. She reaches out with her bottle.

Geek smiles. Clinks his bottle with Nikki's, then mine. We take long drinks from our bottles.

I shove Griffin forward. "Looks like being a fat, greedy slob paid off for you this time."

"Kiss off," he replies without bite. He wipes away blood from his face. I shove him forward.

"Asshole – wait!" he shouts at me. Then he reaches out to a near table and snatches a napkin. He uses the napkin to soak up his blood.

"So you must know the owner in order to have the strobe lights set up." Nikki nudges Geek.

"I am the owner. I set the lights up long ago for just such an occasion."

"You and I gotta spend more time together." Nikki says.

"I've got all the time in the world, princess," Geek replies as he holds the door open for her.

We exit the restaurant and see dozens of bodies lying motionless on the sidewalks and in the street.

Mots zip overhead, never pausing to gawk at the spectacle of the sleeping street people.

"This isn't permanent is it?" I ask Geek.

"No. They'll be out for five to six hours. Wake up with some disorientation; some will throw up all over themselves. Some will complain of memory loss," he shrugs his shoulders and walks into his vehicle.

Nikki follows, then Satan and me.

"Apollo!"

I recognize that voice. I turn to see Liz. I stop as Geek and Nikki gather at my sides.

Liz stops before us. She hugs Geek and says, "Tell me you're responsible for this. I know you're responsible for this."

"Yes I am," Geek says. He hands her a bottle of beer.

And here I thought he was just taking two beers for himself.

Liz pushes Griffin away and hugs me. We kiss, light and quick but it's heavy with feeling.

I give the girls a quick hug.

"C'mon," Geek says as he enters his mot.

The ladies rush in.

I shove the fat man into the vehicle.

The door zips shut behind me. I note a slight lift. We're on the move. We ease through the antechamber and into the round control room of the craft.

"Those people outside and the symptoms you just mentioned, I …".

"Yes, you've experienced it," Geek finishes my sentence.

I continue. "During the war. One day, every solider lay on the desert sand just like everyone outside. And it happened every day for the next year and half, until all troops were withdrawn and sent home."

The cabin is silent. Geek's smile is luminous.

"You … oh!" Griffin stammers. Then his eyes grow wide and shine with clarity. He says, "Just like this mot, you've created vehicles that travel undetected on the grid and they constantly emit the blue strobe. All over the world, in the jungles, across desert sands, in the mountains, on the seas. You put millions of troops to sleep."

"Yes, exactly, but not vehicles such as this. Hundreds of small orbs, about the size of a golf ball," Geek states.

"I can't stop countries from having a military force. And they can't stop me. The moment I have a clear view of all the players on the field, I put 'em down. As for the gangs and tribes, I've mapped their territories and monitor their activities."

Then it occurs to me. I've seen the vids. "Sans weapons, you let the gangs fight."

Geek nods. "A lot gets settled in less than thirty seconds." He sighs then continues. "At first I couldn't do anything about suicide bombers but thanks to outstanding global intelligence, I have an idea where the assholes nest. So I send orbs into their lairs and put them to sleep as well. In these cases, memory loss could be a beneficial consequence of the blue strobe."

"Countries were a heartbeat away from tossing nukes..." Griffin states, eyes narrow and breath hot.

Geek lights a cigarette "Obviously no one pushed a button", he says with a short puff of smoke. "Everyone blames the other yet not one army has gained an advantage. Then, in rapid action, the Movers and Shakers, all those Powers That Be, realized war is no longer a profitable business and switched gears. The world business machine is now focused on agriculture and science and their pursuits have been rewarded with fat profits. Right now, anywhere on the planet, you can get something to eat. You couldn't say that just a few years ago. There are six aerospace firms that offer day trips orbiting the Earth, or to the moon. There are three mining companies working on the moon, Mars and close asteroids. These businesses are making money or they wouldn't be doing it."

"What you've done is treasonous on every level, you sanctimonious sonofabitch! As a citizen, it was your duty to provide our government with this knowledge."

"The government is a business and business is good, so what's your problem?" Geek says.

Griffin rifles his fist through his hair, huffs and fumes. "It's not about business..."

"It's about power. Yeah, I've heard the riff before." Geek smiles. "Guess who's got all the power now? And no ideology, faith or country was injured in the coup."

"You're a psychopath," Griffin says with a dead sigh, his eyes wide open and mouth ajar.

"Screw you. I opened the door for reason. People started to scream about their tax dollars wasted on a sleeping military.

So the money went to education and healthcare. And, surprise! Educated well-fed people come up with brilliant ideas. Ideas that make money. And there are billions of healthy, well-fed people available to build these ideas and buy the fruits of these ideas.

"I'm a businessman. Everyday billions of people use products based on my patents. And that means a lot of money in my pocket. War eliminates my customer base. Ergo, eliminate war and increase my customer base."

"I remember those early Days of Peace. It was very tense," I say and laugh.

Geek laughs with me, but Nikki, Liz and Griffin miss the joke.

Liz says, "I remember hearing a street preacher in my old neighborhood. He would say that war is the greatest of all sins. War is a sin. Sin no more ..."

"And so ended war," Nikki ends the verse.

Liz looks at Nikki with surprise. "Wow, you've heard that?"

Nikki nods. "Sure. I think everyone has." She finds a seat and plants herself.

"Oh yeah – oww and *wow*." Griffin sneers.

We ignore Griffin. I say, "That whole thing even had me thinking about God and my soul."

"Ha! What a laugh! You're a machine, Apollo. You don't have a soul." Griffin looks at me with disgust.

"He's got more soul than you." Nikki defends me even though she has witnessed some of the evil bullshit that I'm capable of.

"What, you don't know about Apollo?"

"Yes I've watched Geek work on him. I know all about Geek and his Freak. And I'm sure the freak's got a better chance at getting into heaven than you do."

Griffin turns to Geek with a dirty smile. "Geek, enlighten the *princess* on Apollo's true design and mission."

Geek takes his time. Then, "Apollo and the others were not created to wage war on earth."

"You getting the big picture now?" Griffin teases Nikki by stretching his arms to an exaggerated expanse, tops it off with a fat grin.

"So... what, space? Apollo is made to fight in space?" she offers.

"Right. And what would he be fighting in space?" Griffin asks.

I think she's about to say, humans, at least that's what it looks like to me, but she doesn't, she holds silent for a moment before the word spills out in quiet syllables, "Aliens."

Griffin taps his nose.

"Apollo was created for homeland defense and deep space warfare in the event of hostile extraterrestrial contact." Geek presents the official dictum.

"Jesus," Nikki sighs.

"Yeah, exactly. I don't know what this information does to your particular God theory but as you dance with that, you can understand why it isn't common knowledge. The riot that is in your mind *right now* would be experienced by billions and with bloody reprisal," Griffin says.

"You underestimate people. I'm good with it. My God is an artiste vivant. Life beyond Earth is a comforting thought because it confirms that my God is still creating. My God is alive and well."

"You're weird," states Griffin. "Look, religion aside, normal people aren't going to sing la-la rhymes and skip through the tulips if the truth of extraterrestrial life is revealed. There's an old story from the last century that clearly illustrates and supports this truth. Some cretin decided to play a joke during a live radio broadcast; he told everyone in great detail that Martians were invading the Earth. The fake broadcast caused riots in several cities. Some people were literally frightened to death by the bogus radio show.

"So to close the loop for you, we, that is the United States government, will never admit that anything other than terrorists caused the Glass Shore. The truth, or any variation of it, will invite chaos. We will not admit to alien contact until we have to defend ourselves."

"I'll keep pushing the truth about my father. I'll tell people what you just told me."

"Please do. In fact, let me help you. Use this on your next post and see what kind of hits you get. US government has created superhuman soldiers designed for space combat."

I watch her roll it over in her mind. No matter how you spin it, the truth is stranger than fiction. She sighs heavily. She takes a cigarette from Geek's pack and lights one.

Griffin holds out his hand for a smoke.

Nikki looks at him, her eyes are furious. "You're unbelievable," she says with a smooth breath.

"Yeah, from cradle to the grave, little lady, from cradle to the grave." He holds his hand steady, waiting for that cigarette.

Nikki slams the pack into his meaty paw and then tosses the fire at him.

"Thank you." Griffin says, as though she had handed him the cigarettes and lighter with the greatest of care.

"So aliens are real?" Liz asks.

"You see," Griffin says pointing to Liz. "She can't process it. She's normal folk." He lights his smoke.

"I can process it, you dick! Why do we have to be under attack? Why can't the aliens come in peace?"

"That would scare me more than all out aggression," Griffin replies. "Peace is a most deceptive act."

I say. "We're off point. Regarding the Event. The UFO was a construct from Mkeyinc. It's a Malcolm Space production. We've checked out the timelines of his patents and it's pretty evident that the whole thing is one big scam."

"What are you talking about?" Griffin asks.

"He was awarded a patent for True Balanced Metal and the Harmonic Actuator. Both elements make a convincing UFO," I state.

Griffin laughs as he points at me and says, "Conspiracy theorists are such idiots. Apart from the grid, True Balanced Metal is the cornerstone for construction. That's why buildings are so tall. The Harmonic Actuator also has engineering applications."

Geek asks, "So, Space figured out the transportation grid after The Event?"

"He had the concept for the grid long before that, but couldn't make it work," replies Griffin between puffs.

"Then it was exposure to the alien metal," Geek says as he works it out.

"Yes. That's why we allowed you geniuses access to the debris and crash site."

"Alright, I hate being the only stupid one in the room, but if the government doesn't consider The Event as an attack, and it wasn't manufactured, what made the Glass Shore? Was it the nuke or the UFO striking Earth?" Liz asks.

Griffin sighs and smokes as he weighs her query. "A lot of both. The nuke shredded the UFO like confetti. We can't explain why that happened. We estimate height of detonation was less than a thousand meters. The nuke alone couldn't have done the damage so the official guess is that the power source for that UFO had to be amazing."

"It had to be an attack," Nikki states. "The UFO eluded Jump One at first contact."

"That's the first thing you and I agree on," says Griffin. "Others have suggested that the UFO may have been in distress and Earth was a place of refuge. Making the evasive maneuver an uncontrollable action, not malicious intent."

"So it stands to reason that all the visitation stories and UFO reports are true. Unless you want to believe that this is the very first UFO that's ever visited Earth," I say.

Griffin states, "I know what's real. So does your creator." He looks at Geek.

Geek leans back in his chair, arms crossed and says, "Until I look reality in the face all I have is a deranged idea of what's real."

Liz steps up to Griffin, "Enough of this ... stuff. You guys can do this debate without me. I want my mother released now."

"Look at this – giving orders!" Griffin laughs for a breath then he becomes serious. "Sit still and I won't have you put to sleep." Griffin fiddles with his watch.

I have the feeling Liz is about to punch him.

Geek touches Liz's hand – she spins to him. He gives her an easy nod and soft smile.

Liz gets calm. At least she's trying to be calm.

"You're not the only one with special toys, Geek. I just called in the big dogs. This mobile home of yours will be mine shortly." Griffin swaggers about the deck.

"Now Geek, you have deeply disturbed the true nature of

things and you're going to make it right. I'm going to inform the President that you're responsible for the *mind-attacks* on the troops. Of course, I could be lenient and allow you to present the antidote to the President." Griffin sidles up next to Geek. Up close and personal.

"I have the President's ear like no other party member, but oh, that kind of compassion will cost you a pretty penny. I want all of the money you stole from Space."

Geek laughs. "Weren't you paying attention at the restaurant? No signal leaves this ship without my consent. That beacon from your watch is going nowhere. No one is coming to your rescue. This is my universe. I just allow your fool ass to take up space."

Then Geek places the palm of his right hand against Griffin's forehead and shoves him back as if performing an evangelical healing.

Griffin staggers back and bounces off my chest. I spin Griffin around and gauge the punch, then tap his jaw with a quick left. His cigarette flies from his mouth and flips back at me as Griffin loses his footing like a drunken man on a treadmill. He hits the metal floor with a wet slap.

Nikki stands up and walks over to Griffin's motionless body. She looks down on him, takes a long pull from her smoke.

Then she kicks him in the gut. She looks over at Geek, Liz and I and says, "The best time to kick a man is when he's down, its easier, he's closer to the ground."

Geek snorts out a laugh. Liz laughs.

I think it's funny too. So I kick Griffin in the ass.

35

I pick Griffin up.

I carry the fat man over my shoulder like a large sack of dry produce.

"What are you going to do with him?" I ask.

"Hit him with a constant blue pulse. It'll clean his mind in less than ten minutes."

"But he's had that Debbie stuff," I reply.

"It wears off. He'll be ready for treatment soon."

"What about my mom?" Liz asks.

"I'll make Griffin issue your mother's release," Geek replies as though this is an everyday thing for him.

"Wow – thank you!" She gives Geek a big kiss on the cheek.

"Don't thank me until she's home."

Geek opens a thin door with the swipe of a card. I begin to follow him but the door is so shallow that I have to work to get the fat man through the portal.

Now Nikki gives me a helping push courtesy of her foot on my ass. In fact, her foot on my ass is a practice I can do without.

So I tell her, "Get your foot off my ass. You gotta stop doing that."

"My legs are strong. You're a big man. Trust me, this is the best method I found to move you."

I look at her and she's not smiling. She is serious.

Damn woman.

Bright light is emitted from small square panels set in all four walls. The room is near-blinding with pristine, white painted walls, ceiling and floor. The room feels and smells sterile. A lonesome and worn dark brown chair is the room's only occupant. Tired leather straps fall from its armrests and front legs.

"You've done this before, I take it?" says Nikki.

"Yep." Geek replies with a dry moan. Then Geek looks at

me. "Set him here."

I flop Griffin down upon the hardwood chair. Geek and I secure Griffin with the leather straps.

"I've never been in this room." I say to Geek.

Geek looks me in the eyes. "Never had a reason to bring you in here before."

Geek removes Griffin's earphone. "That'll do it. Let's go."

We leave the room.

"I'll monitor him from my workstation and give him the blue wash when he's ready." He turns to Nikki. "So what do you want to do now?"

"I don't know." she says, defeated. "What can I do? You heard funboy; I'm never going to get my father's name cleared. Aliens don't exist unless we're under attack."

"And that's when I go to work." I say, amazed. I turn to Geek. "Why didn't you tell me that?"

We enter to the main compartment.

"Well, I rolled it over in my mind and came to the conclusion that it would be best to tell you when it was real."

"But you built me because it is real. I mean, what makes you think that aliens are hostile? Do we already have enemies in space?"

"Okay, slow down. Our true contact with extraterrestrials is limited to encounters from the last century. Recovered bodies and debris from interstellar vehicles found in New Mexico, Peru, Kyoto and Siberia. In this century, aside from the Glass Shore, we have confirmed sightings from marines aboard interstellar vehicles. Nothing suggests hostility towards humans. The impetus behind your creation is the Boy Scout motto, *Be Prepared*."

"Let me play this out. Mean aliens land on Earth and I get instructions from the Allround, to do what?"

"You'd be instructed where to report for duty: nothing different. Standard protocol. Hell, in that scenario, regular army will have to dance with hostile aliens too."

Nikki stares at Geek and then she looks over to me.

I shrug my shoulders.

"I get the vibe that this makes you mad," Geek says.

"Yeah I'm mad and I'm feelin' betrayed because you didn't tell me about this alien crap before now."

"Damn little brother, it wasn't my intention to betray you. I just can't see how this information is important to your life. And really, what's the big deal? War is war and your role is a combat solider. When the madness hits the fan, you won't think twice about killing the alien. You'll fight on Earth and in space. In fact, you're made for cosmic combat. And you get to wear spiffy, specially-designed outfits for extraterrestrial encounters. And not those bulky terra-workmen rigs, but, dare I say, fashionable one-piece skin suits."

"I want to see these suits," Nikki says.

"I'll try to find the designs for you later." Geek sits down at his workstation and works his many keypads.

Winking into existence, a small display at the upper right over Geek's workstation, offering for our viewing pleasure, Griffin in all of his fat, sleeping glory.

"Gonna pump O-two in the chamber to help bring Griffin around," Geek says.

"Do you have any childhood memories?" Nikki asks me, as though the question has been gnawing at her for a long time.

"Sure, even though I didn't have a childhood."

"And how does that work? Just random programs you call up?"

"Well, no, memories just happen."

"Gimme something now," demands Nikki.

I look at her. I'm blank. Then it all rushes from me.

"I was raised a southern Baptist. When I was eight, nine, or so, I looked forward to Sunday. Sunday was the best day because of dinner. Every Saturday night, my mom and my grandmother would clean their homes from top to bottom. Sunday morning it was all about prep cooking for the meal after church service. Mom and I would leave our house, the smell of bacon following us out of the kitchen and into the garage. We would drive to my grandmother's house a few miles away and find my grandmother's home bursting with the smells of warm cornbread and molasses, collard greens and ham. Then the four of us would ride to church in my grandpa's Olds. Grandpa drove. I was sandwiched between the ladies in the backseat. I always thought that my mom and grandma wore too much perfume and smoked too many cigarettes on Sundays. As I remember, the main reason for the fuss over a clean house and all the cooking was due to our pastor. At sometime during the service, the pastor would announce how he and his family were looking forward to dining at a church member's home after the service. No one knew who would be chosen until that moment. I remember the collective sigh of relief sweeping through the congregation not chosen once the selection was announced. I remember thinking that the pastor had awesome power. He had forced everyone in the church to prepare his or her homes just like my mom and grandma. The pastor, Reginald Desea, had a short and pudgy body with a perfect round face, dirtied by a pencil thin moustache. I remember he had a deep, even, soothing voice – except when he was on the pulpit delivering his sermon and especially when he was announcing his destination for dinner. It was a guttural, trembling bass, foot stomping release as he said, THE LORD IS KING!" I stomp my foot on the floor. "THE LORD IS KING!" Stomp. "THE LORD IS KING!" Stomp. "Who's ready for the call?" Stomp. "Who's ready for the call?" Stomp. "WHO IS READY FOR THE CALL!" Stomp. "Sister Nikki – are you ready for the call?" Stomp.

"The pastor and his family had come to my grandma's house once. He told us the reason for his after-service dinners. It was to help his flock prepare for the true call. You never know when the Lord will call on you. One should always have their mind, soul and spirit ready for the Lord's call. The chance for *dinner* represents the Lord's call. Are you ready for the call? Sure you can ignore the possibility, the pastor may not call on you, so it won't matter if your home is dirty and there is no food for guests. But if the pastor does call on you, where does that leave you? It leaves you with the pressure to account for your housekeeping. It leaves you making a million excuses and reasons that don't make the truth go away. The truth is you're not prepared. Now imagine when the Lord truly calls you and you're not right. What excuses will you offer the Lord? Where do you think those excuses will leave you? But if you take the time to make your home ready for guests, you'll be free of shame and those ties that bind you. Your home will be a beacon, calling out to the Fellowship. You will be blessed with family and friends for all of your days. Now that memory makes me feel good, and it also sends a shiver up my spine. Good for the food and family bit. The chill is from the truth that the Lord will call. Everyone shuffles off this mortal coil. Everybody dies. For those that are ready, the Lord's call will be warm and gentle and joyous. Well, I don't go to church, but from time to time, I will say Grace before a meal. And in the moment it takes me to say thanks, it's also a gut check. I always find my house is very dirty. I apologize and try to do better."

Nikki looks at me as though I have just entered the room with my hair ablaze.

Liz smokes her cigarette and I can't tell if she's just exhausted or over the top confused and overwhelmed by this machine before her. Before today I was a regular human to her. Now, I'm not.

Nikki says, "That's amazing. And I can tell that you feel it – that it's real to you. But it's not real. Doesn't that bother you?"

"No. I've thought about it before, I've thought about it a lot. It doesn't strike a negative chord with me. I'm good with it. I like memories, even if they're not mine."

"We provided lifestyle programs, social skills and such, hoping to compensate for lack of true human contact that occurs in the early mental bonding years," Geek states with pride.

"Automatons are not good soldiers. A good fighter must be adaptable, bold, sensible and insane; so Apollo and his kind aren't strict blind faith warriors. They're independent thinkers, so to that end, Apollo has the same appetites, vices and virtues as every other person. This allows for creative and improvisational thought and installs a hard desire to live – distinct qualities that will help him win in battle."

"You told me before that they are many like Apollo. Exactly how many?" Nikki asks.

"I think there are ten thousand troops like Apollo in service."

"Okay, that's not comforting. How long before they're released to take over the world?"

"They can't. The blue strobe affects them the same way it

does normal humans."

Nikki nods. "Cool. Thanks."

"If you can't join 'em – beat 'em," Geek replies.

"Well … where are all these warriors? Are they just stored at some army base?" she asks.

"Of course not. Most are marines. Those military guys that roam the dark cold heaven in funky big ships, protecting mining colonies and labs."

"Right. Smart ass."

Geek smiles. "The rest are like Apollo, working and living amongst the general population. They're chefs, schoolteachers, firefighters, and police. Stunt work for the movies is a big gig. Their designation is home security."

"And no one knows? Amazing," Liz says. "Are all the super-soldiers men?"

"Of course not," Geek replies.

"Good. Are the girls better?" Nikki asks.

Geek's answer is a quiet smile.

"How do you keep it a secret?" Nikki continues on. "I mean, how many people worked on these guys? Wouldn't someone talk?"

"Because the engineers, scientists, technicians don't know what they're working on," Geek answers. "The technology that is Apollo is integrated in everyday service items. So components for a plumbing, electrical, heating, whatever application are also employed for Apollo."

"But what about final assembly? How do you keep that group quiet?"

"Machines perform the final assembly and that occurs off-world."

Nikki shakes her head. "Amazing," she hisses. Then she says, "Ezra told me about what kind of solider you were but I'm not sure he even knew precisely what you are."

"Yeah, hell, I didn't know what kind of solider I was until today. Ezra seemed to know a lot about everything."

"That's why he's dead." Nikki says.

"I would have liked to have met him." Geek says. Then mumbling, nearly inaudible, "Where's that thing?" His fingers dance over the keypads.

Standing next to Liz at the bar, Nikki presses a depression

in the wall and a three legged stool flips out as a slender wall panel falls into the niche vacated by the unfolded stool. Nikki sits on the metal stool next to Liz. She takes a cigarette from the pack on the table and taps the filtered end on the tabletop.

"You okay?" she asks Liz.

"No. Won't be until I get my mom."

"Working on it," Geek says.

"I didn't mean…"

"All good, Liz. I know what it's like to have a loved one under their thumb."

Silence. I don't know Geek's past. And even Nikki doesn't seem to want to open that door.

"So, may I ask what else you've created? I want to know which tech stock to invest in," Nikki says with a smile.

"Of course. Investors are always welcomed," Geek replies.

"How about playing some music for me?" Nikki says.

"How about a little Satchmo?" Geek says.

"Who?" The cigarette dangles loosely on Nikki's lips, the lighter at the ready.

"Ah, the ignorance of youth. Sit back, young lady; here comes Louis."

We hear a ping. We can all see the blue page appear above Geek's workstation. The message states *substance undetermined.*

Geek replies, "Thanks."

He says, "Friend in the lab. Looks like they can't figure out what Ezra injected you with."

Louis Armstrong says hello to Dolly. I don't think I've ever heard this song.

"No matter, it didn't kill me. I'm built to last," I say.

Now I'm thinking about it. "I'm of a mind that Ezra worked for someone and I feel I should kick that someone's ass for the attempt. We should bury Griffin for all the hell he's caused Liz. And we have to draw blood from someone on Nikki's behalf."

Nikki raises her arms, and waves and claps her hands as she says, "Finally – you're on my side!"

"I've always been on your side. I just don't know how to get to you."

"Oddly, that makes sense." Nikki replies.

36

We watch Griffin stir to consciousness.

Geek pushes a few buttons.

"Welcome back, Griffin," he says.

Griffin squints as he looks about the bright room. He struggles against his arm and leg bindings.

"What the hell is this, Geek? Let me go. Let me go now!"

"Tell me the direct number to whoever is holding Liz's mom. I want her released now and you're going to do that."

"No, screw you. You let me go and I might consider…"

Geek pushes a button and Griffin twitches, mouth agape but he emits no sound.

Now Griffin sits in the chair panting and sweating.

"That didn't feel good did it?" Geek asks, plain and calm.

Griffin's eyes are wide and his shirt grows wet on his chest and beneath his arms. Sweat drips from his forehead, nose and cheeks.

"What is the direct number?"

"Griffin-one," says a broken man.

Geek nods. "On my mark, you will tell whoever answers to release Liz's mother. Any other comment will result in your immediate termination. I don't like you. I have no use for you. So I will kill you. Do you understand?"

"Yeah…"

"Hold that thought." Geek says.

"You hold this thought – fuck you!"

We see the flash on the monitor then feel the blast. Everyone is thrown to the metal deck of Geek's mot.

I'm on my feet in a heartbeat.

Nikki, Liz and Geek are scattered about the cabin.

"Talk to me! Who's hurt?" I ask.

"I'm good," says Nikki. She's shaking it off by the smoking rows of servers.

"Okay," comes from Liz and Geek about the same time. Geek rushes to his workstation. Liz gets to her feet with the aid of the wall.

"Apollo, hit the servers with the fire extinguisher," Geek orders.

"I'm on it. Are we still moving?" I remove the red canister from the wall.

"Yeah, but not for long. And we're visible."

"Did he blow up?" I hear Liz asking just under the hiss from the canister as I spray foam through the spaces of the stainless steel blades.

"Yes he did. I knew he was tagged with explosives, just like Apollo had been. I had buffers up to prevent an external trigger. So this was an internal impulse."

"If you knew he was rigged, why didn't you remove the bombs?" Nikki questions Geek. She's surprised at him.

"I didn't think he was a suicide! He's a party member. He's a Senator!"

Nikki throws her hands in the air. Geek responds by tossing his hands in the air.

Liz looks about the cabin, she looks lost but her eyes are not glazed or twitchy. She's worried and not for our fate. She's got one thing on her mind: her mother.

I set the spent canister on the floor. I check the server wall. No more smoke, no sparks or flares. "I think we're good here."

I see Geek nod. He's driving manually. The traffic monitors display the curious faces of pedestrians. Most seem to be pointing at us. And I see trailing smoke. Not a good thing.

Time to make an exit plan. Before I say anything, Nikki dons her canvas bag. She looks at me with a simple, hard smile that says, 'Protect me, bodyguard'.

I nod. I'm on it.

I look to Liz. She's calm, standing next to Geek. As Nikki and I approach the pair, I can see Liz is working the keypads alongside Geek. What the hell is this? She's like his co-pilot. I missed a lot when he took me offline.

"Thank you," Geek says to Liz.

"Glad I can help."

"You got a place to ditch?" I ask Geek.

"About three minutes away."

We may not have three minutes. "I can see left and right

and front but not rear or above. Can you re-establish those views?" I ask the pair.

"I'll work on it," Liz replies.

"Weapons, Geek?" I say.

He nods. "Weapons not damaged. If you see something, say something and I'll blast it."

I scan the three working monitors, gawkers pointing, most with cameras aimed our way.

Other monitors blink on, but the static is so thick I can't make out the scenes through the mass of pixels. Then the screens clear up.

I don't see any cops.

"You got that Bolt thing, right?"

I look at Nikki and nod.

"Good boy."

We see police units approaching from the rear and descending. Three units in total.

"I spy with my little eye…" Nikki starts.

"I see 'em," Geek states, slightly agitated.

"Are you going to hit them with the blue light? Is it safe for us?" Nikki asks.

"Relax woman! We got this." He shakes his head.

The monitors blink off. "I'll keep us on course," says a calm Liz.

Geek nods. He works his keypads.

"When did you learn to fly this thing?" I ask Liz.

"While you were under repair," she says with a smile.

"What else did you guys do while I was out?"

A collective silence coupled with a quiet laughter emits from the trio.

"Aw … c'mon! You coulda woke me up for that!"

"For what, love?" Nikki asks.

I meet her smiling eyes. I just want to make love to her.

I notice Geek touch the back of Liz's hand. She responds by tapping a few keys.

"How far do we have to go?" Liz asks.

Geek says, "Another click or so. Go to dock msxy. Punch in code; s, a, v, e."

Liz moves to the far left of the workbench. She works the keypads at that station.

We ride in silence. I reach into my right pants pocket and pull out the gloves for the Bolt. I put them on. I leave the Bolt in my pocket.

Nikki rolls her shoulders, like a boxer before the bell starts the fight.

"So what are we gonna do, bodyguard?"

"First, get to a safe place. Second, stay in that safe place. Third, find direct links to Gliddin, Space and The Event. Screw Griffin, I'm sticking with my theory."

"Okay, then what? You heard what that explosive asshole said. What am I going to get from all of this?"

I think about what she said and smile. I'm proud of myself for not laughing.

"We're done," states Geek as he rises from his chair. "I'm going to have to give up the mot. We're about three blocks east of the Canal terminal."

"Underground," I say as I lead the way toward the exit.

"Yeah, that's our best bet."

I nod my agreement. I hear no objection from the girls.

I pull the Bolt out. I look back and see my crew is ready to exit. I note that each of them have similar-styled canvas messenger bags.

The scene makes me pause. It's like an orchestrated ad campaign. Now I want a canvas messenger bag so I can be like the cool kids.

I say, "Here we go."

I open the door.

Twelve rounds hit me before I fire back. I take out seven officers. I rush out of the mot, fire at a POD, it explodes. Guess those things really piss me off. I see over a dozen officers silently roar toward us. I wave at my crew and point them east. We rush down the avenue with Nikki in the lead. She's not shy about knocking people over. It's easier to run straight than trying to dodge and weave, and you only have to knock over three or four people before the collective get the idea and get the hell out of the way. So now we're running a dead heat down the block. I stop and fire at the nearest three units. Glass shatters, metal buckles and one of the police units slams into a building. That causes nine police vehicles to come to an abrupt stop. They don't fire on me because I'm surrounded by people. So I rush down the street.

Two meters into my dash and I'm fairly clear of civilians and that's when I feel metal rounds crash into my flesh. The impacts cause me to jerk-step backward but nothing more. And yet they keep shooting, which annoys me so I stop, spin and fire. I strike five police mots. The vehicles come to a stop in heaps of shredded metal, hot smoke and, sometimes, blood against glass.

I see lights flash but feel no impact on my body.

More flashing lights from six hovering police units.

I see the missile launch and I sprint away. I leap as I hear and feel the pressure of the approaching weapon slicing through the air. I roll on the ground to avoid a direct strike from the missile then bound back to my feet – the explosion knocks me to the left.

My back is hot and bare and I spin and bounce like trash blown in the wind. I stop smack against a mot like wet debris.

All body parts accounted for. I'm still here. Get up.

Crawl.

Stop shaking. Need shelter.

Crawl toward the trash.

Concrete bay. Get beneath the heavy bins.

Don't need total darkness to disappear. Just shade.

Feeling better as I fade. Just need a moment to compose then I'm back in the action. I flex my hands. Re-grip the Bolt with my right.

Six cops in heavy gear rush past me. A few cops scout the area.

One cop drops to his knees, bends over and stares me in the eyes. The barrel of his weapon is aimed at my body as he checks beneath the trash bin. He's probably wondering why he can't see through me, yet, since he can't see me, he thinks it's a trick of the light.

Déjà vu. I'm the hunted. How the mind wanders when under stress.

The cop looks away from me. I watch his boots move as I hear him cautiously lift a panel atop the big metal container. He sets the panel down quietly once he finds nothing of interest.

From what I can see and hear, the foot patrols move on. I

know there are hovering units scanning the area for heat signatures and any abnormal movement. So I'll lie still for a few more minutes. I started this deal in a paper and rubbish warehouse, was kicked to the curb, and am now lying beneath garbage bins.

I need a new gig.

Ahh… what the hell! Mind, my mind…

"…Apollo, respond."

"Geek?"

"You okay, son?"

"I'm alive – what the hell, how are you in my mind?"

"Nikki's computer is amazing. Proto built a marvelous unit for her."

"Cool."

"The girls and I are secure. Liz got us sanctuary in a hash bar."

"I know the one. I'll be there as soon as I can."

"You need anything from me? How can I help?"

"Can you access police frequencies? I'd like to know what I'm dealing with."

"Will do. Hold."

And just like that, the pressure is off. Wow, Nikki's computer in Geek's hands. He may be able to shut down the power grids and such. Cause some civilian havoc, a diversion large enough to warrant redeployment of these immediate troops.

I find it strange that I don't hear dogs. I bet they're en route. I figure by now they know who I am and realize that I couldn't have left the immediate area so completely. They can't find me on any of the sensors and they know I can beat everything but smell so it's time to bring in the hounds.

The pressure…"Apollo, I'm going to blow my ship."

I wanted a distraction. "You sure about that?"

"Yeah, it's better this way. Liz saved everything. I'll lose some of the personal stuff but I'll learn to live without it."

"Right. Okay. Give me a countdown."

"On my mark… ten, nine," the pressure is off.

I take a deep breath. I'm ready … in five.

I see boots rush away from me. I hear frantic, "Negative! Negative!"

37

The concrete ripples and shakes beneath me as the air screams.

Eerie silence floods the scene. I don't hear voices or footfalls or cries… I worm out from beneath the metal bin. I feel the sun on my skin and so I've lost my *shade*. I grip the Bolt tight, ready to unload on anything in a uniform or combat gear. I look up, the sky is clear of police units. No PODs visible. I look right and see the street is clean. I look left and see smoke and burning debris and the parade of uniforms and official-acting people. I look ahead and behind, at the buildings, I see hundreds of eyes looking toward the smoke and fire and cops. I'm sure someone is looking at me but I can't tell.

I leave the trash bay and rush away from the action. I rip the tattered shirt from my body. I hold the strips of fabric as I run down the avenue. My goal is to hit the Underground at Eighth Avenue. Not the same one that Geek and the girls entered but I can work back to Yellow Bob's on that line.

I pitch the shirt in a trash receptacle and keep racing down the street.

I see the entrance a block ahead. I slow, from mad sprint to hard run, to power walk.

I look back, no one or nothing in pursuit. Cool. I break it down to the gait of a normal shirtless person enjoying the day. I remove the Bolt and gloves and shove the unit in my pant pockets.

I look down and see my shoes are dirty and beaten. My pants are oily and worn. And I'm shirtless. I look around. I see three stores to shop in before I hit the Underground. Then again, I can enter the Underground as I am. The cops won't give me a second look as long as I pass the eye scan. But this is me … I can't walk around like this.

On second study, two of the stores, Isabella and Bad Bitch, are for women. So I enter Majestic.

Eye scan as I pass through the portal into the quiet store. No music. The shop is well lit. The walls, high ceiling and floor are brushed stainless steel. No visible rivets or seams so the room appears as one hollowed metal brick. I like this place already. The shop is busy, but it's a large, open space so people aren't standing atop each other. Some clients have two people fawning over them. Others are solo, flicking through wardrobes while standing before the FitMirrors.

"Hello, Jack, I'm Cole," says the pretty, thin Asian man. A small, circular unit hovers just off his shoulder. He doesn't flinch at my appearance. He offers a huge smile and bright eyes. He sizes me up with his hands.

"Just in today, new from Italy, Mr. Robolini's Gray collection. May I suggest…." he places his slender forefinger against his playful lips. The floating unit at his shoulder emits a ray over my body.

I'm now suited. I look at myself in the mirror. The classic soft gray jacket and pants, thin black tie, white shirt, black shoes, with a black bucket hat. This is good. And I'm not in a real shopping mode right now. Yet I know this collection came out last month, so 'just in today' my ass.

Damn, now I'm in shopping mode.

I look deep into the pretty little boy's green eyes. "Cole, show me something from Marin Inaki."

His eyes light up, "He's my personal fave! This is so exciting." He sizes me with his hands once again. He steps back, his little head tilted to the left.

Now a white light washes over me, courtesy of the style unit at his shoulder. I'm wearing a green knit turtleneck pullover. The jacket and pants are a shiny off-olive color. The jacket has no pockets or buttons. The shoes are camel with a long flow and blunt toe.

"This is sweet," I say.

"Yes it is!" I think he's more excited than I am.

"I'll take it."

"Yes! Just follow me to the dressing rooms."

I do. We walk quickly through the store.

Cole opens a door for me and I see the clothes hanging from a hook with the shoes on the floor.

"Take your time," he says.

"Thank you."

I see that they even provide underwear. What the hell. I strip down and put the new clothes on. The turtleneck is a thin knit: very light and flexible. The material for the jacket and pants is so soft I feel it will melt in my hands. The tags say eighty-percent wool. So what's the other twenty? And like I care.

Digging the hell out of the shoes. Snug and comfortable. Those style units are spot-on when it comes to fitting.

I look in the mirror. I like it a lot. I bring the jacket together and the magnetic lining hems shut. Yeah, this is working for me. Spin. Looking good from the rear. Back to the front and I pull gently on the lapels and the jacket swings open.

"Price," I say to the mirror.

Little yellow tags appear next to each item in the mirror. The jacket is seven nineteen. Turtleneck is two fifty-nine. Pants, one sixteen. Shoes are six forty-five. Socks, thirty-two. Shorts and t-shirt combo, fifty-two. Not a problem.

I reach down and retrieve the Bolt and gloves from my old pants. I place the unit into the pockets of my new pants. I look around for my wallet ... and it floods back to me.

My wallet is – was – on the dresser in Geek's mot. Dammit.

Okay, it's not a problem. I can get another Lifecard with little effort. Don't stress. This can work.

I exit the dressing room. Cole is waiting for me. His eyes light up as if we're lovers meeting after a long absence.

"You are fabulous," he says softly but with much intensity.

"Thank you."

We walk over to the check out.

"Should I charge your A1 account?"

"Yes." Of course, the new contacts are registered to the new account that Geek set up. Sweet.

"We're good. Now you go out and kick some ass." Cole says with a sincerity that makes me want to kiss him.

"Thank you for the wonderful service."

"My pleasure."

I leave the store feeling fine.

I turn left – I'm immediately face to glass eye with a POD. I'm amazed that I don't smash it. Damn things just sneak up on you.

Eye scan. Satisfied I'm not the one, the POD floats away.

I hurry toward the Underground, escorted by a *personal* Public Service Announcement. There is a picture of a man and a woman displaying their tattoos. The man's tattoo is of a black widow spider and it travels across this body. The woman's tattoo is of a butterfly whose wings continually change color. The PSA advises men and women against digital tattoos. The body art has been linked to birth defects. Consult physicians for deactivation and removal of units prior to conception or, sperm or egg donation.

The pressure returns. Gotta be Geek.

"Apollo?"

"I'm here and about to enter the Eighth Avenue port. I'll work back to Yellow Bob's."

"Good. We'll stay put. See Ed at the bar and just say, housekeeping."

"Okay, you know, communicating with you is very uncomfortable on my mind. It's like pressure. Not like the normal Allround communication."

"Well, I'm hijacking that signal and of course there is a lot of resistance. The pressure you feel is probably the result of my breach on the Allround's security protocols and defenses."

"Right. Sure. I'll see you in ten."

"Cool."

The pressure is off.

I think dark brown … and grow my hair to shoulder length. I darken my skin a few shades and lighten my eyes by the same degree.

I step over a small gold Masonic stamp in the concrete as I mix with the horde and walk through the VIP-Cola advert that curtains the down ramp to the gates of the Underground.

Cops hang about and watch the swarming crowd.

I approach the gate and look for the slender Control booth. There, at the far right.

Without a Lifecard, I have to give blood. I always take that unit for granted. The card has a rough face and back, collecting dust-like skin particles from indiscriminate contact. The card immediately analyzes the owner's DNA.

The information is passed to the central computer and one is allowed or denied access based on health in the time it takes to flash the card.

Without the card … blood is the cost of admission.

Three cops stand about and stare me down as I approach the Control booth.

I slip my forefinger into the oval slot in the wall. My finger is immobilized, prick, a cool spray.

I look straight ahead. Eye scan.

Now we wait.

Three cops are getting paid to watch me and they're not saying a word. The least they can do is make annoying small talk, if just amongst each other. Quiet cops don't set right with me.

I receive a green light. My finger is released. The cop on my immediate left steps aside.

I walk a few paces then step through the clear, shimmering barrier.

38

A screaming guitar, in the drop behind the drum and bass, forms a nice dance beat, part of the *tunnel groove* that defines the Underground. I gotta say, the best DJs in the city are at this Underground terminal.

I turn left, into the bazaar. No name brands or knock-offs here and no chain stores of any kind in the Underground. Just hand made wares from families or solo artists. One-of-a-kind, not to be found anywhere else: rugs, clothing and accessories, drugs, black ink tattoo artists; jewelry and sculptures made of wood, glass, ceramic, metal – anything that's been discarded has some paint splashed on it and is now called decorative art. And of course, paintings on canvas, wood, glass, ceramic and metal. Books and magazines, all manner of archaic media and the apparatus required for listening or viewing the material.

The food courts are hopping. I see lines at the noodle kiosks and falafel shops, Brazilian stew pots and Asian flash grills. With all the good smells pulling at me, I can't believe I'm drawn to the dirty water dogs. And I'm not alone in my culinary yearning, I see over a dozen people eating and standing beneath a beautiful wrought iron sign that simply reads: HOT DOG.

As I near the hot dog stand, I note that the walk-in closet back at Bobby's place is larger than this guy's shop. I nod to the lone man behind the short counter.

"One with onions in that spicy sauce … yeah, that's the stuff."

"Drink?"

"No."

The tall, Latin server passes me the foot long tube of mystery meat topped with wet red stringy onions. Mouth watering and tasting the cumin, I'm about to take a bite when I notice that the guy waits for payment.

"Scan my eyes. Either one," I instruct the vendor.

He whips out his pen, points it at my face and presses the black button on the unit. I see a solid thin red line.

He checks his monitor … then nods with a big smile.

I bite my dog and walk away.

"Excuse me, we'd like a word." The voice is small but firm and full of self-importance. I take another bite. I'm gonna finish this meal. And so I turn to meet the voice and see it belongs to a thin and proper man that stands as high as my nipples. He's got two friends with Bang sticks at the ready. All three men wear tidy blue uniforms with the large and daunting insignia of the Underground Police.

I walk and smile and say, "Yes?"

The little man stays in step with me. He's not sure what he's dealing with so his manner remains polite.

"We noticed that you don't quite photograph, nor do you produce body heat. Yet you were cleared. No doubt that you're a healthy normal male. Forty-two years of age. Single. No children. Baptist. Claims adjuster. Blah-blah-blah … You're not military are you, Mr. Jack Barbarosa?"

I continue to smile. Who gave me that name? Had to be Nikki.

"There is coding within your visual signature. That would indicate active military. Yet you do not register as active military. So we have a point of confusion."

Looks like Geek, Nikki or Liz – whoever set up my profile forgot to update the blonits. I usually appear as retired military. So what line of bullshit do I feed this guy now? And I can't take aggressive action because that will turn the place into a war zone.

I finish my hot dog.

Then it hits me and I do my best to keep from smiling. Let's see if this sticks. I say, "There is a man over there that went undetected by Paws. My job is to follow him. I'm an Ambre agent."

I can see from the glint in his eyes that he's running the line. Then the little guy stiffens. He breaks free of his trance and nods.

"Sorry to inconvenience you," he says. He's not happy about it. He pulls away from me like fresh Velcro, keeping a hard eye in the direction of my alleged target. His buddies secure their Bang sticks as they leave the scene.

The crowd relaxes. I feel hundreds of eyes on me, every one of them questioning how I was able to make the UP quietly go away. Hell, if the crowd knew what an Ambre agent was, they'd rush away from me as well.

I hang out for a moment, look about the bazaar. Then I continue through the mall on my way to Yellow Bob's. The problem is that I'll now be tagged for the entire time I'm down here. So I have to hook up with my crew without making true contact.

I see a blinking red light above a trash bin. All near the receptacle take a few steps back, making sure they are now standing outside the yellow circle. The bin slides into the wall. A new bin juts from the wall as I walk by. The light stops blinking.

The tunnel music slides from Basque downbeat to insane beat and guitar.

"So how long did it take you to realize you're an Ambre agent?"

The voice – you must be kidding me! No, no, no… I turn and see Griffin walking at my side.

Practice thinking. Do not open mouth until process reaches a satisfactory conclusion. Repeat.

And all I can ask is why? What did I do to deserve this?

My personal Satan observes the silence.

"You sent a clone to the restaurant. It was a clone that committed suicide."

"You're talking to a clone now. You've never met the real me," Griffin says.

I find comfort in that.

"You didn't answer my question. How long did it take you to realize you're an Ambre agent?"

"I didn't realize anything. I just ran a line of bullshit and it was golden."

"It wasn't bullshit. Ambre is my division. You're my point man, but somehow you keep forgetting that fact. And yet you fulfilled the assignment. You did the job no one else could. You got next to Nikki. You are the only person she truly trusts. We've had a dozen agents in her play but she always seems to catch on and all goes ice cold. But you, she likes you.

"And then you got the Project Blue Book file but didn't bring the prize home to papa. I thought it was all lost when Nikki kicked you to the curb, but you lived, and found her again and led us to her. Then you saved her ass!

"We can't seem to override or erase Geek's original programming. You ... are not like the rest. In that sense, you've become a true human: a pain in the ass."

"That's twice I've found cheer in your words. Keep it up and I'll kiss you."

"You see, that's the crap the bugs me, sarcasm is not part of the encoding!"

Griffin pulls out a pack of cigarettes. Tugs one free from the pack and quickly lights it up.

Pressure....

"Okay, we've been listening. We're no longer in Yellow Bob's. Moving down the line."

"You're listening?" I send Geek the thought.

"Looking and listening. I've got real time feed on you. Like Griffin just told you, they can't override my program. You always have been, and always will be, my tool."

"So ... I'm really an Ambre agent? My assignment was to get next to Nikki and secure the file for Griffin?"

"No. To secure the file for me," Geek states.

"You know, she killed Ezra," Griffin says to me between puffs. "Ezra was our contact."

"Sorry I lied to you, Apollo."

What the hell? "How are *you* talking to me?"

"We're all online with you, Liz too," Geek says.

"Hi Apollo. Like your outfit. Ask that asshole about my mom."

I ask Geek. "So what do you want me to do?"

"Keep walking and talking to him. Do whatever he asks."

The pressure dissipates as the tunnel music crosses over to bouncy Côte d'Ivoire pop. And Griffin and I cross over into a wonderful FunRow.

Multitudes of beautiful women and men stand before colorful doors for rooms of eight square meters or less. All rooms have their own theme, from Tiki beach with real sand, real water to simulate surf, gas torch lamps and blazing overhead heat lamps, to concrete closets with silver steel bars and black rings set in the walls, ceiling and floor. In some cases, patrons are required to furnish their own toys; which can be purchased at the sex shops sandwiched between the studios.

A tiny blonde dressed in a sky blue ball gown with hot white pearls and bright white heels waves at me. She opens her blue door to reveal a terrace with a Manhattan at night skyline. I note service for two at the glass table by the railing, while a shy Spanish boy-toy in white tie and tails and holding a wine bottle stands at the ready. I could jump into that fantasy.

"You got nothing to say?" Griffin asks.

"I'm ... just ... taking it all in."

"Stop looking at the women."

Like that's gonna happen.

"When did Nikki become an assignment? I've known her for years. I've killed dozens of people for you. I remember each and every order – direct from you. I never received an order in any effect to track Nikki and secure files."

"This is just insane ... I'm arguing with a machine," Griffin says.

"Screw you! You're the real *artificial* life form. Damn clone. In fact, that's all clones are good for – sex. Expensive as all hell but you make great sex toys."

"And you're a great tool that's good for nothing. Pull out your cell phone right now and contact Geek."

I shake my head. "Lost my cell in Geek's mot. Along with my wallet. That's why I had to give blood at the gate. No Lifecard."

Griffin nods. "Okay, didn't understand that ... I thought you were reaching out to us. It helped me find you. That's how I got to you so quick. So where are you going to meet them?"

"Reaching out to you?"

"Shut up. Where are you meeting Geek?"

"I'm not. I came down here to hide. We did that scatter thing."

"Here, call Geek." Griffin hands me his phone. We stand in the middle of the strip. I glance over at the tall brunette cheerleader standing by a neon yellow door. She blows a bubble and quickly snaps it. She smiles, I smile then politely turn away.

Now I face a sex shop called Magical Thinking. The slender window adjacent to the business entrance displays herbal and pharmaceutical enhancements and aphrodisiacs in pure root, pills, powder, liquid and ampoules.

Suddenly under pressure… "Apollo – turn off his phone," Geek orders.

"Why?"

"Because when you turn it on again, it'll display his IP code. I can track that to true Griffin's real location."

I turn off the phone. We hear the tiny familiar beeps that indicate disconnect.

"What the hell?" Griffin snaps at me.

"Wrong button. Can't stop looking at pussy," I say with my eyes on the sour-faced redhead looking for someone to punish.

"Idiot!"

I reboot the unit. We hear the universal uplink ping.

And there's the IP display.

No pressure.

"Got signal. Now waiting for green light," I advise an anxious Griffin.

I watch a couple exit a studio with a silver flecked door. The guy walks away with a smile in his step. The girl fusses with her hair. The set is a dark alley, trashcans along both walls and litter on the ground. I see a knife on the ground. Then the lights come on in the studio. I see two guys in yellow suits enter the studio through a hidden back door. They begin to *sanitize* the set. Housekeeping, not a way I want to make money. Like pulling a watch from a giraffe's ass. I pass.

I punch in Geek's number.

NO SERVICE appears on the tiny monitor of Griffin's phone.

"He must have lost his cell too," I say.

"Call the others," orders Griffin.

"What about Liz's mom?" I ask as I dial up Liz.

NO SERVICE appears on the screen.

"What about her?"

"Why not let her go?"

"Why would I do that?"

"Because she has nothing to do with anything."

"You got one more call to make."

I call Nikki.

NO SERVICE appears on the screen. "Nada. No one is home. Now, if you were to pass legislation that would allow civilians to have access to similar mental communications as the military, police and fire, then we'd be in contact with someone at this point." I give the phone back to him.

Griffin laughs at me as he pockets his phone. He smokes his cigarette with glee.

"That'll never happen," Griffin states. "What I can't believe is that with all the new body modifications Geek has made with you, that he didn't put in a direct line. I can't believe he can't contact you."

Griffin looks me in the eyes and says, "Hi Geek. I'm sure you're monitoring this *Creep*. You've got one hour to come to the Flatiron. You, Liz and Nikki. If you're a minute late, I'll kill Liz's mother. Then I'll really start messing things up. I want you. I want specific operational details for that special blue light. I want the Jump One file. One hour."

Griffin turns and walks away.

"What about me?"

"What do you think?" he says without looking at me.

Well, I think I ought to be there.

I wonder what Geek, Liz and Nikki think? I'm sure they'll tell me in a moment.

I also think I have time for a quickie. But I always think that. Trouble is, either I follow Griffin, back to the main exit, or I continue down FunRow and sex will happen.

Let me follow Griffin. If I keep my eyes on him it will keep my dick in place.

Standing before a matte green door is a very pretty Asian woman with the hottest eyes … she wears a simple silver teddy. Damn! But I keep walking.

Two plain-looking girls dressed as Americana housewives are engaged in a shouting match in front of an orange door. Now they grapple and punch and buttons fly from white blouses and pearls shower down … The tall, firm blonde with big red lips tosses her cigarette to the ground and pushes the thinner blonde into the studio and four clients rush to follow the fighting girls into a clean kitchen set with the morning sun streaming through rose-patterned drapes over a porcelain sink.

Keep walking and keep your eyes on Griffin – how the hell did the fat clone get so far ahead?

I pick up my step. I can see the start of the bazaar. It's like a sick race to make it out of FunRow without paying. I've never made it out of one before. Never even thought about trying to. What's the point? I like to cruise a FunRow as long as I can and until that particular fantasy just slaps me in the face and grabs my dick with a vengeance.

Real funny thing is that human behavioral scholars design most of these fantasies. The FunRow is actually a working lab for behavior therapy. Therapists will recommend studios to their clients. The actors are provided scripted flowcharts and costumes and speech cues; aromas, fabrics, mementos and fetishes that will best succeed with the client. The client may have a wonderful sexual encounter, or just a heartfelt conversation with a kindred spirit, all with the belief that they have been in charge or control of the event.

And I win. I guess. Off FunRow with no cash or dreams spent. I wade lightly through the static bazaar crowd because I don't want to catch up to Griffin.

Can't believe that Geek hasn't reached out to me.

I rush through the barrier, exchanging rocking tunnel music for the normal din and flutter on the public platform. It feels like every law enforcement agent on the platform is looking at me. I'm sure some will physically tail me while command watches me on the monitors.

I walk up the exit ramp. Before me reads, *Mkeyinc Inc. Business at its Best*. I laugh as I walk through the shimmering mercury advert.

The sun is fading. Soft amber streetlights wash over the avenue. Once again, I marvel as I glance up at the buildings. A harsh setting sun forces colors to dance off the faceted panels of the ultra tall buildings. It's like looking at stars, only not.

"Apollo!"

Nikki. I look around and spot her waving hand on from a cab. I bull ahead, bumping into a few people who aren't moving fast enough, or are just in my way.

I get into the cab. Geek, Liz and Nikki. I relax because this is home. I'm not angry with my family even though they have all *used* me in some capacity during the last twenty-four hours. I appreciate the proper use of tools.

"You got the message?" I ask, completely aware of the answer.

Geek nods.

"Oh yeah," says Liz.

"He's an asshole," says my future wife. Nikki and I lock eyes. Her eyes are the greatest. With her at my side, I could be happy watching grass grow.

Silence. I look at the citizens on the street. Happy, smiling people at work, walking tiny pets, or walking and talking.

"So did you figure out where real Griffin is?" I ask.

"He's here in the city. Having dinner at Ernesto's."

"What are we going to do?" I ask.

"Kidnap him," Nikki states.

I nod. "Okay. Trade his life for Liz's mom. I get it."

"A little deeper than that," Geek says. "No disrespect Liz. Securing your mother is important but not the main goal. We've thought this out and it's a viable course of action."

"We?" I start and Geek pats the air in a calming fashion.

"Everybody works for somebody. I work for somebody. Griffin is the party nominee for the next presidential cycle because he has a lot of power. As does my boss but he's in the minority pipeline. So we've figured out how to make this work for us."

"Do tell," Nikki says.

"Offer Griffin's clone the chance for life," Geek replies.

Silence. Liz's face is twisted in disgust. Nikki shakes her

head.

I get it. "Clones only live for three years. We offer this clone access to real Griffin's DNA. He makes a new body when required. We erase owner protocols so that the clone gets to make his own decisions. He gets to live his own fantasies."

Geek nods. "Politically, we'll make his decisions. That's all we care about."

The girls still don't like it.

Liz says, "Won't people get suspicious if Griffin goes against the party?"

"What about Griffin's internal security?" Nikki asks. "Clones have a direct link to the master. Once we offer the deal to the clone, real Griffin will immediately be aware. And clones are registered and tagged with life clocks. So how do you make a new clone without the million and one steps required by the government?"

"Plus real Griffin must remain alive to initiate new clones. You can't clone the dead," I state.

Geek replies, "Griffin's clone was not coded nor had a life clock. My old mot would have made me aware of that. I will ask the clone where he was created.

"As far as the party goes, Griffin and Gliddin are the independent thinkers for their party. They've been at the helm in one way or another for better than twenty years. Griffin has reversed his positions many times in the past. As he goes, so does the party."

Geek looks at me. "Not another clone. More like Apollo sans the body enhancements. We'll promise Griffin's clone fifty years of independent life. I've been told his current lifecycle ends in eighteen months."

"We're here." Liz states as she quiets the destination alarm.

We stare at the restaurant from the comfort of the cab. It's a small, angular building of glass and gold trim that suggests a very small interior but I've read that the dining room is very spacious. Seating is for fifty, usually high profile, people.

"You want me to kill Griffin on sight?" I ask Geek.

Liz and Nikki snap their necks to stare at me. They both know who I am. I guess the simplicity of it just shocked them.

Geek shakes his head. "No. I'll see to his disposal if the clone takes the deal. This is snatch and grab. He must be knocked out immediately because, as Nikki pointed out, his internal security will post alarms.

"You're also going to have to deal with the bodyguards by the limo."

I follow his gaze and see the two guys standing by the smooth black vehicle. The bodyguards look like standard issue. This shouldn't be a problem.

Geek studies Nikki's laptop. Nikki peers over his shoulder. Liz looks at me.

I say to her, "It'll be okay. You'll see your mom soon."

"What if the clone doesn't take the deal?" she says.

My reply is firm. "Everything wants to live. It'll make the deal."

"Not to rain on the party but the other clone did blow itself up instead of making the deal," Nikki states.

"I don't believe it was a suicide," Geek says. "I continually monitored location pings from the unit as well as searching signals to the clone. I think it was programmed to self-destruct if it was out of contact for any length of time. And the web around my mot didn't allow contact."

"This one will make the deal," I say to Liz.

She smiles. "Thanks, Apollo."

"He's on the move," Geek says.

I look at the front entrance of the restaurant. "I don't see him."

Geek points at the laptop. "I'm tracking him via GPS."

"Courtesy of his phone's IP code?" I ask.

Geek, Nikki and Liz nod.

Damn techies.

I exit the cab and walk briskly in the direction of the limo. I put on the appearance of a hurried man seeking a short cut through the parking lot.

I look around; see few potential witnesses. I look up; the immediate sky is clear of surveillance drones and police vehicles.

The guy on my left, standing near the rear door, checks his phone. I deliver an uppercut to his partner on my right. Phone guy looks in my direction to see my fist coming at him.

I open the back door and dump both bodies into the cabin. I get in.

I look for witnesses. Only my family saw the action.

I watch the front door for the fat man.

Silence. The bodyguards were lightweight but I didn't break any bones with my punches. I imagine they have enhancements but obviously are not designed for combat. I push the two quiet bodies deeper into the cabin. Give the fat man some legroom.

I see a well-stocked liquor rack. I could go for a quick shot. Wonder what's in the fridge? I open the black door. Standard stuff: OJ, chilled liqueurs, couple bottles of white wine, chocolate, Resurrection Paks.

What the hell – how does he move so fast? Right at the door.

Well …

Griffin looks around in disgust then opens the back door.

I grab him by the tie and punch him in the face. I pull the heavy man into the vehicle and close the door.

I look around for witnesses.

None.

I look down and see the fat man sleeping, his lips bloodied. I pitch him atop his bodyguards.

Nikki, Liz and Geek rush toward the limo.

I move to the front of the cabin. Where are the controls?

The trio roar into the limo.

"Go." Geek orders.

I see the landscape change. Of course, voice activated. Just like cabs. Practice thinking.

"Destination please," asks the pleasant female voice.

"Just run with the pack," Geek states.

I didn't realize civilians knew that term. It's a police phrase for auto drive. In auto drive, without specific direction like fastest route or shoreline, mots will always go with the flow. Cops use this system to find *hot* spots. The run usually snares teens hanging out and trying to have fun but sometimes they net a real score.

Nikki studies the liquor.

"I'll take a drop of the whiskey," I say.

She looks at me ... Then turns to Liz and Geek. "Since I'm here, what're you drinking?"

"Let's keep it neat, just pass the bottle," Geek states.

We all nod like plugged-in kids.

"How did you plan to keep Skippy asleep?" Nikki asks Geek. She cracks the seal on the whiskey bottle.

Geek seems indifferent. "I guess.... Just let Apollo punch him out when he rouses."

"That's a plan I can get behind! I'll joyously beat his ass for an eternity."

Nikki hands the bottle to Geek. She reaches into her bag, roots around, then pulls out an ampoule of Night: a legal sleep aid.

"Brilliant," says Geek. He takes another pull from the bottle. Then hands it to Liz.

Nikki places the red end of the device against the side of Griffin's neck. She taps the other end with her thumb. Done. She tosses the unit on the floor.

Griffin will be down for hours.

Liz passes the bottle to Nikki. Nikki has a drink. She passes it to me.

Geek holds his phone. I see his thumb working the keypad as he holds the phone on his lap. He looks at his phone as he speaks.

"Griffin."

"Hello Geek."

"Call home," Geek says.

"What?"

"Call home," Geek repeats himself as though spelling out the words.

"I think he shut off his phone," Geek says. He looks up at us; then stares at Griffin's still body.

A buzz is being emitted from the fat man.

Nikki searches the body. She finds the phone in the inside pocket of Griffin's jacket. She tosses the phone to Geek.

Geek points the phone at Griffin's body. He presses the green button.

"Do you get the big picture?" Geek asks. He continues. "If you alert security, we will kill him and you'll spend your short remaining days grooming your successor. Or...."

40

"I'm listening," replies clone Griffin.

"The offer, download you into an Apollo-type body and you assume the life of Griffin. Guaranteed lifecycle of fifty years."

"I want a full century," bargains the clone.

"Your reality is eighteen months of duty and no ceremony upon demise. The offer stands at fifty years. And remember, those will be your years. Sure, you'll push our agenda but everything else is yours. You can indulge in drunken vacations. You get to develop your own sexual fetishes. You can enjoy real food. And you can sleep, perchance to dream."

"Real life," states the clone.

Geek nods. "The best you'll ever know," he states as he stares at the phone.

Silence.

"So how do we do this?" The clone asks.

"First. Release Liz's mother. Tell her to call her daughter once she's clear. Once that's settled, I'll call you with further instructions."

"What happens to me? What happens to this body? I've got tight security protocols."

"We know. Clone you, will live out the contract. You may want to even issue a new one."

Silence.

"I'll set the release in motion."

"You do that. I'll call you later."

Geek shuts down Griffin's phone.

Liz gives him a big kiss.

Nikki takes the bottle from me. She takes a short pull from the bottle. She hands the bottle to Geek.

Nikki asks, "Who do you work for and what's your agenda and how do I fit into it? You said that you wanted Apollo to secure the Jump One file for you."

Geek drinks from the bottle. He sighs. "I work for my

brother. You know him as Carroll G. Thorosen."

"You asshole!" screams Nikki. "So, what, you gonna have Apollo kill me now?!"

"No," I state.

Pause....

"No is right," Geek says.

Geek and I lock eyes. I wouldn't do it if he did ask me. And now he knows that. He winces – slight – and now I know he's afraid of me. He wonders if I'd turn on him at Nikki's call. I probably would.

Geek has another drink of whiskey.

"This is politics and this is family and it's all the same thing," Geek says. He passes the bottle to Liz.

"Malcolm Space, yes, that Space, was to marry my half-sister, Elizabeth Selene Hudson-York. Elizabeth, Carroll and I share the same father. Instead, on Carroll's staid insistence, Elizabeth married our cousin, Denson Weller Randell. Their child, Fury Selene Randell, was the heir to the family fortune as her mother was unable to bear other children.

"Fury was promised to marry Albert, the Swedish prince. That would have placed two powerful families in alliance and secured a major power play."

"Did no one know that Space was romancing Fury? Where's her prince in all this?" Nikki asks.

Geek shakes his head. "Didn't have a clue she was dating Space, or sleeping with Bobby. Amazing. The prince and his family are pissed-off. Yet, from what I gather, they could've handled the affairs ... but Space had to kill her!

"Very bad decision on his part. The act forced the committee en masse to sanction his death. Apollo you will perform this kill."

"You want me to kill Space? He's in jail."

"He will be transferred at some point in the future. Make the hit very loud and messy."

I nod. This I can do.

"What about me?" Nikki asks smacking the seat with the palm of her hand.

Liz passes the bottle to Nikki. She takes it and just holds it as she stares at Geek.

"We apologize for destroying your family. Honestly, we

truly are sorry. We promise, in time the truth will be told. We will do right by you.

"For the now, you will be placed on a committee at the Institute for Social Relations. Your new purpose in life is change the way the world thinks about extraterrestrial life."

"What ..." Nikki's voice is weak.

"Have a drink," Geek suggests to Nikki.

Nikki takes a big swig. She passes the bottle to me.

"Your story has become part of the grand plan. The grand plan is called Star Domination. Major points of SD have been established, such as one power structure, increased education of the people, a fruitful and dutiful working class, consolidation of population centers for better civilian control, and everyone working to expand into space and conquer the stars. Denson Weller Randell initiated the building blocks during his presidency. We were a heartbeat away from a unified family ...

"But all you really need to know is that the UFO encounter with Jump One was real, but no one feels it was an attack. For one thing, it has not been followed up."

"Then what happened to the Apricot Wind?" I ask.

"Records indicate that the Apricot Wind was in the immediate vicinity of the nuke strike at the UFO. As best we can tell, that attack caused a power burst on the Apricot Wind. Major systems upon the vessel were crippled and the spacecraft crashed into the North Pacific Ocean.

"Gliddin wanted to use The Event as a reason to beef up the military and launch an attack."

"Attack? On whom?" I ask.

"We made contact with alien life just over two years ago. The planet is in the Canis Major. There is an ordinary dwarf star that is believed to be evolving. As are the natives of the planet. We could slaughter them like pigs. And the life does not look like us, or anything else you can imagine. Their appearance will easily strike fear in humans.

"Griffin was going to use The Event as evidence of an alien attack from this planet."

Silence.

Geek nods. "Right. So, what we're going to do is keep it under wraps. We're going to pump up the Marines and technology and we are going to secure the planet – because it is habitable. We want to claim that planet as ours. One day this planet will die. We need to be prepared."

"Are we going to destroy the natives to claim this planet?" Nikki asks. She seems to be teetering between shock and anger.

"No. That's Griffin's plan. Ours is to work with the natives."

"No matter how you spin it, this can't be good," I say.

Geek sighs, then, shows the ace card. "Gold has been discovered on the planet. I know, we're telling everyone the discovery was made on an asteroid but that's not the truth. The planet is mineral-rich and untapped. The natives don't have the tools and knowledge necessary to extract the minerals.

"This new planet is ours and we're securing it. But without the hype and fury. Nikki, you will continue to rail against the government and deliver nuggets of truth from time to time. More and more details and evidence will be presented and finally, we'll trot out a whistle-blower with solid proof. By then we'll have established colonies on the new planet and will be able to tout massive wealth via its natural resources."

"Mot stop! Let me out." Nikki rises to a stoop and looks at me.

"Let's go," she says to me.

The limo door opens.

"Is my father alive?" she asks Geek without looking at him.

"I believe so."

Nikki brushes past me as she exits the limo. "Time to be free," she whispers.

I look at Geek.

He nods.

I make my way out of the limo. The city is so bright at night.

I slip on my black leather gloves.

"Call me when your mom is clear," I say to Liz.

She nods. We kiss.

"Nikki," Geek calls out.

"What!" She storms back to the limo. "What do you want? What other orders do you have for me, my lord, my master!"

"Apollo belongs to you now. We'll only call on him when necessary."

Nikki begins to speak but remains quiet. I see the rise in her chest subside.

When she does speak, it is with calm, bright eyes. "He's always belonged to me. So maybe I won't let him answer any calls." She turns and walks away.

I grab the Bolt. I can feel it meld with my gloved hand. I pull it out and fire once, blasting Geek in the face.

May the gods help us all.

"Good boy. You do understand me." She kisses me.

"It was time for this puppet to cut the strings." I say, then exhale slowly and long, until my lungs are empty. "He probably has a clone, or two."

"I'm sure he does. Your point being?"

"Just stating a fact. I'll keep killing until there's no more Geek."

"Perfect." She takes a long drag from her cigarette.

Liz scrambles past Geek's still body. "So what's the plan to get my mom?"

Nikki points to me. "Change," she says.

It takes me a moment, then I realize what she's taking about. I think about it and become Geek.

Liz nods. "Excellent. So let's do it."

Manhattan glows, whirls and pumps around us. I love the feel of the city at night. I take Nikki by the hand and she squeezes hard, a promise to never let go.

Nikki smokes her cigarette. I can see my lady is busy in thought. She's so exciting in bitch mode.

"I'm not happy about this," she tells me.

"I know."

"This is not over."

I nod. I know a storm is on the way, I'm content at Nikki's side. I loved it when she told Geek I've always belonged to her.

I always will.

I'll forever respect Geek, my father and creator, but I choose to obey and honor My Love over all else.

A large oblong *personal* approaches us. The ad scans our eyes then says, "Hello Jack and Diane. What would you like to see?"

"Show us something in shoes," Nikki says.

I bend a little to give her a kiss. My girl knows my passion.

A silhouetted man and woman walk by as our *personal* displays summer footwear from HTML Noir.

Nice shoes.

END

A Proposal for Economic Recovery and Stability

[DRAFT COPY – NOT FOR PUBLICATION]

© Denson Weller Randell *09.04.2048*

Our nation, our society, cannot grow strong and prosperous with a skill set that peaks at operating a joystick to control a remote unit or click a mouse to order an item.

There is no future in a machine world. This direction of convenience and leisure is akin to lemmings leaping off a cliff.

I offer a simple framework for conversation toward rebuilding and stabilizing the working class. We will see positive results regarding the economy within five to ten years. We will see positive results by way of a strong middle class with solid footing soon after that and going forward.

Children and Young Adults in Education, Training & Environmental Improvement Schemes

[AJ- No bullets or numbering here]

At age twelve, students will be introduced to the basic trades: carpentry, drafting, and masonry, electrical, plumbing and painting. They will be introduced to basic concepts of the trades as well as advanced math courses pertinent to the trade. Students will study/work at real operating sites. Students will work projects from design, to purchasing materials, to physical labor, to final inspection of the project. (No, twelve-year old children will not operate power tools or scale steel girders or pick cotton. There are numerous age-appropriate work site functions that will allow students to learn the skill as they safely participate on the work site. Note the Habitat for Humanity youth programs.)

Trade and labor unions will be responsible for training. Students will apply for a general apprenticeship. Students will receive a stipend for projects completed. Unions will collect dues from the stipend. Banks will hold monies and administer earned allowance to student.

Private institutions and banks will sponsor the projects. (Put bank and lending institutions to work. They must issue loans at low interest and without special attachments or conditions.) The projects should have commercial value such as: new housing / inspection and repair of homes, apartments and other living abodes; the construction of roads, bridges, and parks; and the production of essential material goods and food.

Reclamation and recycling services are vital. Clearing and cleaning away decrepit buildings and structures. Removing debris and trash from fields, forests, rivers, beaches, ponds, lakes, marshes and estuaries. Students will receive stipends for participating in these projects.

Students will also be instructed in basic life support, CPR, and other First Response programs. After completion of such courses, students may apply for apprenticeships in firefighting and law enforcement and of course volunteer as support staff in hospitals. (First Response certifications must be renewed every two years.)

[AJ- Seems to be less indented than other bullets]
At age sixteen, a student may commit to a trade, applying for formal apprenticeship with a chosen union. Students will then enter GED track, allowing the student to spend more time studying the trade. At this time, students will also be introduced to other trades such as machinist (tool & die), welding, farming, fishing, forestry, landscaping, sanitation etc.

[AJ- Seems to be no indent here at all]
At age eighteen, a graduating high school student may have

acquired up to six years of general trade experience. This person will be able to work anywhere in America as they pursue careers and dreams and further education.

If student continues education, loans will be guaranteed frozen at rates to be determined later. *[AJ- Later? Would this not have been detailed?] [DWR- This is a working proposal. I still have to run it by AG committees. Values will be determined later.]* By this time, students will have money in the bank and the ready ability to make money, so loans will be low risk. Cash incentives will be offered to students who are admitted to top colleges and universities, as well as students who are accepted into Annapolis and West Point *[AJ- Why would cash incentives be needed here?] [DWR- So they can build savings accounts and/or invest in stocks]*.

The Adult Workforce:

This program can also be applied to the immediate available workforce. Adults retrained to learn a trade or craft. This workforce can be directly employed to inspect, repair and maintain roads, tunnels, bridges, levees, dams, parks, etc. These projects have no end because maintenance is a never-ending element. (All structures require upgrade / retro-fit due to improvements in technology and age of structures.)

New technologies in energy, transportation, irrigation, farming, etc., will necessitate new construction.

This program can also be a tool of rehabilitation for non-violent incarcerated civilians. (Regarding violent offenders, case reviews will determine if program should be extended to these individuals.) While serving sentence, an inmate will be given a stipend for work and educational trade programs, just as a student. The bank holds the stipend and will distribute monies toward union dues, cost of inmate's incarceration including all outstanding costs to any property damage related to inmate's arrest or other incursions to private or public property and financially awarded civil suits. All remaining monies will be deposited into the inmate's bank account.

The system will fashion a path for former incarcerated

individuals to safely re-enter the general population and contribute to society.

This program allows artists, musicians and others the freedom to pursue their craft while remaining gainfully employed.

Long Term Aspirations:

Extra stellar commerce and space exploration.

Currently we have very talented individuals, already working in harsh and dangerous environments (commercial divers working on offshore oil derricks, and coal miners), who can easily adapt to the required working conditions of space. These rugged individuals will build the space stations – military and civilian – in orbit.

At this time, existing space debris, dying satellites and such will be repaired/upgraded, recycled, or collected and destroyed.

Only experienced trade and craftsman will be afforded the opportunity to work in space. An applicant must have six years of experience in trade/craft before an application for off-planet labor will be considered *[AJ- Again, detail needed]*.

Mining asteroids for required materials should be a viable procedure. Once cost-effective transport and supply lines are in place for mining facilities, numerous commercial enterprises can be created.

Profitable Commercial Ventures:

The removal and repair of satellites and other orbital debris.

Mining and space exploration.

Orbital restaurants.

Weekends in space.

Trips to the moon. (General stargazing.)

Concerts and sporting events.

Romantic getaways that offer facilities allowing couples to experience zero-g intimacy.

Regarding Armed Services:

Only enlisted servicemen and women will be allowed to work on orbital military installations or space exploration vessels. All functions to be performed by enlisted servicemen and women. This will lower operating costs and maintain enrollment and stimulate 'recruitment into' the armed services.

Cancel all existing and proposed contracts with any and all Private Military Companies, sometimes called or classified as Private Military Contractors, Private Security Contractors, Private Military Corporations, Private Military Firms, Military Service Providers, and generally any business considered a participant in the Private Military Industry.

Regarding Logistics and the Use of Educational Technologies:

All educational material should be switched to e-reader format. This will enable teachers to present current and relative learning tools to the classroom. E-readers will also eliminate the burden of carrying out-dated and heavy schoolbooks. E-readers should be manufactured entirely in the United States. (No foreign contracts.)

Schools must be updated with Wi-Fi technology. A standardized learning platform should be developed for the classroom and the wireless desktop units should be manufactured in the United States. The desktop units will communicate with the e-reader, allowing teachers to assign and elevate onsite exercises and homework with less stress and a more comprehensive outlook. This system conducts students to work assignments at their own pace and will grant educators inclusive one-on-one time with struggling students.

Classes will be staggered to accommodate students' trade/craft work schedules. (Perhaps as much as two days – 12/16 hours – of work.) Students should also be encouraged to participate in music, sports, clubs and organizations.

In Summary:

Peace is profitable! Remember, a large end of the American economy is balanced on one event – Christmas. The birth of Jesus Christ: the Prince of Peace. I say again, peace is profitable. Bank on the Lord and watch your interest grow daily. And the dividends are amazing.

– End of document –

Elsewhen Press
delivering outstanding new talents in speculative fiction

Visit the Elsewhen Press website at elsewhen.press for the latest
information on all of our titles, authors and events; to read our blog; find
out where to buy our books and ebooks; or to place an order.

Sign up for the Elsewhen Press InFlight Newsletter at
elsewhen.press/newsletter

Elsewhen Press

an independent publisher specialising in Speculative Fiction

ARTEESS: CONFLICT
JAMES STARLING

Arteess: Conflict is the first in a new science fiction series where much of the action takes place inside a game. But surviving the game is not child's play. We learn of science, betrayal, power and progress – from the perspective of innocent, but nevertheless accomplished gamers.

Created as an experiment into the nature of time itself, the virtual world of Arteess exists, in the near future, as a private digital realm. A full-body virtual reality experience where the talented, the shrewd and the lucky are invited to participate in an international war zone of nomadic factions. We are introduced into the world of Arteess alongside the Shard squad, a group of friends specialising in conflict arenas. Though each member possesses unique talents, they are ultimately defined by their personalities, their own personal battles and the moral choices they make in the consequence-free virtual environment.

Surrounded by sociopathic technicians, facetious pilots and a potentially insane commander, they must carve out a place for themselves while surviving the onslaught of rivals and the antics of the rest of their own faction.

James Starling is, by any definition of the word, a gamer. From the mean inhospitable streets of a lovely little community nestled deep within the Devon coastline, James finds himself caught between two distant generations. Dragged along with the modern and the technological, he revels in the virtual environments and endless community entertainment of this millennium's gaming scene. However you view it, he's certainly caught up in the rush of gaming to the point where it's become a bit of an obsession.

Bridging the chasm-like void between literature and gaming, James brings together both the disturbingly amusing black humour of the gaming community, and the focus, scope and monumental scale possible within modern literature. He's quite fond of the end result… *Arteess: Conflict* won the Silver Award in the Teenage Fiction category of the 2013 Wishing Shelf Independent Book Awards.

ISBN: 9781908168306 (epub, kindle)
ISBN: 9781908168207 (240pp, paperback)

Visit bit.ly/Arteess-Conflict

Elsewhen Press

an independent publisher specialising in Speculative Fiction

BOOK 1 OF THE BLUEPRINT TRILOGY

FUTURE PERFECT

KATRINA MOUNTFORT

The *Blueprint* trilogy takes us to a future in which men and women are almost identical, and personal relationships are forbidden. Following a bio-terrorist attack, the population now lives within comfortable Citidomes. MindValues advocate acceptance and non-attachment. The BodyPerfect cult encourages a tall thin androgynous appearance, and looks are everything.

This first book, *Future Perfect*, tells the story of Caia, an intelligent and highly educated young woman. In spite of severe governmental and societal strictures, Caia finds herself becoming attracted to her co-worker, Mac, a rebel whose questioning of their so-called utopian society both adds to his allure and encourages her own questioning of the status quo. As Mac introduces her to illegal and subversive information she is drawn into a forbidden, dangerous world, becoming alienated from her other co-workers and resmates, the companions with whom she shares her residence. In a society where every thought and action are controlled, informers are everywhere; whom can she trust?

When she and Mac are sent on an outdoor research mission, Caia's life changes irreversibly.

A dark undercurrent runs through this story; the enforcement of conformity through fear, the fostering of distorted and damaging attitudes towards forbidden love, manipulation of appearance and even the definition of beauty, will appeal to both an adult and young adult audience.

Katrina Mountfort was born in Leeds. After a degree in Biochemistry and a PhD in Food Science, she started work as a scientist. Since then, she's had a varied career. Her philosophy of life is that we only regret the things we don't try, and she's been a homeopath, performed forensic science research and currently works as a freelance medical writer. She now lives in Saffron Walden with her husband and two dogs. When she hit forty, she decided it was time to fulfil her childhood dream of writing a novel. *Future Perfect* is her debut novel and is the first in the *Blueprint* trilogy.

ISBN: 9781908168559 (epub, kindle)
ISBN: 9781908168450 (288pp paperback)

Visit bit.ly/Blueprint-FuturePerfect

Elsewhen Press

an independent publisher specialising in Speculative Fiction

The Janus Cycle
Tej Turner

The Janus Cycle can best be described as gritty, surreal, urban fantasy. The overarching story revolves around a nightclub called Janus, which is not merely a location but virtually a character in its own right. On the surface it appears to be a subcultural hub where the strange and disillusioned who feel alienated and oppressed by society escape to be free from convention; but underneath that façade is a surreal space in time where the very foundations of reality are twisted and distorted. But the special unique vibe of Janus is hijacked by a bandwagon of people who choose to conform to alternative lifestyles simply because it has become fashionable to be "different", and this causes many of its original occupants to feel lost and disenchanted. We see the story of Janus unfold through the eyes of seven narrators, each with their own perspective and their own personal journey. A story in which the nightclub itself goes on a journey. But throughout, one character, a strange girl, briefly appears and reappears warning the narrators that their individual journeys are going to collide in a cataclysmic event. Is she just another one of the nightclub's denizens, a cynical mischief-maker out to create havoc or a time-traveller trying to prevent an impending disaster?

Tej Turner has just begun branching out as a writer and been published in anthologies, including *Impossible Spaces* (Hic Dragones) and *The Bestiarum Vocabulum* (Western Legends). His parents moved around a bit while he was growing up so he doesn't have any particular place he calls "home", but most of his developing years were spent in the West country of England. He went on to Trinity College in Carmarthen to study Film and Creative Writing, and then later to complete an MA at The University of Wales, Lampeter, where he minored in ancient history but mostly focused on sharpening his writing skills. When not gallivanting around the world trekking jungles and exploring temples, reefs and caves, he is usually based in Cardiff where he works by day, writes by moonlight, and squeezes in the occasional trip to roam around megalithic sites and the British countryside. *The Janus Cycle* is his first published novel.

ISBN: 9781908168566 (epub, kindle)
ISBN: 9781908168467 (224pp paperback)

Visit bit.ly/JanusCycle

Elsewhen Press

an independent publisher specialising in Speculative Fiction

The Lost Men
An Allegory
David Colón

In a world where the human population has been decimated, self-reliance is the order of the day. Of necessity, the few remaining people must adapt residual technology as far as possible, with knowledge gleaned from books that were rescued and have been treasured for generations. After a childhood of such training, each person is abandoned by their parents when they reach adulthood, to pursue an essentially solitary existence. For most, the only human contact is their counsel, a mentor who guides them to find 'the one', their life mate as decreed by Fate. Lack of society brings with it a lack of taboo, ensuring that the Fate envisioned by a counsel is enacted unquestioningly. The only threats to this stable, if sparse, existence are the 'lost men', mindless murderers who are also self-sufficient but with no regard for the well-being of others, living outside the confines of counsel and Fate.

Is Fate a real force, or is it totally imagined, an arbitrary convention, a product of mankind's self-destructive tendency? In this allegorical tale, David Colón uses an alternate near-future to explore the boundaries of the human condition and the extent to which we are prepared to surrender our capacity for decisions and self-determination in the face of a very personally directed and apparently benevolent, authoritarianism. Is it our responsibility to rebuke inherited 'wisdom' for the sake of envisioning and manifesting our own will?

David Colón is an Assistant Professor of English at TCU in Fort Worth, Texas, USA. Born and raised in Brooklyn, New York, he received his Ph.D. in English from Stanford University and was a Chancellor's Postdoctoral Fellow in English at the University of California, Berkeley. His writing has appeared in numerous journals, including *Cultural Critique, Studies in American Culture, DIAGRAM, How2,* and *MELUS. The Lost Men* is his first book.

ISBN: 9781908168146 (epub, kindle)
ISBN: 9781908168047 (192pp paperback)

Visit lost-men.com

THE AUTHOR

Stefan Jackson was born in North Carolina beside the calm eddies of the Trent and Neuse rivers, but spent the latter part of his childhood in southern California. In 1994 he moved to Brooklyn looking for a change, drawn to the energetic confluence of the Hudson and East rivers of the Big Bright City. There he met a lovely woman who became his wife, and they have an enchanting daughter. And a cat.

He now lives in Queens, where he writes stories, plays drums, coaches pee-wee girl's basketball, works the cubicle life, cooks breakfast, rides the F line, laughs and rests his head in the land of jazz.

Stefan has had over two-dozen original short stories and comic scripts published in small press publications and on the web. *Glass Shore* is his first novel.

Stefan says "Cheers to the first fifty years. Hoping the next fifty are just as kind."

www.ingramcontent.com/pod-product-compliance
Lightning Source LLC
Chambersburg PA
CBHW030802200726
48285CB00014B/448